A Sign Change

Lol Marson

A Sign of Change

Author: Lol Marson

First Published in 2022

ISBN 978-1-915164-68-1 (Paperback)
978-1-915164-67-4 (E-Book)

Book Cover Design, Illustrations, and Layout by:

White Magic Studios
www.whitemagicstudios.co.uk

Published by:

Maple Publishers
1 Brunel Way,
Slough,
SL1 1FQ, UK
www.maplepublishers.com

A CIP catalogue record for this title is available from the British Library.

Index

Foreword

Nigel was forced to leave the family home because of accusations of financial irregularities at work and personal money issues. Taking only a few belongings and an old tin bread bin, he took refuge in a rundown cottage on a country estate. Close to the cottage was the 'Manor House' which was being revamped.

When the Old House was complete, ready for the unknown owners to move in, Nigel would have to vacate the cottage. His time frame was only months. During this time he needed to remain aloof, but due to a certain purchase this would prove difficult. However Nigel could not lose sight of the promise he had made, change had to be made and true Names of men exposed.

Chapter 1

Moving In

After over two hours of driving Nigel turned left onto the drive. Five hundred yards in front of him is the Old House, a once grand country house of a rich landowner. Parked outside the house are around six builder vans from a company called Bye, Bye builders whose motto is: 'Pleased to see us go.' As he makes his way up the slight incline passing the dilapidated four space single garage, his instruction is to take the right fork and proceed to the cottage.

The tarmac soon runs into a dirt road. Within fifty yards the cottage is in sight, and he has reached this journey's end.

Not what he had foreseen. Only six months ago, Nigel's life had been turned upside down and now he stood in front of his temporary home. Fortune had not smiled on him. Fleeing the home he had been brought up in and now finding himself having to make a life on his own, he had made a promise to right the wrong.

The two up two down looks in need of some TLC. Inseted in the wall is a stone dated 1865. Nigel knows this humble dwelling will have to be home for now; he hopes to be in a better position in a couple of months give or take. But in the meantime, keeping a low profile was the order of the day.

Nigel enters the building by the old wooden door that still retains the lift and latch door handle. The first room is the sitting room measuring about 12-feet square. There are a number of pieces of furniture - a sideboard, an armchair, a small table with two dining chairs and a smaller table which sits an empty vase, an open fireplace. On the other side of the ornate fire surround is a coal scuttle, loaded with coal, a few sticks and a rolled-up newspaper perched on top.

Continuing through, passing the steep stairs he arrives at the kitchen which is smaller than the sitting room and someone, to save space, had fitted a folding plastic door. Looking around, he notices the gas cooker had three burners, a grill and an oven - it all looked clean enough. On the wall over the sink was an Ascot style water heater with its long spout hanging over the pot sink. Cold water was dispensed from the brass tap firmly bolted to the wall. A few cupboards adorned the back wall, and the work surface was a lift down flap on the free-standing cabinet. A few provisions had been supplied which Nigel was grateful for.

Venturing up the steep stairs, holding the rail just in case of any uneven steps, on reaching the top, and looking up, he sees the grubby loft hatch. This would later prove to be invaluable to store one of the few possessions he managed to bring with him, a safe haven for the bread bin and its contents. Each of the two rooms had a step up to access them - left or right first? - he asked himself.

In his mind Nigel had to make light of the situation. Right it is - surprisingly the bedroom was a very similar size to the room downstairs, he thought - one ¾ bed, table with light and a set of 4 drawers. The bed had been made and the quality of the bedding was OK, thick and functional. The bed had a mattress cover, flannelette bottom sheet, top sheet the same absorbent material, two thick over blankets and a bed-spread (fluffy blue).

Hardly containing his enthusiasm, he crossed the small landing at the top of the stairs and viewed the bathroom – Phew! an inside toilet!! A small sink with one cold tap, bath with one cold tap, the hot water was provided by a larger version and what looked like a newer version of the Ascot style in the kitchen. This was mounted on the wall between the sink and bath. It, too, had a long spout for dispensing the water. This time you had to point it over the sink or bath depending on where the hot water was required. Well, thought Nigel, it is getting dark. He will leave exploring the outside till tomorrow - could overdo the excitement, he thought.

He took the two suitcases from the car, both bulging with his clothes, the ex-Walkers crisp box holding his shoes, and a bottle of spirit bearing the same name as the crisps. An old bread bin lay under a blanket - this could stay there tonight but he needed to find a safe and secure place to keep it whilst at the cottage. But for now, the safest place would be under the blanket in a locked car. That was it, really nothing else to take in.

1865

He was soon unpacked and returned the cases to the car as there was not enough room in the cottage for empty cases. He locked the car and double checked it was locked. The light was diminishing fast, and for the first time he felt the cold air.

Making the fire was the first job, as the room could warm up whilst deciding on tea. Making the fire was simple enough as his grandma had only this form of heating in her house, and he lost count of the times he would help making it or removing the ashes. As he set the fire, his thoughts returned to his grandma, he so much adored all those years ago and how the loss was still in his mind.

OK! He thought - move on, let's strike a light and warm up. He had briefly noticed the-foot-long tapers in the kitchen earlier, so the matches must be close by. Not too many drawers or cupboards to open, but unfortunately not a sign of a match anywhere. The cooker was all gas that did not have its own ignition system. That too required an external flame. It was clear that heating would be required so finding a resolution was now the first order of business.

The builders would have left by now, so cannot ask them. The only other solution was to drive the few miles to the village and find a store that sold matches or a lighter. Back upstairs for his coat and hat, back down to collect the car key off the sideboard and into the car. Starting the car, he had a thought - going back into the cottage he collected a taper back to the still running car. He pressed the onboard cigarette lighter. 10 seconds later up it popped.

Nigel removed it and there was a red-hot element glowing in the dark. Taking the taper and offering the wick to the glow, he saw a flame was born.

Guarding the taper flame with one hand he made his way inside. The paper, wood and coal lay in wait. Nigel first lit the paper at one side, then in the centre, then the other side. Within moments, the paper was ablaze and starting to take hold of the wood, which had been a door or window, as two sides held paint, and which helped to accelerate the flames.

Remembering to turn off the car engine, Nigel removed the key, closed and locked the door and returned inside the cottage, closing the wooden door and putting across the thick velvet curtain that would retain some heat. Likewise with the window. However, these curtains were not so thick but would help a little to prevent the heat escaping via the old, ill-fitting frames and single glazing.

It had been sometime that he had eaten. So venturing into the kitchen to take stock of what was available, he found some supplies had been left for him - tea bags, sugar cubes that looked like they had been relieved from a local restaurant, a small tin of assorted biscuits, a tin of soup, a tin of baked beans with sausages, Carnation milk, cheese wrapped in grease-proof paper. Likewise a ½ lb. butter and bottle of sterilized milk all positioned neatly in the free standing cupboard. A tin bread bin sat on the floor. On opening the lid, he found it was empty. That's OK, thought Nigel. What's in the fridge?

A quick scan around soon revealed - No Fridge! Mmm, that needed to be sorted before spring. His situation had changed but not to the extent of drinking warm milk. With tummy rumbling what is it to be first? A brew! If it's good enough for Chimps, it is good enough for me, smiling to himself. Next he needed the kettle. This was alongside a tea pot in the wall cupboard along with a few slightly damaged pans (but clean). A few plates and bowls, knife, fork, spoons, tin opener and other paraphernalia were in the drawer which had been lined with a piece of wallpaper to help keep clean.

Firmly grabbing the kettle from the cupboard, he saw it came with a whistle, yet another thing that reminded him of Grandma, but in a nice, happy way. Kettle part-filled with freezing cold water he placed it on the blank space where normally there would be a fourth burner. Picking up the part- burnt taper he relit it from the now burning coal in the fireplace.

Shielding the flame, he returned to the cooker, turning the knob and offered the flame to the burner - nothing! OK, try a second burner, No! has to be the third one, No! I don't have any gas; this needs to be investigated first thing in the morning.

Moving back to the sink, he saw his reflection in the window. Sadness entered his eyes and for the briefest of moments the past year and particularly the last few months came flooding into his mind, but this was not the right time for self-pity. He had made a promise that only he knew about.

His rumbling tummy reminded him that part of him still required attention, so the thought of warm food was off the al-a-carte menu, however still in the cupboard were the biscuits and cheese. That will do for tonight and to help wash it down, one could have a cup of ice cold water, a glass of sterilized milk or a small Scotch. Biscuits buttered and a piece of cheese cut from the block and a drop of Scotland's finest, time to retire to the warmth in the next room. Soon the food was eaten and the small glass empty. Placing a little more coal on the fire and ensuring the guard was clipped to the fireplace, time for bed. He hoped that the extra coal would keep the fire in until the morning.

Making his way to the bottom of the stairs he decided to close the kitchen door. After somewhat of a tussle he managed to close it. He was about to close the sitting room door to help keep a little heat in until the morning, then with a smile decided to leave it open. Look! he thought, "central heating", with the heat going up the stairs, and these being in the middle of the cottage, that's central!

Nipping to the loo before getting into bed, Nigel hoped that the night-time pee would wait until first light. Whipping off his clothes, at a speed that would win him a gold in the Olympics he was in bed. Perhaps flannelette bedding was not a bad idea by someone. Nigel closed his eyes and spoke out loud, "I love you."

Nigel's wish came true, the need to get up in the night did not arise. However, perhaps, now would be a good time. Grabbing some clothes he tried to dress in bed but that was proving difficult, so he thought, on a count of 3, it is time to get up. 1,2,3 - out he jumped and as quickly as he took the clothes off last night they were back on this morning. After visiting the loo, it was downstairs. And investigating the cooker that had denied him a warm meal last night.

Nigel was very cold, the air was bitterly cold, but turning into the sitting room gave him some warmth. He rushed over to the fireplace, unhooked the guard and with the poker gently moved aside the grey ash. There was a shining red ember and he carefully placed a couple of sticks paint side down. Within moments the flames lifted and a few more sticks and lumps of coal were added and the warmth could be felt again.

As he stared into the flames, he noticed that the jumper he was wearing was steaming. The clothes had become slightly damp during the night. Something he would need to resolve at a later date. For now it's some form of breakfast. Scotch was not on the menu at this time of the day, so water or milk?

Sliding the kitchen door back seemed a lot easier than closing it the night before. So Mister Cooker! what is your issue? Nothing stood alongside the cooker, so it was easy to look behind. The gas pipe went straight down to about 6" from the floor and then passed though the wall.

Nigel opened the outer door and spun his head around the corner. There sitting, basking in the cold morning sunshine were two large gas bottles tethered to the wall behind an open mesh cage. Taking about 5 steps towards the cage he noticed a valve on the top which read 'open/ close.' Moving the handle to the 'open' position, he had the two gauges spring into action moving the needles to 'full'. Nigel stared at the gauges somewhat with disdain. If only he had come out last night! Never mind.

Back inside, a re-run of the night before, lighting the taper on the fire in the front room, returning to the kitchen, a turn on the knob offering the flame to the burner. However, the air in front of the gas blew the taper out. Try again, relighting the taper. This time waiting a few seconds after turning on the gas emanated a gentle pop and a blue flame danced around the ring.

Fresh water was replaced from the night before in the kettle and on the ring, it went. Within 30 minutes tea was in the cup via the tea pot, the beans and sausage were on the plate and Nigel sat in front of the fire, and ate and drank like a Lord.

It was now time for his Lordship to wash up and try to remember the sequence for lighting the Ascot type hot water heater. A button had to be held in to release the gas. (Let the air out first). The gas was then lit using the taper. The flame heated up the thermocouple. Once hot, the pilot light would remain on.

Pilot light button released, the blue flame could still be seen via the small, sight window. Now with his turning on the tap, within seconds the array of burners performed its duty and hot water descended into the bowl. A quick search under the sink revealed a white plastic bottle with a baby in a nappy that would make do, a squirt of the green stuff transformed the water into a foaming mass. The clean pots and pans were left to dry naturally.

Moving back in the sitting room Nigel opened the curtains. The Sun had now moved round and started to defrost the car. It was clear that a trip into the village was needed, to stock up supplies. Not knowing the area at all and having been in the car for hours yesterday he decided to walk.

Best boots on, hat, scarf, gloves, he walked out through the back door and stepped out into the clean fresh morning air. He turned back to look for a lock. No lock. Well, nothing to take anyway. Looking up at the sky he found a new day awaited him in more ways than one.

A few steps away from the cottage he thought about the sticks and coal. So turning back, he walked down the outside passing the gas bottles. At the back of the kitchen was an outbuilding about 6 feet square, without a door. Nigel was able to poke his head in. Nestled in the corner was a space for a fire - this was obviously the wash house once.

Looking down the garden, which was overgrown, he saw a building with two doors side by side. Next to that was a ramshackle shed. Lifting the latch, he opened one of the doors. There, inside was a heap of coal, some chopped up sticks, an old door and a glassless window frame and an axe. Great, there seemed enough coal for the remaining weeks, thought Nigel.

Now the other door. Lifting the latch Nigel thought that the last owner must have found a consignment of this type of latching handles as apart from the sliding kitchen, all the doors had lift and latch handles. Pulling the door back revealed in all its glory the outside Privy, the black ornamental tank proudly displaying a crest. Protruding from the side of the tank was the arm that held the magic. Once the wooden handle was pulled, a cascade of water would travel down the rusty pipe and dispose of the bowl's content. The wooden seat was thick and looked extremely sturdy. This needed more investigation, but not now!

Moving over to the shed, Nigel did not have to lift the latch as the door had long since fallen off and lay rotting on the floor, devoured by the vegetation. Inside were old gardening tools, trays, and moss growing on pots, a broken weathervane, just rubbish really. Then Nigel spotted a wooden step ladder, and fighting to retrieve it from the rest of the rubbish, finally stood it in the sunshine. Not a tall set, possibly 5 feet to the top tread. Well, that's lucky thought Nigel. Carrying them inside he left them by the kitchen door.

Picking up his car keys and proceeding to the car and unlocking it, he removed one of the cases to expose the blanket covering the old bread bin. He carefully removed the bin from the blanket and replaced the case.

The bin was an old, hinged bread bin, metal handles on either side, the word 'Bread' in bold brown letters that stood out from the dull yellow surround. The bin had a hasp which clearly had always been part of the tin, not added later. What was new, was the padlock threaded through the staple, a key to which he had on the car's key ring. Opening the lock and lifting the lid, he exposed lots of formal type paperwork and a photo. Nigel removed the picture and stared at it for some time, finally, speaking, 'I made you a promise and I will do my best to keep it.' Nigel returned the picture and replaced the lock, firmly checking it was closed.

Taking the bin inside and up the stairs, placing it on the bedroom step, he returned to the kitchen to collect the step ladder. On reaching the landing Nigel opened the ladder. The steps were slightly wider when opened than the space available. With some trepidation Nigel gingerly stood on one tread, taking a deep breath on to the next. He took a moment to consider the situation. Someone could be really, really hurt, and that would be me, but the safety of the contents of the old bread bin was paramount. Two more steps and he could push open the hatch. He could now see inside the loft. Just dark and grim, the only light was from where the roof failed to meet the walls.

Climbing back down he picked up the bin and slid it up the ladder, gently ascending. Almost at the top of the steps he tipped the box on its end, giving the handle a quick thrust and the tin was in the loft. Taking one more step up, he could see the tin had sat itself between the joists. Perfect, thought Nigel. Replacing the hatch caused little disturbance to the grungy paint work and with no finger marks left, no one would know what was up there.

Taking the steps back to the shed, he thought about chopping them up, so that no one could use them. When the time came for Nigel to take it down, he could purchase new ones.

No! thought Nigel, they have done the job, so let them sit in the shed.

Walking back up the muddy road that was frozen an hour before, he was soon on the tarmac. Bye, Bye builders were already working, renovating the Old House. Nigel passed by without any words being exchanged between himself and any workmen.

Walking down the drive, stopping only to look at the ramshackle building that once possibly held cars costing a small fortune, he found viewing inside was simple enough as the door seemed to have gone some time ago. One of the garage spaces had an inspection pit, which was half full of all sorts of rubbish.

Continuing down the drive, Nigel recalled he had turned left onto the drive the day before and had not come through any village therefore he guessed a left. He had to cross the road as only one pavement was available to walk safely. This side of the road had only a grass verge.

Crossing over gave a clearer view ahead. At a short distance a Pub could be seen and after a short walk the steeple of the local Church came in view. It was a pleasant walk not a lot in the way of traffic to spoil the ambiance.

Nigel now found himself outside the Pub, 'The Cooper's. It looked a run-down place. The car park was all chewed up, old barrels left out that had seen better days, now just gathering rainwater and growing moss and grasses. The signpost was still there but the swing sign was gone. The only information on the Pub's name was a few letters still screwed to the wall and those letters missing had left a mark which could still be read. Behind the car park was a grassed area leading down to the river, the remains of what was a flower bed was still visible. To the other side, broken and rotten children's swings and slide. Nigel was not a big drinker but could not help thinking - why in this day and age, was the Pub not being looked after?

Continuing the walk, passing a few old houses on the right he found the Church now came into view. In front of the Church gates, sitting in the middle of the road was a small brick and tarmac triangle and majestically standing in its centre was an old black and white signpost proudly displaying three arms pointing in different directions but not displaying any words. Useful, thought Nigel.

The full extent of the High Street was now in view, shops either side extending along for about two hundred yards. The Post Office was first with its newly painted post box and twin phone boxes; two steps led you into the Post Office, to the side was a wooden ramp with a gentle slope so people who had difficulty in walking could access more easily. On the rail was a small plaque - 'Helping to make life easier' - donated by Bye, Bye Builders. Next shop along was the wool shop, with its display of thick wool jumpers and sweaters. Need to revisit this shop, so checking the opening times - open four days a week, closed Wednesday and Sunday, with half day Saturday.

Next came a house, a nice double fronted building with a whitewash finish. Next, an Iron Mongers', all sorts of paraphernalia outside, hanging off bars and rails, a tin bathtub, 2 or 3 rat traps, clothesline, similar to an upside down umbrella, a large two-handed wood saw, and other items, some Nigel did not even recognise. The table below was an array of paint and decorating stuff, nuts, bolts, screws, hingers, window latches, mortise locks, and yes! a latching door handle the same as adorned the doors of the cottage.

Ready to move on, Nigel's eye caught something under the table court. He instantly had a love for this shop and whoever the owners were. Under the table was a sign which clearly read in large letters 'Fire Guard'. There sat on the floor a metal frame criss-crossed with strands of wool all different colours and thickness. In small letters was written, 'Item reserved. Please see the wool shop for more information'.

Still grinning as he walked along, he next came across the Funeral Director's solemn window display, but very tasteful. Adjoining was a large arch with two fine looking gates, where he guessed the next customer would pass through for the last time.

A couple more houses came before the next shop. This was the traditional Butchers' - outside hung wood pigeons, pheasants, hare, rabbits - Nigel was not keen on any form of suffering and hoped that the end came quickly for these animals. Still it did not stop him pushing open the door.

'Morning,' someone yelled, 'Be with you in a moment.' This gave Nigel a chance to have a quick look around, no shopping list so quick thinking was the order of the day. Too late! There stood a mountain of a man about 6'5". Must have been 20+ stone and hands like shovels, 'What can I get you?'

'Not sure,' said Nigel.

'What meal are we looking for?' asked the butcher.

'That's good thinking,' thought Nigel. 'Breakfast for 3 days, please.' Nigel knew he needed to keep provisions slight as the cottage did not have a fridge, but the cold weather should keep it OK.

'No problem,' said the butcher. Within 5 minutes holding a white carrier bag. Nigel was on his way down the street, not a clue what was in the bag, other than breakfast food.

Next a Uni-sex hair salon. Farther down the street, what looked like a farm agriculture show room/workshop. Not in the market for a tractor. That can wait. Way past the farm place on the other side of the road looked like another Pub. That too can wait, thought Nigel.

Crossing over, the first shop he came to was directly opposite the Funeral gates. Sitting proudly over the shop window, written in bright red letters 'Antique.' With the items on display it looked more like 'a rag and bone yard'.

The next shop was a bit of a mish-mash establishment - push bikes, prams, push chairs, dolls, teddy bears, toys and jigsaw - all shared the window space. Next, and possibly the smallest, shop sold electrical goods. One lone washing machine was in the window, but he could see on shelves down the premises radios, a TV, food whisk and other boxed goods. He may need to revisit this shop at a later date.

Possibly the biggest shop on the street was the Florist's with its beautiful displays of flowers. Its perfume could be detected yards away. Nigel had an empty vase, so was soon inside choosing a mixed bunch.

Next to The Newsagents an 'A' board sat outside the main door enticing you in with the latest news story. The last stop on the trip was the general store. Here Nigel required supper for tonight and a box of matches. Entering, he collected a battered wire basket and started looking around for something to titillate the taste buds. Progress was a little slow whilst trying to balance the increasingly heavy white bag and a bunch of flowers. Two potatoes were first, a tin of beans, small can of cooking oil, a steak pie in a box, a small loaf, perhaps a small pudding, apple turn over cake, and to polish off, a tin of the Black Stuff.

Now, with two bags one in each hand and flowers under an arm, it was off, back to the cottage. No time for sight-seeing. Not only had the sun gone low but with the weight of the shopping bags, slowed progress. Never mind, thought Nigel, the treats inside would make it worthwhile.

Finally passing the Pub and crossing the road onto the drive he thought someone had increased the incline, positive it was not that steep before. Putting the bags down for a moment he could change over weights and put the flowers under the other arm.

As he was about to set off, a Bye, Bye builders' van turned into the drive, and passed him without a second look. Nigel thought about the sign outside the Post Office, 'Helping to make life easier.' Really! By the time he reached the back door of the cottage the sun was casting its final light of the day and the temperature dropping, not that Nigel was aware. He was warm enough at the moment.

Inside the kitchen, the bags were placed on the floor and the flowers in the sink. Grabbing the kettle, he filled it with water, whistle on. Placing it on the spare burner space he rummaged in the bag for the matches, soon found. The ring was lit and the kettle was on.

Whilst the water came to the boil, time to investigate the breakfast bag. All the items were wrapped in white waxy paper, except for 6 large eggs, so each had to be unwrapped to identify the contents -6 sausages each the size of a baby's arm, 6 slices best back bacon, two rings black pudding and 3 kidneys.

Each was laid in turn on the free-standing cupboard's lift down table. Well, thought Nigel, pretty sure, I asked for 3 days' breakfast. If this is the standard breakfast for the butcher, no wonder, he is a big lad.

Wrapping the food back up he placed the breakfast items into the tin bread bin and placed it just inside the kitchen door, cold enough on the floor. Kettle now whistling, a drop of water in the pot to warm it, empty it, then two bags in the pot, pouring in the rest of the water. Whilst that was brewing the rest of the shopping could be put in the cupboard, the Guinness could sit by the bread bin for now.

Next job was, cleaning out the fire in the sitting room and re-setting, ready to light. The cold ash had to be taken on a sheet of newspaper in order to carry it outside. The chosen route being the front door, less chance of mess. This worked well enough, the package was left by the gas bottles. Sort that tomorrow, thought Nigel.

Back inside, the trusted method of fire laying complete, cup of tea made, time to get supper ready. Tonight's feast - pie and mash with beans, the potatoes peeled, cut up and placed in water, pan on the burner.

The pie was removed from its box and placed on the baking tray, with oven lit. Nigel needed to check the cooking instructions and adjust the setting on the oven knob. In, the pie went.

Next go light the fire in the sitting room. Fire guard in place, Nigel had a wry smile thinking about the woollen guard at the Iron Mongers'.

Returning to the kitchen, supper well on its way, change of plan, thought Nigel. The can will remain unopened and another cup of tea would be better. Beans opened and half placed in a small pan the remaining beans in the tin are popped in the tin bread bin. Potatoes now ready, using a fork (nothing else available), adding a knob of butter to the pan, time to mash, Nigel started to hum very loud, even the odd Lar-lar. The sound of a fork on the pan goes straight through him. Nigel really hates the scraping sound.

A check on the pie, it looked done, plate placed in oven to warm, check pudding details. This needed less heat and a shorter time. Time was a bit of an issue as the only clock was on the car dashboard.

Meal plated up, dinner on the knee in front of the fire, strong cup of tea, what a fine moment!

Supper finished, a quick dash to the kitchen to retrieve the pudding which looked OK, that too was quickly eaten. Nigel allowed himself a short time to let all that food go down before retiring to the kitchen to wash-up. During the washing process it dawned on him that he too had not had a proper wash for two days, and the thought of washing in the bathroom at a possible 3° or less was not a pleasant prospect.

Then there were the clothes washing to be considered. Whilst a small fridge may be fitted in the kitchen, a washing machine was well out of the question. Let's figure that out tomorrow. Putting another few lumps of coal on the fire and securing the guard in place, time for bed, leaving the sitting room door open for the central heating to work, it's up the stairs, nipping to the loo then cleaning his teeth, with the same speed as the previous night and Nigel was soon in bed. "I Love You."

Chapter 2

Early Years and the Man in the Hat

Not sure how long he had been asleep, but he woke with a start, sitting upright in bed, not sure what that was about, thought Nigel. He had recently had many sleepless nights but for totally different reasons. Lying back down he needed to clear out of his mind whatever it was that woke him.

Nigel was born late 1939, the only son of Nelly and Jim. The early years for obvious reasons were not good for a lot of Europe, but he was too young to remember much. Rationing had left him slight of build, but his parents always made the best they could with what they had.

As he lay in bed thinking about his young life not a lot to really focus on, Junior School was OK. They provided a small bottle of milk a day and sometimes a bottle of really nice orange juice. He had a friend, Harry. They would walk to school together and play in the playground. Sometimes go down the Canal at the back of the allotments, but the friendship ended when Harry and his family moved.

Big School was OK. Nigel was not the academic sort. He liked sums, and woodwork, but all the other lessons just average. When it came to Sport, he would not be the first to be picked or last, just average, most of his homework marks were 'B' or even 'C'.

The one thing he was grateful for, was home life. He came from a loving family although the "Love" words were never said, perhaps didn't need to be, he thought, as he lay there. You know Love is in the Family, in the home and everything you do together.

Home life was very routine. His dad had an allotment every Sunday Morning. Mum would make up a big flask of tea, Nigel and his dad would attend to the vegetables. They could not afford a lot of shopping so the allotment helped with all sorts of veg. But one little corner was reserved for flowers so that during the summer they could take some home for Mum. In another corner Dad grew unusual vegetables, like white carrots or red broccoli but they always tasted good.

Sunday was Sunday roast, cheap cut of beef or chicken, or as Dad would say, sheep's waistcoat. Whatever it was, it always tasted great. Sometimes in the summer Mum would gather fruit and bake a pie, the best pies in the whole world. Monday would be chips, Tuesday pancakes, etc. etc. Routine!

Once a week Grandma would come for dinner, she only lived four doors up the street. She would bring Nigel a small bag of sweets. He and his dad would go round to her home to help do little jobs, Nigel's job being to make the fire ready for lighting, under strict supervision of Grandma, of course. During the summer Nigel's role changed to cleaning the front windows. Dad would always say, 'Make sure you get the corners, Son, it's not a port hole.'

Then one day Dad and Mum seemed sad. Dad put on his coat against the cold, Nigel jumped up and grabbed his scarf and gloves. It's all right Son, Grandma's OK for the fire today. You stay with Mother. Later Dad returned with a beige tin with a lid with the word 'Bread' written in brown letters. Nigel would not see this box again for almost twenty years, Grandma would never bring him sweets again.

Things soon went back to the routine - Dad to work at 7.15 everyday, home at 5.15. Dad worked for the council in the parks department. Mum did 'Out work'. At the time Nigel was not sure what that meant, other than a Man delivered a big box every Friday and took one away, and Mother used to sew a lot.

The routine continued. The annual treat was the three of them would take a picnic each day, one day at the seaside, one day at the Zoo. Mum's favourite place was a big house outside of town, they had to take two buses. This was Nigel's least favourite place to visit, but Mum loved it, it wasn't a mansion, but a very big house with lots of flowers and small bushes.

Mother would say, 'I would love to live in a house like this.' 'I am not cleaning all those windows,' Dad replied. Nigel could not remember how old he was, but still at school.

One Saturday morning Dad was discussing veg. with other men on the allotment, so Nigel walked down to the Canal. Mother had given him a few pieces of bread to feed the ducks and if lucky, the two swans would be there.

Breaking the bread into small pieces so it lasted longer, the ducks and swans paddling over, ready for the up-and-coming treat, Nigel tried throwing a piece to each bird, so they all had some.

Nigel stopped feeding the birds as he felt uneasy. Turning around, he saw, there stood Raymond.

Raymond was without doubt the unchallenged school bully. He was in the year above Nigel, but everyone knew Raymond.

'There are some rats over there,' said Raymond.

Nigel looked across at the other bank, 'Those are Voles not rats! They have smaller faces and only a little tail. Sometimes they hide it under their body.'

Raymond looked down at the birds, 'I think they're really pretty.' He continued to look at them for a short time and turned to walk off. Stopping, he turned back, 'Don't tell anyone what I said.' 'I won't,' said Nigel. With that Raymond walked off.

Nigel went back up the hill, Dad was packing away ready for home. Now Saturday afternoon was another routine. 4 o'clock Wrestling on the TV - one of the few times Mum and Dad would jump up and down. Mum would sometimes get vocal if she did not like one of the people in the ring.

Then 5 o' clock the mood would change. Mother would put the kettle on and Dad would sit at the dinner table, not to eat. Far more importantly, checking the football pools.

Week after week Dad would turn to Nigel, and say, 'Told you they wouldn't draw.'

You see, every Tuesday evening, Nigel and his dad 'studied form' on the pool's coupon, which teams would draw a football match with whom for the three points. And of course, if Dad picked a score of 3, 'told you' would ring out, but if Nigel or Mum picked teams without collecting maximum points, Dad would say, 'You need to do better.' Twenty-four points or the jackpot never did come their way.

Nigel lay between the sheets still wide awake. He couldn't remember the year, but a few things changed. Nigel was allowed a few pence pocket money, to help him learn the value of money. The local Scout leader came round and asked if Nigel would like to join the Scouts. This meant Subs and Nigel didn't fancy paying for them out of his pocket money. Mum and Dad agreed to pay if he liked it. Soon, Nigel was invested and had a new green jumper, new blue and white Scarf, a new berry, new trousers - this was the first time ever that the clothes he stood in were all new.

Nigel did not make a lot of friends at Scouts but enjoyed the company of others. He worked to get his badges which his Mum would sew on. One week he was presented with his birdwatching badge. When Scouts had finished he made his way home with his new badge held tightly in his hand. Mum will have that sewn on next week. Thinking of sewing, he thought, ' Why has the man with the big box stopped coming?' but Nigel never did ask Mum.

Walking up the street, turning the corner into the alley he came cross Raymond and two of his bully boy mates. 'Ha it's a Brussel Sprout,' said one. 'What's in the hand?' said Raymond, little point in Nigel refusing to open. It would only be forced open, so he only opened it enough to show part of the badge. Raymond pulled Nigel's fingers and looked at the bird beautifully embroidered, 'I like that' and took it from Nigel's palm and walked off with the other two boys laughing.

Nigel lay in his bed well over twenty years later, still remembering that sick feeling.

There was a slow walk home, what was he to say? Mum and Dad did not know about the badge so would not ask, however Skip will ask why it had not been sewn on. He thought and thought and decided to tell them he had lost it. Not a lie, but not the truth.

Nigel entered the house. 'Are you OK?' said Mum.

'Yes, thanks.'

'Would you like a glass of milk?'

'Yes please, I will nip and put my pyjamas on.'

Upstairs Nigel took off the uniform and threw it on the bed. He should have done more to keep that badge.

'Nigel!' shouted Mother. 'One of your friends is at the back door to see you.'

Puzzled, Nigel went downstairs to the back door.

There stood Raymond. 'I am returning this. Don't tell anyone.'

Raymond stretched out his hand and presented Nigel's badge.

Nigel remembered the badge being the correct way up and the little bird emblem being perfectly positioned in Raymond's palm. Nigel carefully took the badge, looked at Raymond, 'I won't,' said Nigel.

The more Nigel tried to get to sleep the less he was inclined. I will nip to the loo and when I get back to bed it will still be nice and warm, that will help me go back to sleep, thought Nigel. As he jumped back in bed he curled up under the blankets, his position only served to remind him of something else.

Coming to the end of his time at school with only a few weeks left before starting work, Nigel was walking down the alley at the back of the shops, when he heard an unusual noise.

Taking a few steps closer and looking around by the bins he could see a boy rolled up like a sleeping dormouse, sobbing uncontrollably. Nigel did not have any idea who the boy was as his hands were cupped around his head. Then the boy sat upright still bent over. This time he rested his head on his knees.

Nigel had never seen anyone so upset, the boy could hardly breathe for crying. Nigel took out his handkerchief and gently tapped the boy on the head to offer the hanky.

The boy lifted his head, Nigel was shocked. The boys' eyes were red, like an alien from the movies. His nose was running so much, the slime was all over his face.

The boy took the hanky, it was only that at this point Nigel knew the face was Raymond's.

Not knowing what to do Nigel placed his back up against the wall and slid down next to Raymond. No words had yet been exchanged for two reasons - Nigel did not know what to say and Raymond could not gather air to attempt to speak. Eventually both boys sat with their backs against the wall with knees up to their chests.

Raymond cleaned his face and looked straight ahead. 'Dad's left us. Mum said she can't cope with me anymore, fighting and getting into trouble. She is sending me to live on a Farm with my Uncle and Aunty and their two boys. She said she's not talking about it and I am going.'

Raymond's breath seemed better. The tears stopped. He cleared his nose and offered back the handkerchief. Nigel just shook his head. With that Raymond sprang to his feet, chest out and started walking away. He stopped. Before he had time to turn around, Nigel said, 'I won't.'

That was the last thing he remembered thinking about. He must have finally dropped off to sleep.

What woke him was the sound of a big throaty engine outside the bedroom window.

Quickly putting on some clothes he looked out of the curtains to see a tractor in front of his car.

Going downstairs he slid back the door curtain and opened the door. The driver had got out of the tractor and was looking at the car.

'Morning,' shouted Nigel trying to be heard over the tractor's engine. 'Sorry, didn't know this track was used.'

'Morning,' said the driver, 'I sometimes use this way. I live on the farm,' pointing back up the track, 'and save going through the village, especially Market Day.'

'Market Day?' asked Nigel.

'Yes, every Friday, it's not very big even in the summer, with less traders turning up when it's cold, but all helps to keep the village going. What are you doing here?' asked the farmer.

'Well, currently freezing to death. I will get my keys and park by the side of the cottage. That will give you access.' Nigel dashed back inside to retrieve the car keys. Luckily, whilst the weather was extremely cold no defrosting of the windscreen was required.

With the car started, Nigel backed alongside the cottage and waved to the tractor driver, he could continue his journey.

However, the driver seemed not to be in a rush.

Nigel sat in the car as long as he dared, finally turning off the engine. He was going to have to get out of the car. He was not going to get away with that bitter cold excuse.

'Why are you in old Arthur and Millie's Cottage?' asked the farmer.

Trying hard to think on his feet, he needed to deflect the conversation away from himself.

'Is that who lived here before?' asked Nigel.

'Yes! The last owner of the Old House ran it as an Old Peoples' home. This was no home, it was solely profit over people. Part of the consent by the authority to run the home was, there had to be someone on site at all times, but not in the Old House. In case of fire, there should be people outside the building who could raise the alarm. They offered the job to Arthur and Millie.

'The Bastard' that ran the home promised a beautiful little cottage with the position, but what did he do? Put in a couple of old water heaters, a bathroom, a reconditioned cooker from the shop on the high street.

He made them pay rent, but they had to move out when the Police eventually investigated the home, not a home, it was never a home, only an Old House to rip people off, but the authority finally found out what he was up to and came after him 'The Bastard'. '

'What happened to him?' asked Nigel.

'He did a runner to Spain, last we heard. The house has stood empty for years. It was auctioned off last autumn and the builders started work on it end of year. No one knows what it's going to be, but someone is spending a few bob.'

'Let's hope it not the last chap coming back!' said Nigel.

The farmer scowled.

'Only joking,' said Nigel. With that the farmer returned to his tractor and set off on his way.

Nigel raised his hand to wave goodbye but didn't receive any recognition. 'Don't think the farmer was so happy with the last remark,' thought Nigel, 'but still the thumb screws were off for now.'

Nigel returned indoors ready to make breakfast. Getting the produce out of the bread bin and lighting the grill, Nigel was feeling rather smug with the morning's events and whilst some parts of the goodies were cooking, minus the kidneys, he went to check on the fire.

Lucky me, he thought, I still have embers, a couple of sticks and the last few lumps of coal and warmth was installed once again.

Soon all the ingredients were assembled on a plate. Tea in hand, he returned to the sitting room to enjoy.

Breakfast finished, washing up done, coal scuttle filled, the next job could not be put off any longer, you need a good wash Mr!

Only two options - strip wash with flannel and the sink, or bath?

Sink! Nigel felt better after washing and changing clothes.

It was not that bad, but not an experience he would like to repeat anytime soon. So, Friday is Market Day let us go and have a look.

Donning his hat, coat, scarf and gloves, Nigel decided to walk to the village. The builders were again on site. A number of vans, tools and the usual bits and pieces were spread round the front of the Old House. The work men went about their business but as Nigel walked by, not a single acknowledgement.

Not such a bad thing being invisible, he thought. Continuing down the drive he crossed the road. Passing the Pub, he could see several cars parked by the verge, and turning by the Post Office on the other side of the High Street, he saw there were several Market Stalls.

First Nigel needed this side of the street, The Iron Monger.

He stood outside viewing the wares, then he spotted what could be useful. He thought to himself, don't be silly. How would I fill a tin bath when it's in front of the fire?

On his pushing the door open, the sound of a tinkling bell told of his entrance. A chap in a brown overall greeted him with a bright, 'Good morning, can I help?'

'Hope so,' said Nigel. 'I need something to warm a bathroom, please'.

'I can sell you an electric fan heater, but it shouldn't be used in a bathroom. I have paraffin heaters,' showing Nigel an area at the rear of the shop, 'I can sell you a single burner or double.'

'I will take the double,' said Nigel.

'It comes in a box, and you will need to assemble it at home,' said the shop keeper, 'you don't need any tools. It all clips together. The only other thing you need is paraffin, and I've sold out at the moment.'

That's useful, thought Nigel.

'Only joking,' said the shop keeper. 'How much do you need? A gallon?'

The box was manageable, not too heavy, the gallon of fuel posed a bit of an issue.

'Do you need a hand to the car?' asked the keeper.

'Thank you,' said Nigel.

'Where is it?' asked the shop keeper.

'About a 1½ miles up the road, it's at home.'

The shop keeper looked a little taken aback. 'Only joking,' replied Nigel.

However, it was going to be a challenge. Turning around Nigel spotted a very large tartan shopping bag on wheels. 'If these two items fit in the bag, I will buy the bag.'

'Don't worry,' said the man, 'after that joke they will fit.'

True to his word, both items were in the bag, the heater sticking well out over the top of the wheelie bag, but it was OK.

A quick look around the market, a purchase of underwear and socks, a couple of potatoes, a jar of home-made jam and a pot of honey, all of which could be put in the side pockets of the wheelie bag. Off we go, thought Nigel.

Passing the village notice board that he had obviously missed the day before, he read the advertisement: 6 till 7 every Saturday the Fish and Chips Van would be in the market plaice. There are more Comedians than on TV around here, thought Nigel.

Ready to cross back over he could see the Church gate. To the left-hand side was a thermometer type gauge showing the progress of some latest fund-raising efforts, the height of the red line possibly reflected the temperature, as it seemed not to have risen very high. Perhaps it's new?

On the way back, Nigel thought that over the last few days he had spent perhaps half his cash money so he needed to be aware that he would need money next week.

Turning onto the drive ready for the incline that didn't seem any less steep, rounding by the old garage building, he heard a booming voice, 'Hey mate, you left your Granny behind,' whilst pointing at the wheelie bag. Another wag shouted, 'That, a big sporran.'

Nigel had passed the builders on a number of occasions without being noticed. He just grinned at them and continued his way.

Back at the cottage, cup of tea in hand, time to assemble the heater. Instructions came in the form of drawings, simple enough. Moments later, work done, there stood a perfectly assembled heater.

Now, to add the paraffin. Should it be filled outside and then carried upstairs or filled upstairs and risk spilling it on the floor?

A sip of tea and a re-look at the instruction: 'Important - fill on a hard non-absorbent surface.'

The tank had two dials to indicate fill level. The whole thing in essence was two single heaters in one cabinet.

The fill cap had a device that would help prevent over filling. A sort of float that as the fuel rises, blocks the fill hole off, worked well enough. Finding an old rag from the shed, Nigel wiped down the small amount of fuel he had spilt.

First, he took the cabinet to the bathroom, positioning the heater against two walls. Less chance of a mishap. One of the many safety devices was a spring loaded cap that had to be raised through 90° against a small hook. The idea is, if the heater is knocked, the hook had a very small perching area on the cap which would release and extinguish the flame.

It took Nigel several attempts to get the hook to hold the cap, but once both were done, the caps sitting proudly upright, it was time to test it out.

The wicks looked damp. A slight smell of paraffin was in the air. Match lit and placed against the waiting wick, the prettiest blue flame ran around the circumference of the burners.

Gently lowering the chimney, the flame still seen via the little window, he placed the front of the cabinet into positions. Job done!

Nigel was sure he could feel the difference already. Let's give it a few hours, he thought.

Back outside, tidying up the packaging and storing the remaining paraffin in the toilet, he thought it would be safer than with the wood and coal.

Nigel looked at the packing and thought over the period he was likely to be here. What about the rubbish? Doubt, the bin man comes here anymore!

Putting his teacup back inside and grabbing his hat, coat, scarf and gloves, closing the door behind him, he decided to walk up the lane in the direction that the tractor had come from. It led to the woods. He needed a stick for supper!

Nigel could not have been walking for long when a black Labrador dog came bounding up, circling round and round him. The dog seemed friendly, unlike the chap that stepped out of the woods, definitely an outdoors person, well-worn wax jacket, moleskin trousers, clodhopping wellies, a cowboy stye hat, and a shot gun draped over his arm.

'This is private land, what are you doing?' he barked.

'Taking a walk, looking for a stick for supper,' replied Nigel.

'What!' the man barked. Nigel repeated, 'I am looking for a stick for supper.'

'This is private land, get off to where you came from you idiot,' growled the man.

'Whose land, is it?' inquired Nigel. 'Whose land am I trespassing on, yours?'

Nigel had never been confrontational. He hated any form of bullying or aggression but something about this chap, told Nigel to retire.

'Have a nice evening,' said Nigel, as he turned to go back down the lane.

'Hope you enjoy eating your stick for supper,' said the man.

Nigel turned back, 'I am not going to eat the stick, I don't have a toasting fork to toast bread, so I am going to use a stick, and you thought I was going to eat the stick for supper, now who's an idiot?'

Back at the cottage Nigel's first job was to check on the bathroom. On his opening the door a cascade of warm air hit. There was a slight smell, but he could live with that.

The light was starting to fade. Carefully he went downstairs.

He removed the ash from the fire, cleaned it out, put the silver white dust on a piece of newspaper and carried it carefully outside, tipping it on the previous fire remains.

Paper, sticks and coal stacked correctly in the fireplace, with paper lit, the flames were dancing around the coal, fire guard in place.

Time for the first proper wash in days. Back upstairs, he swung the water heater spout over the bath. Pushing in the bath plug, he turned on the water. A small dooming sound indicated the gas had lit. He waited a few moments.

Nigel tested the water. 'Blimey, that's hot.' It would seem the old heater still worked well.

He went into the bedroom, collected some clean clothes and undressed in the warmth of the bathroom. The bath was reasonably full, but now required some cold water, it was far too hot.

In he climbed and spent a most pleasant time. Some bath salts, or bubble bath would have made it extra special, but as he lay there considering the upheaval of the last few months, Nigel thought, 'I can't complain.'

Bath over and dressed, he was soon downstairs in the cold kitchen.

I am going to get another one of those heaters, a single one for the kitchen. The slight smell puts me off buying one for the bedroom. I should be able to afford it.

Pot of tea made, cup ready, he took the bread and butter, his pot of honey and put them in the sitting room.

Back to pour his tea, and then settle down in front of the fire with his newly found toasting stick, he proceeded to make honey on toast, food of the Gods.

It had always been a favourite tea-time meal at home with Mum and Dad - a bit of a treat and dependant on Mr. Webb's bees.

Mr. Webb had an allotment, a few plots up from his Dad's and he kept a hive behind the shed. If the bees had been 'good little boys and girls' as Dad would say, he would give us a jar. But we did not have butter, we had margarine, but still lovely, nevertheless.

Licking the melted butter and honey from his fingers, a small Scotch is in order he thought. Sitting back down in front of the fire, toasting another slice of bread reminded him of his Scouting days.

When he went week-end camping, Nigel didn't mind a weekend but not for a week. Mum and Dad said he could go; they could afford the few pounds. It wasn't until later he discovered why things had changed, but changes at the time were magic, going on a train to the country side, spending three days at the seaside in board and lodging. The Zoo was much the same, the trip to the Big House, Mum and Dad paid to go inside. For Nigel the furniture was old (older than at home) paintings of people in big frames on the wall, and a man taking them round telling stories of the Big House, but the best bit of all after the walk round, they could go into the tea room.

They would sit at a table with a white tablecloth, and fancy cups and saucers, and plates, not dinner plates, smaller - all the crockery had the same pattern on them.

Nigel remembered, as if yesterday, a Lady in a black dress and white pinny with a white hat came over and put in the middle of the table, three plates on a stand.

The big plate at the bottom was filled with sandwiches with lots of different fillings.

The middle plate had scones, either side of which was a little pot of thick cream, and jams in the other pots.

On the top plate were tiny little cakes, not all the same, some had pretty patterns on them.

Then the lady came back with a big tea pot, a jug and a bowl. When it was on the table Nigel could see what was in them - milk in the jug and square sugar in the other.

They all had the same pattern as the rest of the pieces on the table. The pattern was a pretty blue bird sitting on a branch with a few leaves.

The cups were very thin, you could almost see through them.

The lady returned and picked up the tea pot and poured Mum's tea. Mum had not even put in the milk and sugar.

The lady then poured Dad's tea, again no milk or sugar. She then turned to Nigel and asked if he would like a glass of milk.

'Yes please.'

As Nigel sat by the fire, he smiled, thinking back of that day when he thought he had to drink tea without milk or sugar and a glass of milk was better.

Dad picked up the jug of milk and put some in Mum's cup, then put some in his. The sugar bowl came with a pair of tweezers with little hands on the end, this was for picking up the sugar.

They both had one square each.

Nigel remembers watching Dad trying to drink his tea. The cups had little handles and Dad could not get his finger through the gap, so ended up holding the cup in both hands.

Nigel's milk arrived. Not sure what to do next, Nigel sat looking at the food. 'When the Lady gets back, I am going to ask for cake, the biggest one.'

He looked over at Mum, tears filled her eyes. What's the matter, Mum?

'It's all so beautiful, really nice and beautiful, what a privilege to live in a house like this.'

'What!' said Dad 'And who's going to clean this lot?' Mum just laughed.

Of course, the lady did not need to come back to serve the food, it was all ours. Mum explained what needed to be done.

This special trip went on for years, though as time went on Nigel did not always go.

The fire was getting low indicating bed, so a prod or two with the poker, a lump of coal to the back and the guard in place, time for bed.

Quick nip to the loo, clothes off in record speed and in bed. It somehow felt nicer, perhaps because I am clean, thought Nigel.

'I Love You,' said Nigel.

Chapter 3

Meeting with the Vicar and a History Lesson

Morning soon came round, it was getting light. So time to get up, grab a few clothes on the way to the bathroom. On opening the door he found the room was still warm!

Morning ablutions done, Nigel's first job was to put the kettle on and check the fire. Sure enough a few embers were visible, a couple of sticks and lump of coal will have that sorted thought Nigel, fire guard put back on, now to the kitchen to make breakfast.

Looking into the bread bin on the floor, there were still plenty of options, but it had to be eaten, not right to waste food.

Not the kidneys thought Nigel, so a selection of meats were soon in the frying pan. A knife and fork were taken into the sitting room in readiness.

Twenty minutes or so, the food slid on the plate along with an egg, second cup of tea, off we go to have breakfast in the sitting room.

Nigel never had a big appetite, and it did not take long to finish off the breakfast.

Back in the kitchen to do the washing up which included last night's plate, drinking glass and pots, all done and left to drain.

Wonder what the time is, add a clock to the list Nigel thought. That's a clock, a heater, bath salts. Better get some milk, and tea tonight. No! it's going to be fish and chips.

Poking his head out of the back door, he saw the sun was trying to shine. There was a nip in the air but not freezing cold, still need hat, scarf, gloves etc. to keep out the cold.

Walking down the lane, he realized there had been a frost in the night. The ground was hard under his foot.

The tarmac was a little slippery, so caution needed. The builders were at work even on a Saturday.

'Morning,' one of them shouted, 'not with your Granny today?'

The bag! I forgot the bag! Spinning around back to the cottage, bag collected and off again, as he got to the builder, 'Thanks, I had forgotten it,' shouted Nigel.

Nigel walked over to try and talk, if only to be sociable, but trying to be careful not to give anything away.

One of the men was a thickset chap. Nigel walked up to him.

'Morning,' said Nigel,

'Morning,' replied the builder, 'look, sorry about the bag, just in jest!'

'Don't worry about that, glad you did say something otherwise I would be carrying the shopping back.'

Nigel stood about 5' 8" and slight of build. The builder must be 6' 1" and built (as they say) like the outside privy.

Nigel looked down at the wheelie bag for a moment, looked back at the builder, 'You don't think I have an image problem, do you?'

'No mate, I am thinking of getting one myself,' replied the builder.

'That's good,' giving a sideways glance.

'I am Nigel,' putting out his hand. 'I am Love,' said the builder shaking Nigel's hand.

'Love?' enquired Nigel.

'Yes, I am one of the owners of Bye, Bye Builders so I got the Name, Love, as in bye, bye Love. My brother's nick name is Baby, as in bye, bye Baby.'

Not sure what to believe, Nigel changed tack, 'What's happening here?'

'A miracle, that's what's happening. About three months ago after over sixty years as a family business we were done, finished, going to the wall, bad debts, inflation made work drop off. Baby and I were ready for finishing, laying off all the local lads, bad times!

'Then came some chap, asked if we could put the Old House back to a house to be proud of. At first, we turned it down, we hadn't got the money to pay for the materials up front. Then the chap came back with a solicitor, a very short man in a pin-striped suit and bowler hat, he put money on the table and here we are.

'That's not the whole story. After this we have work to do on the Pub across the road.'

The builder continued, 'There are strings. The Solicitor takes 15% of the profit for 5 years. After that we give him back the same amount of money, he gave us a few months ago. The only thing we have to commit to is to take on an apprentice every year for 5 years.'

'Is that a good deal?' asked Nigel.

'No issues at all,' said Love.

'Suppose the chap that gave you the work is going to live here,' said Nigel pointing at the house.

'Hope so, we need someone decent after the 'Bastard' that had it last.'

'When will the house be completed?' asked Nigel.

'We are hoping to finish our part in two weeks, then the sparky comes in, then the plasters.

'We hope to sign off in 8 weeks or so. As I said we will be over at the Pub in 2 weeks for about 6 weeks, then back here to finish off any snagging.'

Then Love's expression changed. 'You're living in the Cottage, aren't you, Nigel?'

'Yes,' said Nigel.

'I don't know what your arrangement is and it's no business of mine, however when this house is finished, we start modernising the Cottage.'

'OK, thanks for the information, I will leave before you start. I better be on my way, having shopping to do. Should I nip into the Iron Mongers' and reserve you a wheelie bag?'

'You're OK, thanks,' said Love.

With that Nigel was on his way into the village, passing the Pub. He thought, I wonder what that's going to look like after Baby, Love and their team have finished. Will need to keep an eye on the reopening. That will be my notice to move out of the cottage.

Nigel turned the corner by the Post Office.

Will need money somehow, need to think carefully about that.

He walked into the Iron Mongers' to the sound of the little bell. 'Hello again,' said the shop keeper, 'What can I get you?'

'The heater you sold me yesterday - I would like another, but one with only one burner, please,' said Nigel.

Soon the heater was in the wheelie bag. 'Do you have any paraffin?' asked Nigel.

'I am surprised you need more,' said the shop keeper.

'Oh, I don't need any. Just thought I would ask.'

'Is that all?' said the owner.

After paying for the heater Nigel was on his way to the Junk shop. The door of the shop was open, the place was rammed either side of the walkway, floor to ceiling.

'Yes?' came a voice.

'Oh, Hello, I am looking for a clock,' said Nigel.

'What sort?' came the question from nowhere.

'One that tells the time,' retorted Nigel.

'Funny!' growled the voice, 'Grandfather, Grandmother, wall clock, one that sits on the sideboard, one that chimes the hour or half hour or no chime at all. What sort?'

'One that sits on the sideboard, chimes!' Nigel answered.

'One over here,' said the invisible man.

'Where is 'over here'?' said Nigel in a tired voice, now running out of patience,

From behind an old cooker up popped a well-weathered little face, 'Here.' The man put a clock on the cooker. Wooden, half round top, the man turned the hand, and the clock chimed the hour. On turning it still further to the half hour the clock chimed once.

The shop keeper told Nigel how much he wanted.

'Do I get the key in that price?' asked Nigel.

The old man's shoulders started to move up and down, his little face grinned, exposing his ill-fitting teeth. He then started to laugh out loud.

'You outsiders are not all daft. Yes, I will give you the key.'

The old man was still chuckling as Nigel left the shop.

Calling in at the general store Nigel got his bath items and other bits and pieces, including supper for tomorrow night. Not for tonight, tonight was chippy night.

Exiting the shop, he heard the sound of clattering as the Iron Mongers and the Junk shop started to close up and move goods back inside.

Nigel had temporarily forgotten it was half day closing on a Saturday, although 2 o'clock was hardly half day, but hey, what do us, outsiders, know?

Passing the pub, he saw three cars were in the car park, not far off. Chucking out time, thought Nigel. Let's hope they are not drinking and driving.

Crossing the road, ready to tackle the ever-increasing slope up the drive.

As he approached the garages, he noticed a gulp lorry was sucking out the stinking water from the pit.

As Nigel looked on, one of the younger builders, possibly early twenties, came over to Nigel,

'You don't want to fall in that.'

'No,' said Nigel. The young man continued, 'It needs to be cleaned out. We are starting on the garages tomorrow. We are replacing the lost bricks, and redoing the roof, then cladding the outer walls with posh polished wood, then fitting some right grand doors. It should look great.'

'Thought Love told me, [if that's his name] you would be moving over to the Pub next week,' said Nigel.

'Yes, that is his nickname. The rest of the team are, but me and two others have been given full responsibility to finish this job. I will be foreman.

'Love and Baby said as more work is coming in I have to show I've got what it takes.'

'Do you think you have what it takes?' asked Nigel.

'I think so,' the young chap said.

'Go home and think you can. And come back tomorrow knowing 'you can'. It will help!'

Nigel bid his goodbyes and continued on.

Around the back of the cottage Nigel started to assemble the heater.

Not going as well as yesterday, he thought. No tea.

Shortly after a cup of tea at the ready, the heater was primed and put in the kitchen.

It took four attempts to get the safety damper to sit at 90° but it held on by the smallest of margins on the hook.

With match in hand Nigel gently lit the wick trying not to knock the damper. Wick lit, carefully fitting the chimney in place, front in place, all done!

Three of the four rooms could now be heated, that will be enough for the next few weeks.

Placing the clock on the sideboard, Nigel needed to nip to the car to ascertain the time. Almost 4 o'clock. Winding up the clock and setting the correct time, Nigel stood staring, mesmerised, waiting for the big hand to reach 12. After what seemed like an age, the clock rang out - Dong, Dong, Dong, Dong.

Before the light faded Nigel refilled the coal shuttle, with coal and sticks. He cleaned out the fireplace taking the ash outside and tipping onto the pile. Returning inside, he made up the fire.

Whilst he was OK for coal and sticks, paper was running out.

Wait a moment! I can save the chips paper from tonight and use that tomorrow.

Time for a wash, best clothes available. Having packed so fast, he didn't have time to think about nice clothes.

Washed and dressed, Nigel heard the clock sound out 5 o'clock. Going downstairs he checked the temperature in the kitchen.

A slight chill was still in the air. Need to close the door. That will help. A second battle with the sliding door ensued. Close run thing with Nigel taking two hands and a foot to close it.

He needed to light the fire in the sitting room. Just because I am going out no need to come back to a cold house.

Check. Hat, coat scarf, gloves and cash - OK off I go!

The outside temperature was not too bad, considering the time of year. Walking past the old garage but stopping for a moment, Nigel looked directly at the garage and said, 'You're going to get a new hat and coat starting tomorrow.'

Good grief, I have been here less than a week and I am talking to bricks and mortar.

Crossing the road and passing the Pub, Nigel noticed the outside light came on suddenly, advertising the Pub was about to open.

Turning the corner, he saw the Chips van parked opposite the Funeral Director's.

The van was possibly an Ex-furniture van that had the top half of one side hinged.

Inside were deep fat friers on the back wall. At the front was a small shelf with two lots of Salt and Vinegar pots placed in the centre. On board were one chap and two ladies - the chap being the frier and the two ladies serving at either end of the counter.

Two small queues had formed. Nigel and another gent joined at the rear of each. The other chap was dressed in a long black coat, a black hat and highly polished shoes.

Nigel's queue moved ever so slightly faster than the other.

Nigel was at the counter. 'Yes please,' said the young lady.

'Fish, chips and peas in a tray, and wrapped, please.'

'Salt and vinegar?' enquired the lady.

'Just a little of each, please.'

Moments later, Nigel was walking off with a piping hot parcel.

Mmm, thought Nigel. Not really thought of the next phase of the plan.

Do I take them home by which time they could be cold, or sit on the bench and eat until the cold air cools them too much to eat?

Nigel stood motionless, staring at the parcel.

'Are you OK?' said a voice behind him.

He turned around. It was the Gent with shiny shoes that had stood in the other queue. Fortunately the street light lit the area well enough to show the man's face, and the dog collar.

'You're new around here,' he said.

'Yes I am,' said Nigel, 'I am not sure where to eat my supper - here or take it home and it could be cold by then.'

'I am the local vicar. I live in that small house over there. Please join me in the warmth. I promise not to talk about Churches, God, or pass around the begging plate or try and rope you into the choir. And I have put away the thumb screws so eating over there is better than cold fish and chips?'

'OK, that's really kind,' said Nigel.

A short dash over to the house. The kitchen was nice and warm. Should we eat at the table here in the kitchen or in the other room?' asked the vicar.

' I've not eaten at a table for almost a week. Here, would be great,' said Nigel.

'Before we start, my name is Nigel,' holding his hand out.

'Well Nigel, you can call me Vicar, Reverend or Paul, or Reverend Paul,' shaking Nigel's hand firmly.

Both men removed their cold weather clothing.

'Would you like a plate?' 'No thanks, just off the paper.' So both men sat down, unwrapped and started digging into the feast with their wooden forks.

Not a lot of conversation passed between the two of them whilst they were eating.

The final few bits of food finished, the vicar asked if he could clear away the paper and tray.

'I will keep the paper if you don't mind,' said Nigel.

Looking rather puzzled, the vicar cleared away the trays whilst Nigel folded the newspaper.

'You are welcome to stay for a hot drink. Or if you are feeling uncomfortable you can leave anytime.'

'Well, that would be rude not to repay your kindness. Are you a drinking man, Paul?' inquired Nigel.

'I don't mind the odd pint, but drinking with a vicar can get second looks, so I tend not to.'

'Come on then, Paul, let a vicar and a not so daft outsider get some looks. I will explain on the way. Is the Cooper's, OK?' said Nigel.

'Fine,' replied Paul.

Walking toward the Pub they passed the big cash raising thermometer by the Church gate.

'What is that for?' asked Nigel.

'Now Nigel, I promised, no begging plate and no Church talk. Maybe some other time, or not.'

At the Pub the fire was blazing in the fireplace. There was a chap sitting close to the fire, with four young people sitting on the other end of the bar.

'Evening, lads,' said the landlord.

'What would you like, Paul?' asked Nigel. 'A pint of bitter, please.'

'Two, please,' said Nigel.

'Evening, Arthur,' said the vicar, to the gentleman sitting by the fire.

'Evening, vicar, don't see you in here very often. Been dipping your hand in the collection?' asked Arthur.

'If I was to spend the money from the collection you lot put in, I would have to spend it abroad. Always know when you've all been to Spain.'

'Not me, vicar. I don't have a pot to pee in. One pint a week for me and two magazines for Millie. That's our treat.'

Good grief! Arthur and Millie. I am in their old cottage, this could be awkward, now what? thought Nigel.

Finishing the final drop of beer, Arthur stood up fastening his coat, 'I bid you good evening, gentlemen.'

'Good night,' both replied.

'How long have you lived in the village, Paul?' asked Nigel.

'About twenty years.'

'What can you tell me about the history and the people of the village?'

'You're going to be sorry you asked that question. The history and the people of the village is a passion of mine.

'I will start with the Old House across the road. The history of the building had not always been documented, like the small cottage and other buildings in the grounds. The house was built around 1860 by a Mine owner. Scandal and bad dealings forced the family to move out around 1910.

'A few years after that the army commandeered the house to help the soldiers of the 1st world war to recover from their injuries. Not many of those brave men made it. Around 1920 it was closed, and the remaining men sent off home. A couple of men stayed in the village.

'After that they closed the house. It had a few more years sitting unused. Its next occupancy was children (all boys) who were sent by various methods by bad and non-caring people who only used the situation for their own bank balance- its unwritten rule, Money, Money, Money - whilst the Children's home lasted, over 25 years. The home was closed after many reports of sub-standard housekeeping and food hygiene. Fortunately it was only for profit the boys were exploited.

'The house was again left for many years before it become an Old People's home. If the boys were a cash cow the old people and relations were taken to the cleaners by a smooth talking conman. After years of being run on a profit over people basis a Police investigation forced it to close, with the conman taking off abroad, beyond the arm of the law.

'The old house was shut down and boarded up and left to fall down. Years of Court cases and arguments followed until the administrators were called in. The house, land and all associated buildings were to be sold as one lot by auction about 5 or 6 months ago. No one knows who owns it, but word has it, it was so cheap, almost a steal, but good luck to them.

'The builders have been working on it for the last 4 or 5 months. Baby, Love have been lucky. Due to the inflation and bad deals, they could have gone down. That contract came just in time. They're working on this Pub next, then there is a small cottage to update.

'Arthur and Millie lived in the cottage but fell foul of the conman like so many others, including this Pub. I will come back to that later. If you walk up past the cottage there is a green lane. The lane forks - one way leads to 'The Captain's House'. Not a large property but really nice. He owns the shooting and fishing rights around here.

'The other way on the lane takes you to the farm. It's run by a young couple, who, I think, will not be there much longer. They're working so hard, but with inflation as it is, and the loss of their Father under distressing circumstances, and the new Old House owner asking for rent, could be the tipping point.

'If you go through the farm you come to the road. Turning right you would come to the Church Hall, used for the usual activity, but not at the moment due to the heating not working. It's like an ice box in there, so Scouts, Brownies, Women's Guild, Wedding receptions etc. are all cancelled until the weather warms up, really sad!

'We come to the church, currently only a few in the congregation, due to the lack of heating. You have been to the Church house. Then we come to the High Street.'

'Can I stop you there, Paul?' interrupted Nigel.'Finish the pint, we will have another, and we can carry on.'

'My round,' said Paul.

'No! I will gladly pay for all this information,' said Nigel.

Returning with two pints he retook his seat.

'I am interested in what you tell me, what about the people of the village?' said Nigel.

'OK, I can do that.' Leaning forward on the table, Paul started as if giving a Sermon.

'There are three old families in the village, 'The Hutchinsons' that's Arthur's family, the man who sat there. His father ran the small farm behind the house. It was the original garden to provide food to the Old House. Then the garden provided extra food for the sick soldiers.

'When they left, Mr Hutchinson continued to grow veg. and fruit and give his produce to the poorer people of the village. He took on one of the soldiers. By all accounts the poor soul suffered shell shock due to shells exploding nearby, but Mr Hutchinson and the soldier then helped as much as they could.

'They both kept the garden going whilst the House was run as a Boys' Home, growing mostly potatoes, to fill up the boys. Sometime when the boys were there, Arthur took over the running of the garden. You will have to ask him when that was. The garden was still producing food during the closure providing support to the poor with fresh fruit and veg.

'Once the last owner arrived the Garden expanded, so it "could provide good wholesome food to the residents", Millie was taken on as the housekeeper, even though she did not have any formal training.

'After a few years the house had extra rooms put up inside. More and more residents, extra staff were taken on, but not to Millie's standard.

'It was also discovered around the same time that the food grown in the garden was being sold and sub-standard food brought in.

'Millie and Arthur 'lived in', but that took a room in the Old House. Two more paying residents could have their room. They were moved out to the old cottage with a promise of modernization.

'It never happened. If it wasn't for old Mr Bye, the Builder, they would have died in the old place. They were eventually moved to a council house at the bottom of the village.

'Whilst we are in the Pub,' continued Paul, 'there's the 'Millers'. Unlike a lot of Pubs, the Millers own this place lock, stock and barrel. I think the current owner is fourth generation. It seems the Pub started life as a Parlour Pub, serving Ale brewed by the old lady of the house. Must have been good tasting stuff as the Pub is still here, but only just!

'This is strange fact,' continued Paul.

'Not long after the Old House across the road was sold, word has it, the Millers were approached by a gentleman with a proposition to revamp The Cooper's. Possibly a lifeline, it had not been doing that well.'

'Damn right, there, vicar!' came a voice from behind the bar. Then appearing from around the corner was the landlord. He bent down in front of the fireplace, picked up a piece of coal and placed it on the fire.

'That Bastard, excuse my French, vicar, almost did it for the family and this Pub.'

The landlord continued, 'There isn't any excuse. It was my fault. He was so convincing. I was investing in expanding the Old House, more residents, more income. He even showed me accounts and solicitor's letters - bogus.

Liars from start to finish. I even took a loan from the bank. Now with the interest rate rise, and the new Pub the other side of the village offering half decent food, it was becoming impossible.

'Then came a gentleman from out the blue. We talked and talked more. He put some plans forward, offered to invest, 'real money'. I tell you, I thought long and hard. Was someone trying to take what little I had left?'

'He then came back with a solicitor, a real one! Very distinctive, short, noticeably short man. He wore a pin-striped suit and a bowler hat. He went through the details a few times, making sure I understood and I signed on the dotted line. Two days later my loan with the Bank was paid off.

'Days later, an architect came. We discussed the changes to be made, we agreed on what the old place should look like. To be honest at first, I thought it to be too radical.

'The final plans are due next week for sign off. When the Bye Bothers have finished over there, they're starting here. I will have to close for a few weeks, that's better than closing for good.

'I make no bones about the deal. I have to try and employ people from the village where possible. The gentleman takes 15% of the profits for 5 years. Then I get the option to pay back the money at the cost I borrowed it.'

The landlord returned behind the bar.

'I hope he makes it,' said Paul.

'He will, I am sure. Seems a decent chap,' replied Nigel.

'Before I move on,' said Paul, 'after the hospital closed one of the men lived in a spare room in this Pub, being looked after by the landlady and the regulars of the pub. There was a Farthing jar on the bar.

'When the soldier was fit enough, which I think it took about two years, the money in the jar was given to him to help him put his life back together. The Government or the Army should have done that!' snapped Paul.

Before he could continue the landlord reappeared from behind the bar with two pints, 'Here, lads, you can help to celebrate my new good fortune, and I need to make sure all the ale has been drunk, good health.'

Nigel looked at the full glass and the half he had left from the previous pint. I am not going to manage that, thought Nigel, I drank the first one too quick. Must have been the salt on the chips.

No such thoughts from the vicar, the remainder of his pint, downed in one and the next lined up at arm's reach.

'The next family,' continued Paul.

'A moment, Paul, what happened to the soldier that lived here?'

'Not sure, he left the village.

'The next family are the farmers. That's not their name, it was they do, 'farming'. They're are the Snows. I think they have been here the longest, not a lot to say about them really, good people!

'There are a number of Snows on the Village War Memorial, dedication to the ultimate sacrifice in both Wars the family made.

'Mr Snow was found shot dead in a field. After Police investigation it would appear that the gun had gone off by accident whilst he was going over a stile. No evidence of anyone else being involved. That was many years ago, and the family have struggled ever since. As I said earlier the new owner of the Old House will be looking for rent.

'That's about it, really, not much else to tell you about,' said Paul.

'There would have been a lot more if it had not been for Sargeant Darwin. That wretched Old People's home would still be open, ripping off the old and their relations.'

'If that Bastard was still here someone would have shot him.' said a voice from behind the bar.

'How come, how did the Sargeant find out about the Old People?' asked Nigel.

The landlord reappeared.

'Darwin has always loved fishing and wanted to rent the estates a one-acre lake for the local fishing club. It lies to the left side of the house just down the hill. About twenty yards from the lake is a damn big hole. People say it was made by a German bomber who was losing power and was going to crash, so to lighten the load he dropped one hell of a bomb. Sorry, vicar. It made a massive hole. There isn't any sign of a crashed plane hereabouts, so I guess it worked, and no one was hurt, so all's well.

'Are you not enjoying the beer?'

'Very nice,' said Paul.

'Good,' said Nigel, looking at about 2/3 of a pint left in the glass.

'Anyway,' continued the landlord, 'the deal was that the second hole was also to be made into a lake. This was going to be the responsibility of the fishing club. Agreement made, work started on the second lake with the help of Mr Bye and his digger.

'According to Darwin he had fished the lake some years before. The Sargeant went one Sunday morning, set up his gear and started to fish without any success. Then one of the old boys from the house came wandering down, stood alongside Darwin and said, 'They're all dead, nought left, lad.'

'Sorry,' said Darwin.

'They're all dead, gone, the waters bad,' said the old man before turning around and slowly making his way back to the house.

'According to the Sargeant when he was telling the story, he continued for a few hours still without any bites. So being of an inquisitive nature, he used his flask to collect water from the lake, packed up and went home.

'Being a member of the local constabulary, he knew people in the Lab. and asked one of them to test the water from the lake.

'According to Darwin it took a few days for the results to come in. The contents of the water were bleach, washing detergent, household soap and human pee.'

The landlord pulled up a stool, sat down and leaned over the table. 'That was the start of the end,' he said, 'whilst the house was a family home the loo pits were OK. Likewise with the soldiers, they came and went, allowing the latrines to recover.

'Again, with the boys, they went to school and used the toilets, and of course, there were times the house was closed. The pit recovered.

'Now an Old People's home, he put more and more people into the building, building smaller rooms so he could get more in. Older folks don't get out as much, well not at all, but that's another story.

'Eventually, the effluent started to flow above ground, and into the road and the drains. The Council was soon on the case, and to cut a long story short, made him put in a proper cess tank.

'The Council gave him the minimum size of the tank and the location it was to be buried.

'What it transpires he did was, he got a smaller tank, had that buried with the manhole cover showing as it should, then had a second manhole placed up about 30 yards from the first manhole making it look like the tank was much bigger.'

'Yes, but it would overflow,' said Nigel.

Leaning still further forward, the landlord's voice dropped to almost a whisper, 'The crafty sod had a pipe put in, so the solids sank to the bottom of the tank, the liquid waste as it filled up ran down an extra pipe into a new hole in the ground. This was covered over with railway sleepers and covered with turf laid over it, invisible! This meant less pumping out, cheaper to run.

'His trick was undiscovered for years, but he got greedy. More residents meant more washing, taking baths and showers, more laundry, more cooking, and eventually the waste filled the new hole and unseen, had time to seep into the lake killing the fish and marine life. The owner had no idea. Why go down to the lake?

'That was the start of the end. The Council came over, the environmental people came over. Investigation after investigation found that at any opportunity he would rip off the old and their relations. He would steal from anyone, here sits the proof.

'Then one day, gone! Not to be seen again. They think he ran off abroad.

'Well! must carry on,' with that the landlord stood up, replaced the stool and returned behind the bar.

'We must leave it there. It has been a most enjoyable evening, but work tomorrow, so best be on my way. I hope we can do this again,' said Paul.

'Yes,' said Nigel, 'perhaps next time only two pints.'

'Are you a bit wobbly, Nigel? Do you have far to go?'

'No, not far, Paul.'

Stepping outside, he found the air temperature had dropped.

'Which way are you going?' asked Paul.

Pointing in the opposite direction to the one Paul was going to go, 'That way,' said Nigel.

'OK, good night,' said Paul.

'Good night,' Nigel replied.

Setting off over the road Nigel could not remember the last time he drank three pints in one sitting. Still perhaps it will help me up this drive, he thought.

As he progressed up the drive, the beer was taking its toll and along with the cold, Nigel needed to step out a little more. As he was passing the old garage, a voice boomed out, 'Who goes there?'

'Who goes there?' said Nigel, 'Who says 'Who goes there' anymore?'

A bright beam of light lit up Nigel's face almost blinding him. 'Me,' he said, 'Who goes there? I have to ask, that's what they told me to say.'

'Shine the light somewhere else,' said Nigel.

'Where?'

'Anywhere but in my face,' snapped Nigel uncharacteristically.

The man pointed the torch downward and Nigel took a few moments for his eyes to readjust.

'Who are you?' said Nigel.

'I am the new night patrol man. I have to look after the house and grounds. It's the first night, best make sure no one steals from the house before it's finished. I am Dave.'

'Hello Dave, I am Nigel. I live in the cottage and I really need a pee.'

'OK, see you tomorrow, good night,' said Dave.

Nigel bounded through the door into the warmth and dashed upstairs, just in time.

Feeling better and back downstairs, what an evening! thought Nigel. I need to digest all that information tomorrow. Sliding the door curtain across, he put another lump on the fire, and fastened the guard in place.

Nigel retired to bed, just as the clock chimed 10.30, not being as quick getting undressed as previous nights, perhaps due to the drink.

Nigel finally slipped under the sheet. 'I Love You', he said out loud. He would be up several times before morning.

Nigel awoke to a dull day. Then he heard the first chime of the clock, another 9 after that. Good grief, 10 o'clock!

He went to the bathroom. It was a little chillier than it had been, on close inspection he saw the flames were out. Checking out the gauge, he found it needed refilling.

Nigel quickly got dressed and went downstairs and started making a brew. Think I will have just toast!

Venturing into the sitting room, he found for the first time the last lump of coal had not done the trick. The fire was totally out. Never mind, forget the toast, a slice of bread and butter will do with the tea.

Breakfast was a stand-up affair in the kitchen, as that was the warmest place.

Returning upstairs, he collected the heater and carefully took it outside. Removing the front allowed the tank to be slid out.

Nigel retrieved the paraffin from the outside toilet. He kneeled in front of the heater and unscrewed the cap. The smell of the paraffin really got to the back of Nigel's throat.

I am going to be sick he thought, screwing the cap back on and retreating a few steps to take in fresh air. Think I will fill that later!

Nigel took a moment, time to have a walk and get some fresh air.

Returning inside, winter attire on, he set off towards the house. No builder's vans today.

But as he moved toward the house a voice shouted, 'Morning Nigel, I can do this! Did you enjoy the evening in the Pub, with the vicar?'

'Yes thanks, how do you know?'

'I sat in the corner with some friends, watched you wobble out,' said the young man. 'See you, later.'

Nigel approached the house and stood looking at the front of the two-story building. There were 5 windows across the first floor. Each window had 24 panes of glass, each about 12"x 9". And 2 windows either side of the door on the ground floor, had the same number of panes but with the glass smaller in size.

There were two steps that led to the front door. This was a really large single door which shone with its dark blue almost black paint. There was a big brass letter box, a door knob that must have been 5" in diameter, and a door knocker shaped like a hook.

The window frames had been painted a high glossy white. The glass had not been cleaned, guess due to the builders still working on the inside and the plasterers due. They will create dust and dirt.

What a grand looking house! If the inside looked anything like the outside it will be a place to be proud of and somewhere the village can be proud of too.

Nigel continued to walk past the house. The land dropped away slightly. In the distance he could see the lake. There wasn't a path to it so he took a straight route across the grass.

Approaching the lake which was pretty big, he thought, that's what a 1 acre lake looks like.

Further to the right was the bomb crater, which was egg shaped now, possibly due to work started and not completed by Mr Bye for the fishing club.

He now walked along the grass keeping the house parallel to his right with the lake behind him.

Must have been a good 10 / 15-minute walk when he came upon the old garden. He could tell it was once a garden. It looked like the allotments Dad and the rest of the chaps worked on.

There was a large green house. About half the glass was missing but the frame was still standing. A couple of brick buildings stool alongside.

From this point Nigel could only see the upper floor of the house due to the slope of the ground. This side of the house had 6 windows which from the distance looked the same configuration as the front ones.

Up the slope behind, the Old House was covered in woodland. Nigel walked up the hill toward the house. As he got closer there, the remains of a wall about 20 yards from the house, most of the area had been slabbed. As this faced South, he wondered if it was once the kitchen garden, then the wall removed to make a sitting area for the soldiers to sit in the sun in summer.

To the left side was a large formidable looking gate with three big black hingers held in place with square headed bolts. The latch was a larger round circle. The metal was twisted, like the cough candy twist sweets.

Shall I turn or return to the front of the house? No! Let's try it.

Much to his surprise the gate swung open to reveal what was once a spectacular garden, the grass was not too high as it was winter.

Viewing the rear of the house, large half glass door, he found it would open out onto the patio. A small wall ran round the edge, the whole area covered around half the width of the house. To the right as Nigel looked at the house two steps led to a large white stable style door.

Turning to view down the garden, he saw some garden statues still remained; some in a poor condition, but considering they were well over 100 years old and various occupants had been in the house there doing all right, someone could clean them and possibly repair?

Nigel sat on the wall looking towards the bottom of the garden some 300 yards away. Even more trees. He wondered what they would look like in spring and summer.

'Ahoy there.' Turning to his left he viewed a lady on horseback. As the lady approached Nigel, 'Hello, you look to be daydreaming. Hope I haven't ruined your thoughts,' she said.

'No,' said Nigel 'just thinking of all the things that have happened here over its history. My name's Nigel.'

'Hello, I am Faye,' she replied. 'Do you live local?'

'No, in temporary accommodation now. Is that your horse?' enquired Nigel.

'No' said Faye. 'It belongs to a friend and if I clean out and do other jobs I get to ride him. Do you ride, Nigel?'

'No, never been rich enough, don't know anything about them, definitely don't participate in gambling on them, and I don't like the idea of chasing foxes and other animals with them. Better get down off my high horse now, sorry about that.'

'Don't apologise, Nigel. Just a word that may help. The chap that owns all the rights for hunting and shooting may not see your point of view and he is not known for his tact and diplomacy.'

Nigel thought for a moment, 'Does he wear a cowboy style hat?'

Faye held her head down and raised her eyes. 'Aah, so you have met him then?'

'Yes,' replied Nigel. 'Unfortunately, we have crossed swords, or in our case it was 'crossed sticks'.'

'Nigel, it's up to you. If you're only going to be temporary here, stay out of his way. Don't mis-understand me, he is not known to be violent, but he knows people who just seem to make life a little more difficult, no violence, just difficult. If you intend to live around here, you need to find some olive branches.'

'Well, Faye, thanks for the advice. There seems to be a lot of woodland around here and if I need an olive tree do you know of any?'

Faye smiled, 'Perhaps we will meet again.' With that, she pulled on the horse's bit and walked off towards the woods.

Nigel took his place back on the wall and stared down the garden.

Nigel had had a few girlfriends, some of whom he had been intimate with, but Nigel not being the exciting type spent a lot of time with Mum and Dad, and time down the allotment, and walking with a Firm's Rambling Club.

When he passed his driving test he seemed to have a few more friends, but Mr Parker helped him understand why he had extra friends.

Next to his Mum and Dad, Mr Parker looked out for him. He had an allotment next to Dad's. His was always tidy, not a plant or leaf out of place. Well, that's how it seemed.

Mr Parker worked at the local Engineering Firm as the chief bookkeeper. Nigel had told Mr Parker on several occasions, that sums were the only subject he was any good at, all the other subjects just average.

Chapter 4

On the Job Learning and Life Lessons

On his leaving school Mr Parker offered Nigel work as a trainee bookkeeper, and it would be possible to attend College for extra training and qualification.

Soon it was time to leave school and time for work.

Monday morning came, Mum and Dad stood at the front door, ready to wave him off for his first day at work. Dad had taken the morning off work as holiday, just for this momentous occasion.

As Nigel sat on the Old House wall, he could feel himself cringe, all these years later. That moment was still with him, his Mum and Dad waving as he walked down the street, he could not wait to turn the corner to stop the embarrassment.

Nigel was told where to report when he reached the factory, and Mr Parker came to collect him.

The office where he was going to work had half panel wall with dark brown wood, the top half was woodchip paper, painted cream colour. Desks were staggered apart. Mr Parker sat at the back of the office. As they both walked between the decks, Mr Parker explained the office layout.

That's the Works Foreman's deck, pointing left, that's the Planner's desk, pointing right, that's the buyers, gesturing left, that's the Factory Managers and that's the Plant Managers, as two more desks were picked off.

That's my desk and you will sit at that one.

In the corner was a desk that looked like it belonged in school, but still, it's mine, thought Nigel.

'First and most important job,' said Mr Parker, 'come here!'

He walked through an opening which possibly at some time had a door on it. It led into a small room and in there was all the equipment required to make cups of tea.

'We all have our own tea, milk, sugar and a packet of biscuits. Each person has their own little cupboard and own cup. Now I am going to show you how to make tea, as I like it.'

Nigel remembered saying to Mr Parker, 'I will bring a cup in tomorrow.'

'I purchased a new cup for you, Nigel,' and reached in the cupboard and handed him a cup with the inscription, 'Nigel'. At that moment a bond was made between the two of them that lasted to the present day.

Over the next few years Mr Parker helped Nigel understand the complexity of bookkeeping, but far more important taught Nigel about people.

Mr Parker's secret passion was watching people, how they walked, how they spoke to others, how they stood. He knew if they were not telling the truth, he would never challenge anyone, he just knew.

'The world of business is very difficult, Nigel. Never mind what the person is offering or suggesting, look at the person, it's the person you will need to trust, read the signs.

'You see, Nigel, these people can take a little of something, a few cups of tea, a little of the Company's time, and no one will say anything.

'This is important, Nigel.

'If people think you have taken even a penny, then as a bookkeeper, or accountant, you're finished, please remember that.'

That lesson was drilled into Nigel, something that he would need more than he ever thought possible, later.

Nigel's thoughts went back to Faye. It was her smile that set Nigel back in time.

Nigel's one and only job was the Engineering Company.

Part of the process on the shop floor was assembly work. This was mostly done by three ladies and a girl. Whenever Nigel had to go onto the shop floor it was like a lamb to the slaughter. The female team would pull his leg, make suggestions that made him blush, and sometimes smile in a luring way. It was Faye's smile that drove away the years and plunged Nigel back almost 20 years.

The words rang in Nigel's ear, 'Look at the person, it's the person you will need to trust.' He didn't know if she had a look that could be trusted.

After about 6 months of working, Mr Parker asked Nigel what he had learnt about the other people in the office, 'They all seem OK, Mr Parker,' said Nigel.

'Most have a little secret. Nothing bad, some think they're getting away with it. See if you can find out what it is without asking.'

Nigel watched for a couple of weeks but could not see anything unusual. Reported the lack of results back to Mr Parker.

'I will give you a clue, Tea drinking, read the signs.'

Nigel still had to maintain a high standard of bookkeeping. Mr Parker checked his work almost daily and Nigel wondered if it was to relieve the tension in his own work, that Mr Parker took an interest in others'.

Nigel had now found a new interest alongside work, it was starting to grab his attention.

Then one day Nigel was on the shop floor, trying to avoid the assembly team, when he watched the Foreman go into the canteen.

Morning and afternoon break ran to a strict time frame. The canteen should be closed now so the staff could get food ready for lunch.

Nigel had a quick look through the glass. The foreman was sat at a table with a pot of tea, in the canteen, the tea normally came in a mug.

Continuing with the errand, Mr Parker had sent him on, Nigel returned past the canteen some 20 minutes later and the Foreman was still there. 15 minutes was the time allowed for breaks, thought Nigel.

Need to be sure of this, so for a few days Nigel checked on the canteen and sure enough the foreman had the same routine, a pot of tea and around 20 ~ 25 minutes' break.

Hesitantly, Nigel reported his observation to Mr Parker.

'Correct! And he doesn't pay, thinks, as the Foreman, he is entitled, no big deal in what he is doing but what does it say to other people on the shopfloor?

'Look at the person it's the person you will need to trust,' repeated Mr Parker.

Over the next weeks Nigel observed that the buyer would have a small nip of whiskey in his afternoon tea just a small drop from a half bottle.

A new half bottle would appear every three weeks at the same time as a delivery of stock for the factory.

'Correct again, Nigel,' said Mr Parker.

Once Nigel had understood a little more what to look for and interpret, the observations became a little easier.

Mr Parker had a meeting every day to discuss cash flow, investment financial issues, etc. This meeting was at 11.00 every day on the dot, and lasted no later than 12.30 lunch time.

Nigel had to make Mr Parker's tea for 12.30.

The Factory Manager had flexibility for his break as from time to time he had to deal with Factory matters.

Like the rest of the office, apart from the Foreman, they all shared the brewing room. Like everyone else he had his own tea, sugar and milk and biscuits.

Nigel's role meant that he sometimes needed to be out of the office, checking details, tallying figures. 12.20 was time to make Mr Parker's tea.

I don't remember leaving the sugar bowl there, thought Nigel. It didn't take long for Nigel to work out that just occasionally The Factory Manager would use other people's stores.

Nigel reported this to Mr Parker.

I know, lad, he has been doing it for years, he only needed to ask, what has that done to his reputation?

'Look at the person, it's the person you will need to trust.' Again those words rang in Nigel's ears, again today his mind spoke that sentence.

Nigel thought for a moment, I could have something to eat now. Only had a cup of tea and a slice of bread, can't think how I lost my appetite.

Nigel continued to walk round the building. He could now see the old garages; the scaffolding people had started to erect poles and boards around the building.

As he looked, a small number of Ford Transit vans came up the drive, and stopped outside the big house's door.

Several men jumped out and opened the backs of the vans. One chap went to unlock the house door and pushed it fully open. Men started to unload sheets of plaster boards ready to carry into the house.

'Hang on, not yet,' shouted the man who opened the door, 'covers first.'

The team stopped in their tracks. A lad appeared with two old looking blankets, walked up to the door and threw them over the gloss paint work.

As Nigel watched the unloading, the man was shouting his instruction to the team to start bringing in materials.

The man then turned and spoke to Nigel, 'Best not spoil Rembrandt's work.'

'Rembrandt?' asked Nigel.

'Yes, the painter,' replied the man.

'Oh yes, got it now. What about the paint work inside?' asked Nigel.

'There isn't any paint inside, only done the outside, managed to complete before the poor weather. Things need to be done inside before Rembrandt comes back. He is almost the last in the chain, all the stud walls, stairs, and woodwork are in. The sparky has done the first fix, the plumbers almost finished, he can continue whilst we board out.

'On the outside facing walls we are using new insulated boards, ordinary boards on stud walls inside, insulating you see!

'When the plumbers finished first fix, we set about plastering, big job!

'When we have done, Sparks comes back in for second fix, along with the plumbers then almost done.

'I understand that a modern kitchen is being fitted with all the latest gizmos, even a microwave machine. Not going to catch me ever using one of those,' continued the man.

'Each room is going to have its own identity. There are some form of viewing shelves at that bottom window over there,' pointing to the bottom left window.

'Some rooms upstairs will have en-suite, that's a bathroom next to the bedroom, private like! Then Rembrandt comes back, it's going to look fantastic.

'One of the last jobs is going to be Snagging. The architect will come back for that, a real stickler for detail, she's a lass, not many in this business.

'Someone put their trust in her, but I think it paid off. She's done the Pub, too. Anyway, must crack on. Nice talking to you. Bye.'

Talking to me, thought Nigel. I hardly said a word.

Tummy really rumbling now, Nigel returned to the cottage, made himself a snack and a cup of tea.

The clock chimed the half hour, 4.30. Best do my jobs. I can tackle the paraffin smell now.

Sure enough, he filled both heaters although the kitchen was still lit. He extinguished it, and filled it anyway. That done, both heaters back in place, numerous attempts to set the safety devices finally paid dividends and all three burners were lit.

Time to sort the fire in the sitting room, the trusty routine for taking out the ashes, stick and coal at the ready.

Paper?

I have the chip wrapping from last night still in my pocket. On retrieving the paper, some of the grease and oil had penetrated to the outside and a slightly slimy residue was left in the pocket.

Mmm. Sort that later.

After he made the customary paper, sticks and coal recipe, the fire was on its way.

Now 5.15. There is still some light, but I will stay in now, I need a list of actions. First, put on the kettle and make a cup of tea.

To make a list I need paper and pen. No pen, so a pencil will do. There's one in the car, pencil retrieved. For paper he tore off some of the chip paper that had not been contaminated with fat.

Nigel thought that he must look at the basics first. Food and drink, currently running hand to mouth, so, I need a shopping list for food and drink.

A check of the current situation revealed that he possibly had enough money for the week.

Nigel thought about what he could buy on a budget - a box of porridge, was first on his list. He could have that a couple of days with the honey, a couple with jam.

Next, milk, a couple of bottles. The outside temperature should keep it OK for a few days.

Stew! Sheep's waist coat, or stewing beef from the butchers' that can last two days.

Sausages one evening and a pie another, root veg from the general store.

Bread? See which is cheapest.

Putting the pencil and paper down Nigel went to the kitchen. Having counted the tea bags, he would be OK till Friday. He was OK with toiletries, it was well stocked when he arrived.

Washing clothes? Now, that's going to be an issue, did not see any laundrette in the village. Don't think I have enough money anyway to put in a machine.

Other than that money should be Ok if I am careful.

Not much of a problem really, he had spent 10 years or so watching his parents having to be careful with money.

Now what happens when the money does run out? he thought to himself.

Perhaps Paul could help, I will see him tomorrow. I also need to use the public phone, best make sure I have change.

He was reminded of the handful of change, Mr Parker once gave him, that helped in a tricky situation.

Mr Parker had helped him a lot, not the handful of change, but his entire career and learning about people.

Nigel was aware some people think it stupid, but they are wrong.

He has come to understand and make informed decisions about people. It helps to define who helps and those doing harm. A skill he needed to put to maximum use whilst in the cottage.

Thinking back neither Nigel nor Mr Parker never let on what they learnt about other people, a little like Nigel and Raymond.

Thinking back, Nigel must have been about twenty. It was one early Saturday morning, he was outside cleaning his car. As he finished the final wipe of the windscreen a voice said, 'Hello Nigel.'

Turning round he saw a big set chap about the same age as himself.

Nigel looked into his face and eyes. The last time he saw them, they were red and sore. They looked like a monster's eyes; however, he knew who they belonged to.

'Hello Raymond, how are you keeping?'

'Really good, thank you,' he replied.

'Just visiting?' asked Nigel.

'No, Nigel, I've moved back in with Mum and her new husband. I like him he's smart and gentle, has his own business, transport and storage over on the Industrial Estate. I work for him. I have to start at the bottom, work hard, keep my nose clean. If I do OK, I can start and move up the ladder and make the tea.

'Not really. I can now drive, I was taught by my uncle on the farm. I passed my driving test, then only a few weeks ago passed my HGV.

'It was tough on the farm, Nigel, but it taught me a lot. Bullying and fighting is foolish and a rubbish thing to do. I hope to be more like you now. Bye, be seeing you.'

Raymond continued walking down the street.

'I won't,' shouted Nigel, in a light-hearted voice.

'I know, you never have. You're a good man, Nigel.'

Nigel grinned, 'Got the cream,' said his dad, coming out the front door.

'No, Dad, just something that someone said.'

'Off down the allotment, are you coming?' asked Father.

'Better do, someone needs to stop you talking all day with the other chaps.'

Nigel nipped inside, collected a coat and joined his dad.

The allotment looked good, not as good as Mr Parker's but no one's ever did. There were a few beautiful flowers in the corner of Dad's plot ready to take to Mum.

Nigel stood looking at them, then heard a soft voice,

'They are really lovely.'

'Yes, they're for Mum. Dad grows them for her.'

'My name's Helen, Helen Parker. That's my dad's plot.'

Yes, I am Nigel. I work for your dad at the factory, not seen you here before.'

'Not really my thing, never has been. I am at University and only home for a few days so Mum said I should come down for an hour and spend time with dad.'

'What are you studying?' asked Nigel.

'History, Design and Mathematics. Three more years. Anyway nice to see you, Nigel. Look after yourself, bye.'

'Yes, bye.'

It would be over a decade before he would see her again.

'Let's get Mum some flowers and off home, should we, Nigel?'

'OK Dad.'

I guess the afternoon was in front of the TV. Watching wrestling. Mum and I would get told off for picking the wrong numbers on the pools. Much the same as ever. How I wish I could do that just once more.

This time he could not contain the tears.

He put a lump of coal on the fire and putting the guard in place, went to bed.

'I love you,' he spoke out loud.

Chapter 5

In Need of Cash

The night was kind, he didn't hear the clock chime that many times. He lay awake in bed for a few moments then got up, washed and dressed.

Going downstairs and into the kitchen, on with the kettle, then into the sitting room, poking the ash revived the embers. A couple of sticks and a few pieces of coal and the fire started to burn.

Passing the clock, 3.30.

3.30? No wonder I did not hear it that much in the night. It has stopped.

Tea made, breakfast would have to be toast and honey, not too much honey as it must last two more breakfasts.

Nigel went to the car to check the time on the dashboard- 9.40. That's late, he thought.

Still no place to go in a hurry.

Back inside adjusting the time, and winding up the clock, it didn't seem so cold as it had been. Still hat, scarf, gloves are the order of the day, granny's shopping trolley, money and off.

Just as he was about to pass the house, he remembered the shopping list still in the sitting room. Leaving the wheelie bag behind he nipped back to collect it.

Back at the wheelie trolley he started to walk down the drive.

'Don't leave that there again, mate, the tractor could not get by,' shouted one of the plasterers.

Funny! thought Nigel.

As he walked down the drive he smiled, that was witty.

'Morning, how's it going?' asked Nigel to the lad up the scaffolding.

'I can do it,' the man shouted.

The sun was shining, still a bit of a nip in the air but nice.

Crossing the road, he could see diggers at the side of the Pub ripping up the car park and a third one digging a trench. Two large lorries were being filled with the spoils. There stood Baby.

'Morning, you're not hanging about.'

'Morning, Nigel. No, we need to crack on. The Pub will have to close. Without money coming in it's going to be tough so the sooner we finish the better.'

'What's the trench for?' asked Nigel.

'It's part of the extension, a restaurant here, a conservatory next to it and a new kitchen there.

' It's no secret they had a similar offer to Love and me. 5-year loan with a percentage of the profit and a chance to buy back.

'I hope they do it. Sorry Nigel, got to sort the digger drivers out, see you later.'

With that Baby disappeared round the back of a lorry.

Continuing his walk, trolley in hand, he turned the corner by the Post Office to see Paul, the vicar.

'Morning, Paul.'

'Morning, Nigel, a beautiful morning.'

'So, it is,' replied Nigel. 'Do you have a moment, Paul?'

'Yes, let's go into the house and Mrs Bright will hopefully have the kettle on.'

Entering the house Paul shouted, 'Hi Mrs Bright, I am back, and I have a friend with me.'

'I will get another cup,' she replied.

'How can I help?' Paul asked.

'I need some money,' Nigel replied.

'Best come into the study.' Both men retired to a small room decked out with all sorts of paraphernalia.

'Best take a seat, Nigel. We do have a social fund, but you have to...'

'Sorry, Paul. I need to stop you there. Sorry, it came out all wrong. When I said I need money, I have money but not enough.'

With that the door opened and Mrs Bright came in with a tray, two cups of tea, sugar bowl and a few biscuits. Both men politely thanked her and she left.

'Can you please close the door, Mrs Bright?' asked Paul.

'Sure! Whatever it is, it's no concern of mind,' she snapped.

'Look Paul, let me start yet again. I have enough cash on me to last me till Friday, so I can buy food and drink for this week. I have some money, but not here, I do not bank with the bank in the village and they will need at least 3 days to clear anything. I currently do not have a permanent address, so I am hoping you can help. Can I have sent to you Postal orders, crossed in your name? You can change them at the Post Office for me.'

'Nigel, it will be a pleasure to help, I will right down this address.'

'Don't bother Paul, I know it, thanks,' said Nigel.

Both men sat making idle chit chat whilst drinking the tea and sharing the plate of biscuits.

'Are you enjoying it here, do you think you will move on?' asked Paul.

'Just for now Paul, I need to park me and mine in the same basket as your Church, God, and collection plates, if that's OK with you?' said Nigel.

'Well, the collection plate. Anyway you don't have any money,' replied Paul.

Nigel laughed. 'So true,' he said.

'Must be on my way, shopping to do, phone call to make, thank Mrs Bright for the tea and biscuits.' Both men reached the front door and shook hands.

'I will see you Friday for the cash, if that's OK?' said Nigel.

'I am sure it will,' replied Paul.

Nigel went on his way. Paul was left thinking, how did he know the vicarage address?

Closing the door, Mrs Bright was collecting the tray, 'I shouldn't give him money. You don't know anything about him.'

'Mrs Bright, I can assure you I will not be giving him any money.'

'Good!' she replied sternly.

Nigel's first stop was the butchers'. He joined the small queue and was soon at the front.

'Morning,' said the butcher, 'what a beautiful morning. What can I get you?'

'I am going to make a stew, I need enough meat for two days, please,' said Nigel.

'Which meat do you require?' asked the butcher.

'A cheap cut of beef or lamb, please. Either... it's all down to cost,' said Nigel.

'I can do you a bit of lamb that should cook up nicely, anything else?'

'Yes, please. Two sausages and a small meat pie. That's all. Thanks,' answered Nigel.

'Hope you've got more shopping to do, damn big bag for these few bits.'

'Yes, just a few more,' he said.

Paying up with high denominational currency Nigel left the shop. He could hear giggling back in the shop, but it didn't sound malicious.

General store next, for the root vegetables, oats, milk and bread.

Now with a pocket full of change Nigel needed the public phone.

Both phone boxes were available. Parking the wheelie bag outside the box, definitely not enough room in there for him and the bag.

Nigel made the call which luckily ended before he put in his last coin.

Nigel could see in the distance, clouds starting to form. Could rain later, best get a move on.

Passing the Pub, Nigel couldn't resist having a look around the back, the trench was almost right across the whole length of the Pub.

Two machines were cutting up the tarmac, piling it into lorries. Earth, rocks and stone were everywhere.

The third machine plunged the back bucket into the trench, pulling great clods of earth, before swinging round to deposit them into a second lorry.

The noise and smell were intoxicating, movement everywhere.

A new and different noise came from the front of the Pub.

Nigel went to investigate, a skip lorry was unloading two big skips, and placing both by the Pub doors. One skip was inside the other. The driver removed the chains from the bottom skip and fixed them to the top one. Back in the cab he lifted the top skip out and placed it by the side of the first. Both now sat side by side.

The driver jumped out of the cab and unhooked the chains. He looked over at Nigel and shouted whilst pointing at the wheelie bag, 'If my boss needs a new skip, I will tell him to contact you.'

'Hello again, Nigel.'

'Hello Baby, what are they for?'

'Some of the inside walls are coming out, and new ones being built, the manky carpets done for, that's going in the skip. Part of the bars will be taken out to make way for a smaller new one.

'A stone floor throughout, and the fireplace will stay in, which is nice.

'When this is finished it will be a Pub the village can be proud of. All the design work has been done by a small team, headed by a young woman - the same team that designed the changes to the Old House.

'She's hard to work for, but she knows what she needs to get done and not afraid to listen.

'It's helped our family business, we have always strived to do good work and with her help we are slowly picking up a little more work.

'I hope we work together even more in the future. See you, Nigel.'

'Yes, bye, Baby.'

Crossing the road, he stood at the bottom of the drive. 'I am sure someone's making this driveway longer.'

With his best foot forward, he was soon nearing the top. A large part of the garage roof was off and the tiles stacked on the boards of the scaffolding.

'Thought you were supposed to be building it up, not pulling it down,' shouted Nigel.

'Hi, Nigel,' came a reply.

'We need to take off the roof to align the brick work. Those clowns that rented it off the last owner used it to repair cars. Looks like they often hit the walls with cars or trucks.

'If that's not bad enough they put in a wooden beam to lift out engines. It wasn't built for that sort of thing, damn lucky the building didn't collapse on them.

'Anyway, it's bent a couple of walls that need sorting. They did a runner when the owner did, left all sorts of toxic stuff around the back, all cleared up now.

'What do you think, Nigel, will be in here when finished? A Rolls Royce, Aston Martin, Ferrari or a Lamborghini?'

'If you don't get it right the new owner may not be able to put a push bike in it.'

'I can do it,' the lad shouted.

'I'm sure you can,' Nigel shouted back.

Outside the house was an array of different vans and a few cars. Leaving his bag behind, smiling to himself, 'I don't think the tractor will be coming.'

He couldn't help taking a look. Standing outside and looking through the open door, he saw men were everywhere, bags of plaster piled high, buckets of water, boards, tools, lots of dust.

I will have a better look some other time, thought Nigel.

Collecting the wheelie bag, Nigel made his way to the cottage's back door.

He decanted the contents of the bag. Most items went into the bread bin that sat on the floor, a couple of potatoes and sausages were set aside for tea.

Eat the sausages today with mash, make the stew tomorrow and eat the pie tomorrow, stew Wednesday and Thursday.

Following the routine Nigel made the fire in the sitting room before starting dinner.

Sausages and potatoes cooked, the spuds needed mashing, not the horrible sound again, need to add a masher to the shopping list, a few Lar-

Lar later, dinner ready, plate in hand, with a cup of tea in the other, Nigel settled down in front of the fire.

Putting the food free plate on the floor, Nigel thought a dash of brown sauce would have been nice. 'Perhaps I will put it on a new shopping list, along with a masher, but can only shop after collecting the cash from Paul on Friday.'

Until then Nigel had three days to fill without spending any cash.

That needed thinking about, he thought.

Now what? A little early to go to bed. Mmm, no playing cards, could have played solitaire, a game he had not played for years.

Nigel did play cards with Mum and Dad. Sometimes he played chess with Dad. This was Nigel's favourite of all the board games.

Mum wasn't keen on chess, she was an ace draught player and very often beat them both, the family was Even Stevens with dominoes.

Anyway, thought Nigel, no cards, best do the washing up.

Pots and pans clean and stacked away, a small Scotch was in order before bed.

Scotch in hand Nigel settled down and watched the flames dance and twist around the coal.

Things are happening quickly he thought, the Pub started, some of the car park has been dug up, there's a trench across the back, skips on the front ready for stripping the insides.

There is a small team on the garage, and men all over the old house. After that they will be starting on this old cottage, and I must leave, still should have at least a month or more.

I wonder if it's possible to find a circular walk around the area. That could be taken care of tomorrow.

Until the early part of last year Nigel was a keen walker. The Engineering Company had a social club with regular activities - Rambling, Darts team, Badminton, and Fishing.

A small group was set up to run one-off events, sometimes more serious than others.

They entered a charity raft race, took part in the local carnival, sorted the Christmas parties.

It was good. Sometimes the Company would offer money to support an event, mostly the Charity ones, but still very good.

Nigel was a member of the Rambling club, which met twice a month at the weekends for walks and one night a month to discuss where the next two walks would go.

Mostly local areas were found, getting to the start of the walk using cars, but every now and then as funds allowed, a minibus was hired and they would travel greater distances.

Over the years Nigel and the club had been to some fascinating places, but never walked this area. Hopefully should be interesting, tomorrow's walk would be the first for well over a year.

As he watched the last few flames disappear into a red glow, time to add a lump of coal, guard well in place, time for bed.

Upstairs in the bathroom Nigel checked on his toiletries, they should be OK until the weekend.

Looking at the heater, he felt the evening was not that cold as previous nights and wondered about turning off one burner to save fuel.

Yes, I will turn one off. Taking off the front Nigel knocked the heater and both safety devices sprang into action and extinguished the flames. Mmm.. guess I will turn them both off tonight!

Quickly undressing, he jumped between the sheets, pulling them under his chin and spoke, 'I Love You.'

Apart from one visit to the bathroom in the night, Nigel slept well.

Washed and dressed, he was downstairs filling the kettle for his morning tea, nipping into the sitting room. The fire was still lit, the customary couple of pieces of wood and a little more coal and the flames started up again.

This morning's breakfast will be porridge with added honey.

If I am walking, I will need the energy.

Soon Nigel was in front of the fire enjoying the feast. Breakfast done, he left the pan and bowl in cold water, so the residue of the oats did not stick, a trick his Mum had shown him.

Luckily, despite leaving home in a hurry Nigel had thrown into the Walker's box a strong pair of boots, not walking boots but they would do.

Stepping outside he was taken aback on how mild it was. Still he went to take hat, scarf and gloves. He thought, you never know.

Walking toward the house, he saw an array of vans parked up and the sound of workmen and their radios could be heard.

The plasterer that Nigel had spoken to before was at the back of the last van. He turned around. 'Hello again,' he said.

'Morning, how's it going?' Nigel asked

'Really well. If this weather holds, and with the architect agreeing to dot and dab, it should dry out in the next few days, don't you think?'

'Yes', said Nigel.

'Nice talking to you,' said the plasterer, 'must get on, bye.'

Mmm. Good idea, dot and dab. Absolutely no idea what he is talking about, thought Nigel.

Chapter 6

Out for a Walk

As Nigel continued along the drive, the young chap, shouted, 'Morning, where are you off to this morning?'

'Morning, I am off for a walk, I would like a circular one, but not sure of the area and I don't have a map.'

'Are you up for about 8 miles? You can do about 12 if you wish,' said the lad.

'Think 8 will do,' was the reply.

'OK, down the drive, turn right. Best cross over, no pavement on this side, better to stay on the pavement on the other side. It's safer. After about ½ an hour there's a road on the right. Cross over and follow that. That will take you to the other side of those woods,' pointing in the general direction of the lake and bomb crater.

'Keep going along the road, again about ½ hour. You will see a broken farm gate. I think there is a signpost that reads bridleway or foot path, can't remember. Look for that, you should see hoof prints. One or two riders use it. Now keep following the path. It runs to the back of the woods which are at the back of the Old House. Keep going, and keep going, and you will come to a road.

'Now if you're feeling good then cross the road, it will take you down to the river. Follow it upstream to the bridge at the bottom of the village. It brings you out by the tractor shop.

'If you don't fancy that, then right turn when you come out of the edge of the wood, that will take you past the Captain's House. Then you come to the farm. You could nip through. There it comes out by the cottage.

'If you decide to continue past the farm you will get to the Church. Turn right and you will be back here. If you're really feeling fit stay by the river and it will bring you out behind the Pub where Baby, Love are working.'

'Sounds OK,' said Nigel. 'I will see how I feel after the 8 miles.'

'The route I have just told you about is the edge of all the land that belongs to the Old House. The extra 4 miles also belongs to the 'The Old House'. It had the fishing rights at one time, perhaps still does.'

'The land finishes at the bridge. It comes up the back of the shops just past the Church and hall, runs left along the road to here, big old estate! I think it's well over 150 acres, what do you think?'

'I think,' said Nigel, 'the chap who bought this place better cancel the Rolls Royces, Aston Martins, Ferrari, or Lamborghini for an old Land Rover, or depending on the job you do. Get that push bike.'

'Cheeky,' replied the lad.

Nigel set off down the drive. He stopped for a moment. He had not really studied the view, the rolling green field down to the river, a small copse lying to the right. With the sun shining it was a joy to behold. A green and pleasant land for sure, so different from his hometown, which he is never likely to live in again.

Crossing the road and staying on the pavement as instructed, he found the Old House soon disappeared, being blocked from view by the brick wall, bushes, trees and then the hedge row.

After about ½ hour a small lane could be seen on the right. The lane was easily wide enough for two vehicles, but he still needed to be careful of any traffic.

Either side of the lane was a grassed verge running alongside the lane, with the tall hedge rows. Nothing to see really.

On the right was a small stream which ran down to the main road then into a pipe, disappearing under the roadway.

As Nigel progressed up the lane it was noticeable that it was starting to rise.

Not being able to view how long the lane and hill was, because of the hedge row, he had little option but to keep on going.

To his right appeared a farm gate. It was in tack. Now the lad had said a 'Broken farm gate'. This would be a good time for a little breather.

Nigel opened the gate and went through to get a better view.

He could see part of the Old House in the distance, and what he thought was a small area of the green house. This must have been the entrance to the garden that supplied the food over the years to the House.

Nigel stayed for a few moments to listen to the birds singing, then having regained some of his breath he returned to the lane, and continued up the hill.

The lane had started to curve slightly to the left and was starting to narrow with passing places for two vehicles to pass each other.

The hedge rows were a lot smaller now, supposed to give a better view of any oncoming traffic.

The lane had started to level out a little. The broken farm gate appeared on the right. There was a sign pointing to the right - 'Foot Path'.

The ground was not too boggy so easy to walk on.

Now high up and being exposed to a slight breeze, it was still very nice. The sun was shining on his back. Lucky to have picked a nice day for a walk.

The farmland to his left was still divided up with hedge rows and the fields were, *field size*. Not being from the country, Nigel did not have a clue how big an acre is, still it looked great instead of the massive fields some farms have.

To his right the hawthorn and thicket hedge, the worn grass showed clearly this was the correct path. Behind the hedge was wood land, still bare of foliage, but the sun would soon shine enough light and warmth to tease the leaves out.

Continuing to walk and lost in the sound of the breeze and the birds, Nigel spied a small gap in the hedge. A port hole size hole. Bending down and moving side to side trying to view past all the trees he thought he could see the Old House off in the distance.

The lad had said the wood ran at the back of the Old House. He didn't think it would be this far back.

As he was about to resume his walk a horse and rider appeared.

'Hello, Nigel,' said the rider.

'Hello, Faye, what a beautiful day to be out and about. Are you off anywhere special?'

'No, just a short ride,' she said.

'We come along here, then through the gate, turn left, a short distance down the lane, and onto the estate. Don't like being on the road, cars come round far too fast. Where are you going?'

'I was told about a circular walk around the estate starting at the Pub and ending back there,' said Nigel.

'Good place to finish, it's got to be 10 to 12 miles. You will be ready for a pint when you're finished,' joked Faye.

'You can't get beer there now. It's closed for a few weeks,' Nigel replied.

'Oh yes, I remember someone saying it is being revamped. What with that and the Old House, some people have money. See you again. Enjoy your walk.'

'Thanks, enjoy the ride.' With that Faye rode on towards the lane.

Nigel continued along his route. The sun was still shining but had gone behind the trees. The path split into two. The left side clearly showed hoof prints, the path to the right went through a kissing gate. Choosing the right-hand side he continued.

The neat hedge had given way to a more overgrown array of plants and bushes. An old barred wire fence was partly buried in the branches.

Nigel walked into the woods. The woodland smell was really nice, but it did not last long.

Over a stile and he was soon out on the road.

There was a fantastic view over the valley with the river snaking its way past under the bridge, downstream, and the road making its way up the hill with a sharp bend almost 90°.

At this point it was easy to see that not every vehicle had made the bend as skid marks, bits of vehicles and smashed plants and bushes lay testament to their failure to make the bend.

Nigel now needed to take stock, was he up to that extra 4 miles or so, or should he take the shorter route?

Whichever, he needed to cross the road to the pavement.

A few hundred yards took him past the 'Captain's House' a modest building, three windows across the top, and one either side of the door, a single step up and a porch with two extremely big wooden supports - all very well kept, clean and tidy.

The property was surrounded by a garden with a small drive to the garage. Add all the features together and with a view, it was a genuinely nice property.

Continuing to walk, he saw the next set of buildings was the farm. This stood well back off the road and looked like a typical farm! The lad had said cutting through the farmyard it would take Nigel back to the cottage. Nigel decided to continue, but which way?

Nigel did not know what time it was, but it seemed that the sun would shine for a little longer and with a second or third wind, he decided to walk to the river.

Going through the narrow slot in the stone wall he headed to the river. Again the farmer had left in the hedge rows, so from the road Nigel had to wind his way over three stiles to access the river path.

A clear well-trodden path ran parallel with the riverbank.

The river at this point was about 100 yards wide and looked deep. Not that he could tell as it was a murky brown colour, he just had a feeling it was deep and cold!

As he progressed upstream, he noticed various points were obviously used by fishermen as the banks had been cleared.

There was still some bird singing. Nigel spotted a kingfisher as it darted from tree to tree.

In the distance there was a sign. Once close enough it read: 'Private waters, day tickets available from The Captain's House or the Iron Monger, High Street.'

And a couple of phone numbers were printed along the bottom.

I wonder how much that cost to fish, thought Nigel.

Moving around the bend in the river, Nigel could see the bridge, not long now!

It seemed a bit of a slog to get to the bridge. Climbing the steps onto the road Nigel needed a few moments.

He knew the bench he almost had his fish and chips was close by, so headed for that. With a sigh he sat down.

The noise from the shops dragging in their wares alerted Nigel. It must be about 4 or 5 o'clock, and he had not had any lunch, but he never intended to be out this long and to be fair, not really thought about food, until now!

OK, he thought, last bit. Striding out, he headed for home, or the cottage anyway!

Approaching the Pub, he could hear the machines working away and the sound of earth, tarmac and concrete falling into the waiting lorries.

As he approached the front of the Pub one of the skips was brimming with all sorts of items - old tables, chairs, carpets, part of the bar, curtains and more.

Nigel wondered if there was anything left inside. As he stood watching, the dart board came flying out landing in the skip.

Then from around the corner came the Captain, distinctive by his hat, and Love. They shook hands.

The captain headed towards Nigel and as he passed, said, 'Are you still here?'

Nigel decided it was best to keep quiet, and moving forward he saw Love waiting for him.

'Hi, Nigel, told you things were going to get better. The Captain wants an extension on his house and larger pens, and is asking us to do it as long as the lass that designed this Pub is on board with us. If we get our finger out, we can start it at the same time as we do up the cottage. Sorry Nigel, it was a bit insensitive. You will need to be out of the cottage.'

'Don't worry, Love, my concern at the moment is getting back to it. Your lad gave me an idea on a circular walk. I think I've been around the edge of the 'Old House Estate'. Now I have to tackle that drive.'

'That's a long way,' said Love, 'the estate's got to be over 150 acres. Must be 10 miles or more. Come, I will give you a lift in the van.'

'Thanks, Love, I've done this much, I have to finish. But thanks, anyway,' said Nigel.

As he went across the road he ascended the drive. The steps got smaller and smaller but finally reaching the garage, 'Made it,' he shouted to the lad.

'When you were halfway down the drive, I shouted at you, 'you can do it,' but you didn't hear me.'

Nigel just raised his hand, too tired to reply. He moved on.

Finally opening the door of the cottage, he sat down, looking at the clock. Almost 5.30.

No! can't stop now, a cup of tea needed, and I have to make the stew for tomorrow and Thursday.

Taking a few moments to think, Nigel decided on a plan of action. Kettle on, more coal on the fire, prepare the veg, and a visit to the toilet, not in that order, toilet first.

On entering the bathroom, he found it a little chilly. He needed to light one of those burners, toilet first! Toilet bits complete, heater lit, kettle boiled, time for tea.

Think I will have jacket potato with the pie, I am not scraping the fork on that pan. Oven on full, potato pricked, in it went.

Nigel picked a selection of vegetables. He peeled and sliced and placed in cold water ready for cooking tomorrow.

For some reason, the fire had remained lit in the sitting room, so only needed a couple of sticks and a few pieces of coal and on it went again.

Turning the oven down he placed the pie on the bottom shelf.

A second brew was in order, but not before washing the pots from this morning's breakfast. Once that was complete, kettle on, ready for that second brew.

Tea poured, he checked the contents of the oven, the pie and potato were cooked. Removing them from the oven and slicing the potato in half, he added a knob of butter. When plated up Nigel retired to the sitting room.

Food and drink consumed, he sat back in the chair.

Nigel thought to himself, been a good day today, possibly the best since I arrived, great walk, nice to hear the birds singing.

There was a real sense of urgency around all the building work. Baby, Love and the team clearly are aware that the Pub does not have any income so need to work hard to try and get it reopened as soon as possible, whilst maintaining the high standards expected by the architect.

Then the Old House with its army of men dotting and dabbing everywhere, the garage too was making progress. I wonder how long the Old House would take to finish and they start on the cottage. Well my packing won't take long.

Which reminds me, he thought, I wonder where I can get my clothes washing sorted? Perhaps I will get some washing powder on Friday and hand wash?

Putting a lump of coal on the fire, fixing the guard in place time, for bed, you had a busy day, Nigel, he said to himself. Evening routine complete, climbing between the heavy sheets, 'I love You' had barely left his lips, and he was asleep!

Chapter 7

In Need of a Toilet?

Nigel woke to the chimes of the clock. Is it 7 or 8 o'clock? Not sure if I heard the first chime or not.

Climbing out of bed, he washed and dressed and made his way to the kitchen. Kettle on for the first brew of the day, then into the sitting room, a poke at the fire, not so lucky today, the fire's gone out.

I will make that in a moment, tea first.

Glancing at the clock, he saw it was neither 7 or 8, but 9 o'clock.

Good job, I do not have to be anywhere important today, he thought, smiling to himself.

Tea made, time for breakfast. Porridge would be the staple breakfast until Saturday when he could purchase more provisions. Whilst the breakfast was cooking, he lit the burner under the veg.

Putting a little oil in the frying pan he browned the meat. Once brown it was placed in the pan with the veg.

Nigel took some water from the vegetables and washed it around the frying pan. This could help with the flavour. It still looked a bit wishy washy, needed body, and he didn't have any gravy powder.

Guinness! Where's that tin? he thought.

Kneeling on the floor, he spotted it under the sink, it had rolled under. Quickly retrieved, the contents were poured into the pan. It looked better, but let's taste it later, he thought.

The porridge was ready, but the fire in the sitting room was not set.

Mmm, thought Nigel, do I turn the breakfast right down and make the fire or stand in here and eat it.

Eat it now, straight out of the pan, no one likes burnt porridge.

Leaning against the sink, pan handle in one hand and spoon in the other, a broad grin came on his face, like a naughty schoolboy doing something he shouldn't.

If Mum could see me now, I would get a telling off, he thought.

Breakfast finished, he removed the ashes from the fire in the sitting room and relayed paper and sticks ready for lighting, but it didn't seem that cold. I will light it later.

Returning to the kitchen Nigel turned the burner under the stew as low as it would go. That's going to take a few hours, which is good, he thought.

He wanted to investigate more around the estate. He couldn't be long or go too far otherwise the dinner would burn.

I would like to see the lake, bomb crater and the old garden, he thought.

It was overcast but not cold, still taking coat, hat, scarf and gloves 'just in case', off he set.

He needed to pass the front of the Old House to get to the lake. There seemed more vans than yesterday, same amount of noise with all the banging and radios as yesterday; must be dotting and dabbing that makes the noise.

From the front of the house, it was not possible to see the lake, but a few yards' walk, and one end could be seen. The more he travelled down the more of the lake came into view. It was pretty big.

Nigel stood looking into the water, trying to find movement. Then to his right he could see small fish, possibly stickle backs - a good possibility that the water had recovered, and life had returned. Nigel stayed there for some time hoping to see other animals, but perhaps too early in the year or too cold for frogs, toads and newts.

He wondered what fish had been in there prior to the poisoning. Suppose Sargeant Darwin would know, but not to ask him, best to keep away from the law, they could ask too many questions.

Nigel walked around the lake, looking back at the house. Parts of it could be seen depending on which side of the lake he was on and the height of the slope.

At the highest part he could see part of the bomb crater.

Walking across, he could see the extent of the blast. The bomb appeared to have landed into the curvature of the ground and possibly because of the hill the main blast was directed towards the road and not the house. At least that's what Nigel thought, but what did he know? Still unsure of dot and dabbing.

However, it was clear what work Mr Bye senior had done before being stopped due to investigation work, and I guess he never came back.

Nigel stood staring at the crater, thinking about the damage that one bomb could do, and why would you need two lakes anyway?

The clouds moved over to allow the sun to peek through. For a few moments the light danced on the lake.

Nigel walked back over to the lake side, this time to the highest point.

He had not noticed before, what a stunning view it was, overlooking the Valley, and with the lake in the foreground, it was a view like no other. Somehow it needed to be given the reverence it deserved.

Nigel now needed to explore the old garden. He had seen it a few days before, but this time wanted to find the green lane he found yesterday. He kept over more to the left, away from the Old House.

The walk took longer than he thought it should. He was about to give up thinking he had made a mistake when he came across what he thought was the old route to the garden.

At this point the ground was fairly level. Looking down at the ground, Nigel could see hoof prints, so it was a fair assumption this was the way from the Lane to the old garden, the one Faye spoke about yesterday.

It was the garden Nigel was really interested to see.

It didn't take long to find what he was looking for, but what he failed to spot before was that the garden was on two levels. Because of the slope and the greenery reclaiming the earth it was not easy to define, bigger than Dad's allotment.

He was wondering how much food could be grown. It had kept the Old House going with all its staff, then the soldiers, then the boy, mostly with potatoes. Forget the OAP, they possibly never saw any of it that went to market.

But nevertheless, good honest food, obviously seasonal, like Dad's allotment, different food at different times of the year, and with that greenhouse, even more produce.

Walking over to the large glass structure, he found despite some panes missing, it looked sturdy and with some trestles inside it could produce some seedling for the garden, possibly tomatoes. Someone could be busy all year round.

The only other thing to look at, was the broken-down building, simple enough structure. It looked as if it had been a single-story house at one time. The windows had been bricked up, perhaps a change of use sometime in the past, the door proudly supporting a lift and latch door handle.

Opening the door and looking in, he saw it was empty apart from a pigeon that flew out of the hole in the roof making Nigel jump.

It didn't seem that deep, the back wall was wonky, poorly erected, so Nigel decided to move out and have a look around the back of the structure.

What seemed to have happened decades ago, it looked as if a tree had destroyed the back of what was a property. The bricks had been put back up on the rear of the house. It looked a bit unstable, but Nigel guessed it had been there for years so must be sort of OK.

He was hoping to revisit the back of the Old House if the gate was open.

He would like to have another look at the garden behind the house. Luckily it was not locked. However not so quiet and peaceful as it was on Sunday. This time all the doors and windows were open and with the men inside working and the radios playing loudly it was busy enough inside.

Passing the stable style door, he could not resist a look inside. This looked like the kitchen, with various copper pipes protruding from the plaster, lots of electrical cables coming out of metal boxes that were buried in the plaster all around the room. These were positioned at two different heights, some low to the floor, the others about waist high.

Numerous cables were dropping down from the ceiling.

There was an unusual smell coming out of the house, not unpleasant, just one he had not encountered before. Perhaps something to do with dotting and dabbing, he thought.

Nigel quickly turned round and made headway down the garden, just in case someone asked what he was doing.

Passing the statues, he spied a small bench to the side of the garden slightly behind a bush, not easily seen from the house.

Nigel decided to take a few moments and listen to the birds. While the sounds of the radio could still be heard it was not loud enough to drown the sounds of the birds singing.

As he sat rabbits ran around the bottom of the garden by the edge of the woods, then without warning darted into the under growth.

'Morning,' came a voice.

'Morning,' replied Nigel.

'Nice to see someone enjoying the surroundings and the wildlife, can I ask what you are doing here?' said the man.

'As you say, just enjoying the outdoors. You look like you're working on the house. Are you dotting and dabbing?' asked Nigel.

'No,' he replied, 'I am skimming at the moment. Just nipped out for a cigarette and saw you sitting here.'

'Yes, just sitting waiting for my dinner to cook.'

The plasterer started to look around.

'I am not cooking it here. It's back at the cottage on low heat,' pointing in the general direction of the aforementioned dwelling.

'You're the chap with the big shopping bag on wheels.'

Yes, that's me,' said Nigel,

'OK, see you,' said the man.

So, there are dot and dabbers and skimmers, still none the wiser, Nigel thought.

Continuing to enjoy the moment he sat for a while.

Nigel decided to investigate the woods in front of him.

The woods had not been managed for some time and the outer area had nettles and brambles, and a few fallen branches.

Nigel made his way past the undergrowth. The wood was a little more open. There was only about 200 yards and Nigel came to a hedge. Peering through he could see what he thought was a path and surmised that this was the path he had walked earlier, possibly where he met Faye.

Now not sure of the time, he thought he should return to the cottage and check on dinner.

Making his way back the same way he came was a little easier due to his flattening some of the undergrowth.

Returning to the garden he was greeted by another worker from the house.

'If you need the toilet there are port-a-loos round there, better than hiding behind bushes,' said the man.

'I didn't need the toilet I am just being nosey, are you a dot and dabber or a skimmer?' asked Nigel.

The man looked at Nigel sideways.

'Neither. I am one of the plumbing team. I am out here writing a list of materials for delivery next week. Those guys in there are really motoring. The plumbing team and the sparks need to be ready to move in.

'It's not going to be my team that lets the project down. The lass in charge will have some one's guts for garters if it's late finishing, and it's not going to be mine.

'If this is late then the Pub will be late and Baby, Love will not be happy. When they say a job will be finished on time, it better be finished on time and to the highest standard.

'Must crack on. You know where the Thunder box is if you need it.'

Nigel took a moment, Baby, Love, dot and dab, skimmers. Thunder box, what are people talking about?

Go check dinner, he thought.

On entering the cottage, he felt the sweet smell of food hit his nostrils.

As he removed the pan lid, steam gently rose up. A quick poke with a pointed knife on the root veg indicated that possibly a couple of hours' cooking should do the trick. Returning to the sitting room, Nigel checked on the time - 3.10.

Still with his hat and coat on, Nigel ventured out again this time in the opposite direction up the green lane. He had been up there once looking for a stick. This time he hoped not to bump into the Captain.

Captain, he thought - a seafaring man or army, he wondered?

Whichever one, it didn't do much for his personality or manners.

Walking along he noticed a metal object hanging from a branch, cone-shaped like an upside-down ice cream cone, only much bigger with a circular trough around its base. It hung about 18" from the floor.

Getting closer to have a look at the base he found it was full of seeds and pellets. What's that for? he wondered.

Emerging from the undergrowth, he saw the farmer he had encountered on Friday.

'Good afternoon,' said Nigel.

'Hello again, needed the toilet, did you?'

What's with the toilet thing? thought Nigel.

'No just looking at the cone-shaped thing over there.'

The farmer bent down for a better view, 'It's food for the pheasants.'

'That's nice that someone feeds them,' said Nigel.

'No,' replied the farmer.

'They are being fed but only to keep them nearby. If you feed the birds then they stay close by, then the Captain and his paying invitees get to bag more birds, makes him a tidy profit.

'The feeder hangs from the tree to prevent rats getting to the feed from the ground, but they only then travel up the tree over the branch and jump into the trough and munch on the grain. I've seen them do it.'

'Do you shoot?' asked Nigel.

'I am not keen on rats. They do a lot of damage and can bring in disease, so we have cats on the farm. They tend to discourage the rodents. Shooting birds is OK if you are going to eat them, not for so called sport.'

'How about you, do you shoot?' asked the farmer.

'Not me, not too keen on guns. Sooner or later people can get hurt.'

Why did I say that? thought Nigel.

'How true that is!' replied the farmer.

Nigel stood there, what a clown, what did you say that for?

The farmer continued, 'What are you doing, taking a walk? Was that you the other day walking the riverbank?'

'Yes, one of the building lads said there was a circular walk around the estate. I did it but was tired by the end, still worth it.'

'Well,' said the farmer if you ever fancy doing it again and get wary, nip through the farm. It brings you out here, that will save a few miles.

'Come through the farm entrance and keep to the right. You will go past the back of the barn and the back of the stables; just follow the fence and you will come out on this path.'

'You have stables, do you have horses?' asked Nigel.

'No, the stables were part of the farm and 'that bastard' sold it off to the Captain. He bricked up our entrance and opened them up his side. He rents them out.'

'What else does he own around here?' Nigel asked.

'He owns the fishing right from the bridge by the road right down to the bridge in the village. It's a few miles, another earner.'

Nigel asked, 'The Captain must be what? About 45 ~ 50? He rents a house, he has fishing and shooting rights, a stable block, where did he get his money?'

'He owns the house,' replied the farmer, 'it's not rented! Some say he was involved in a scheme about time share for a few years. Got out early with a few bob in his pocket.

'You're welcome to use the short cut anytime. Must go, bye.'

'Yes, perhaps, see you Friday.'

Time to go back to the cottage for a cup of tea and dinner.

Walking back down the lane he could hear a horse, it was Faye.

Nigel stopped to have a chat, but Faye just said 'Hi' and carried on.

Nigel stood a moment. Mr Parker had taught him a thing or two about people. She was guilty of something, her look and demeanour were all wrong.

Nigel continued on his way. He decided to go around to the back door so he could smell the stew as he walked in the door.

On opening the door - that's funny, not a lot in the way a food cooking smells and it's not that warm in here.

The heaters were still lit as was the cooker, should be warmer than this surely?

As he turned to close the door, outside, in the dirt, were hoof prints, strong possibility a horse!

A burst of anxiety set in.

A dash to the top of the stairs, close inspection of the loft hatch didn't show any sign of movement, no chipped paint or finger marks.

He still needed to check something, so heading for the old shed, peering in the rickety steps, he found they were still where he had left them.

OK, he thought, let me just put that behind me for a while and enjoy dinner.

Lighting the fire in the sitting room, Nigel returned to the kitchen.

Kettle on the boil, he started to divide the pan of stew, half today and half tomorrow. Tea brewed, stew in a bowl, talking to himself, come on then, Nigel, let's see if you can cook.

The answer to that question was evident, as within less than half an hour, plate almost clean, it just required a thin slice of bread to mop up the last few drops of gravy.

For a chap that does eat much you did well there, he thought.

Nigel sat back in the chair, if only to let the dinner go down a little.

Nigel sat thinking.

Fancy thinking about Mr Parker today, without his help who knows what would have happened. Last year was a nightmare.

I guess as I have led a sheltered life I was not ready. Mr Parker took time to show me options, but refused to make any decision for me, and I will always thank him for that.

I am here in this situation by my own making, so there isn't any point in thinking what could have been!

With that, the same routine followed, a lump on the fire, guard in place, and off to bed.

I wonder why someone wanted to see inside the cottage, he thought, as he sank between the sheets.

'I Love You.'

Chapter 8

Acts of Kindness

The events of yesterday didn't seem to disrupt Nigel's sleep pattern. On hearing the clock chime 8, time to rise and shine.

After washing and dressing, downstairs for breakfast, it didn't seem that cold. He looked out the back door. The sky was overcast, but no chill in the air.

Breakfast was the usual, as new provisions could not be purchased until tomorrow, and it would be Market Day so lots of fresh produce.

Nigel sat in the sitting room and decided not to make the fire although he did put a few sticks on to give a glow and something to look at during breakfast.

Today Nigel decided to investigate the river from behind the Pub up to the bridge in the village.

Pots done, coat and scarf on, there was some deliberation on hat and gloves, but he was throwing caution to the wind.

Passing by the garage, a voice he recognised, but in a totally different tone, 'Morning Nigel, who's a quick worker then?'

'Morning, why have you almost finished?'

'Don't you give me that having ladies around. You not been here 5 minutes.'

'What do you mean?' Nigel asked.

'The lady on the horse. We are working on this roof and can see across to the cottage. She went around the side, tied up the horse and disappeared for about 4 ~ 5 minutes, came out and got back on the horse and walked off down the lane.

Why, didn't you know she was there?'

'No. I guessed someone had been in. You see I can't lock the doors. To be honest didn't think I needed to,' said Nigel.

'Hang on a moment,' said the lad. 'I am coming down.'

Reaching the ground, he went to the back of his van, he re-appeared holding a canvas bag.

'Come on!' Off he marched towards the cottage.

'What are you going to do?' asked Nigel.

'We are going to make it a little more secure.' Within moments the lad was at the back door.

Dipping into the bag he produced two large sliding bolts.

'Which door will you use the most?' the lad asked.

'I need to stop you there; I don't have any money until tomorrow.'

'Didn't ask for any. Anyway, if you need to pay for them you will have to see the new owner of the house. I took them off two doors that were in the skip, so sort it out with them if they ever get here before you leave.'

'Back door,' said Nigel.

'So, we will screw the bolt on the inside of the front door and the other bolt on the outside of the back door. Doesn't matter about the screw holes. The cottage is having new doors and windows anyway.'

Nigel stood in amazement as the lad screwed on the bolt to the door, a few blows with a hammer and chisel and the hasp was in place.

A few trial runs and that was done and locked.

The same workmanship was applied to the back door but this time on the outside.

'Look at that Nigel, nice smooth action. Let me show you what to do on the inside.

I am going to put large wood screw just above the latch on the inside, so at night you can screw it in and remove it during the day. With this in place no one can lift the latch to get in.

When you go out during the day here's a new padlock with keys, put the lock on. Now the cottage is locked up safe and sound. You can have this screwdriver to put the screw in and out.'

Nigel was slightly overwhelmed.

'That's a real kindness thank you so much. Could I ask one more thing of you? What's dot and dabbing?'

'Now Nigel! You are taking advantage, see you.' And he went off chuckling.

Nigel secured the lock and felt much better both for the security and for the kindness the young lad had shown.

Nigel almost skipped down the drive having been shown so much kindness.

He wanted to walk the river and needed to go through the Pub car park.

Only one small skip was now out the front, not much in it.

The car park was without any tarmac just loose stones.

There was still an army of workmen, building walls, putting up wooden frames inside. Outside were new toilets pans, handwash basins, boxes of floor tiles, plastic pipes, new drain covers, all sorts of items.

'What do you think then, Nigel? It is coming on,' said Baby.

The conservatory will be here early next week, that's going to sit on this brick work.

That's part of the new restaurant. You will look out over the garden and river whilst eating. It's going to be great, that lass is definitely forward thinking. We would love to work with her again.'

Baby was really on a high about the project. Nigel could tell it was the way he spoke so passionately.

'Come inside, the landlord won't mind, come on!'

Baby pointed out different features that were being built.

Baby explained how the bar would look. The pub would retain a small, quiet sitting area by the front window with settees and armchairs for comfort.

'Nigel, I can't tell you how much this will mean to the village. It will transform it. If you don't move far away, you will have to come back and have a look.'

'What do you think?' It was the landlord.

'I think this will look brilliant, with the new restaurant on the back overlooking the river and garden. What more could you wish for?

'What type of food are you serving? The lass can't do that as well, can she?' said Nigel.

'No, the investor has asked – asked, not told me but asked - if we can look at engaging a new up and coming Chef. We don't have to pay him for 3 months. After that we pay an agreed wage and as an incentive he takes a small share of the profits.'

'That's good,' replied Nigel, 'if the Chef takes part of the Pub's profit, then you're not paying the investor so much, so the only person losing out will be the investor, but he or she gets their original money back.'

'That's the only worry. In 5 years can we afford to pay it all back?' questioned the landlord.

'I am sure you will be OK. If not, then the bailiffs will have to seize the dart board,' said Nigel.

'We are not having a dart board.'

'You really are in trouble,' said Baby, laughing.

'Must carry on then, Nigel, see you.'

'Before you go, are you dot and dabbing?' asked Nigel.

'Yes, and wet. They're going to be a feature in that wall,' pointing over to the fireplace.

'That is good, then,' said Nigel, making his way out towards the back of the Pub and out to the car park.

As he took large steps across the car park, he thought, I am going to find out what dot and dab is, if it's the last thing I do!

On reaching the river side he watched the water flow peacefully by. The path followed parallel with the water with occasional areas where it was possible to fish. This time there were no signs for fishing tickets, so perhaps it's free.

It didn't take long to reach the village, he had to go under the bridge for the steps up to the road.

On reaching the road Nigel decided to have a look at the only other pub in the village.

The tractor shop as it was called, was on the opposite side of the road. A short walk found Nigel outside The Angel Inn. It had coloured lights around the roof line, three big lights, lighting up the wall sign: "The Angel Inn".

Either side of the doors were the Menu of the day: Leek and Potato soup, Butterfly Chicken, Black Forest Gateau, with a three-course meal, a free tea or coffee.

Not today thought Nigel. A second day stew is in order.

Nigel decided to continue down the river to a point where he could access the farm and take the green lane as the farmer had invited him to do, a short cut back to the cottage.

Walking back towards the river, he heard a voice call out, 'Hi Nigel, wait a minute.'

On turning round Nigel saw Paul coming up the road.

'Hello, glad I bumped into you, the postal orders arrived yesterday. How much cash do you need, all of it? There is a lot there?' enquired Paul.

'Hi Paul, about 25%. Best if you keep the rest if you don't mind. I can call on for more, later. Can I collect in the morning about 10.00?'

'Yes, that's not a problem, where are you going now?' Paul asked.

'Off down the river and then through the farm towards the Old House.'

'What about you, what are you doing?'

'Church work. I've been over to Arthur's and Millie's, -you know, the chap in the Pub last Saturday.

'I shouldn't say this, but the pair are finding things tough, and both of them are too proud to ask for help. They are looking for odd bits of work, but in this climate nothing at all, it's sad!'

Nigel thought for a moment, 'Paul, do you think Millie would do my washing, or is that too rude of me to ask?'

Paul grabbed Nigel's arm, and almost dragged him down the street.

'Come on let's go and ask, great idea.' Paul took off at a pace, 'Come on, Nigel.'

Nigel could hardly keep up. Arriving at Millie's, Nigel thought Paul was going to push the door off its hinges with the force of his knocking.

'Coming! Coming! Where's the fire?' came a voice from inside.

Millie opened the door.

'Hello again, vicar.'

'Hi Millie, I brought Nigel along to see you.'

'Hello, Nigel.'

Nigel just stood and stared, mouth open.

'Does he speak, vicar? Or is it a new form of fly catching?' asked Millie.

'No, I can speak, I do speak,' said Nigel.

'It's the vicar, I suggested something, now I am wondering if it's the right thing or not.'

'Come in, lad!' Once in the kitchen, Nigel felt a little easier.

'Spit it out, lad,' Millie ordered.

'Well, I need a little work done and well.'

Paul jumped in otherwise they could be there all day.

'Millie, he needs his washing done. He's here for a few weeks and needs some help.'

'I don't want it for free, I will pay,' said Nigel.

'OK Nigel, not a problem, but I don't know how much.'

'Don't ask me, the last person to do mine was Mum and I can't ask her.'

Millie stood pointing around the kitchen, 'Pull out the machine, fill with water, add powder, wash, rinse, peg out, fetch in, iron. How about….,' and gave Nigel a cost.

'What do you think?' asked Millie.

'So, let's look at it - pull out the machine, fill with water, add powder, wash, rinse, peg out, fetch in, iron,' Nigel thought for a moment.

'Sorry, Millie can't agree on the cost. You need to cost in, emptying the water, putting the machine back, wear and tear on the washer, possibility of breaking pegs, taking the line in and out, etc. Sorry Millie, it doubles that price.'

Nigel put his hand out. 'Deal?'

'Yes, great, see you tomorrow,' said Millie.

'About 11.00, if that's OK?' asked Nigel.

'Yes, thanks.'

Leaving the house, the boys turned round to see Millie with a big grin and waving. The boys waved back and continued down the street.

'I will stick to the rules, no questions, but there was something about what you did there, not offering more money, that was really nice, it was the way you assess it all. More to you, Nigel, than meets the eye. I will be sorry to see you go.'

'And I will be sorry to leave, Paul.'

The two men continued along until they reached the bridge, 'I am off down the river, Paul, see you about 10.00 tomorrow, have a nice evening.'

'And, you.'

Paul stood for a while watching Nigel walking along the river's path, and without turning around Nigel put up his hand and waved.

How did he know I would still be here? thought Paul.

It was still a pleasant day, so Nigel decided to sit on the bank and let the world pass by.

I need a plan, still have about 6 weeks, possibly 5, the rate every one's going at it.

Not sure if I am going to miss the cottage or not, perhaps 6 more weeks will turn me stir crazy.

Perhaps I could grow a few vegetables to help keep me busy. Nothing grand, simple stuff early varieties, not like the exotic veg. Dad used to grow from time to time. At least I now know why he grew them.

The market may have some plants tomorrow, perhaps broccoli or cabbages. Will need a spade, perhaps a fork, will see what is in the shed when I get back.

That was astute of Paul to pick up on me talking with Millie, this is no time to drop my guard.

Nigel sat for some time watching nature. There was the odd pheasant on the other bank. Stay over there, less chance of getting shot.

Washing sorted that's good. Will need to get another set of sheets and pillowcases, can't sleep in them for the next 6 weeks, market tomorrow!

As he looked up, the clouds were starting to turn dark, best get a move on.

I will try the farm path, something new. Following the path up the hill through the various gates, he reached the road. A short walk along the pavement brought him opposite the farm.

Crossing the road, keep to the right and go between the barn and the stable was his instruction. Sure, enough there was the path, not what Nigel had envisaged, it was much wider, and well-kept for a farm path.

As he was about to exit the pathway, there stood 'the Captain' in his distinctive hat. 'Hi you! You are trespassing, this is my land, and I will thank you to turn back and not to use it again,' he grunted.

'OK, but I only need to complete the last 20 yards or so then I am on the green lane. Is that too much to ask that I continue?' asked Nigel.

'Yes, give your sort an inch and you take a mile. You're living in the cottage, don't suppose you're paying rent, bet you don't have a job.'

'Well,' replied Nigel, 'it is true that I am staying in the cottage, and at this moment I am not paying rent. It is also true that at this moment in time I do not have any paid work.

'However, I will be moving on in about 6 weeks, the builders have given me notice, and I guess they will pull the place apart if I am in it or not, so I will have to leave and move on. Why are you making it more difficult for me than it needs to be in the meantime?'

'I don't know how you found this place,' growled the Captain. 'And I don't care, the new family are moving in the Old House soon and I am damn sure they do not want the likes of you, living next door.'

Nigel interjected, 'Captain, we all make mistakes. Sometimes the outcome of our actions do not match the promise made or one's expectations.'

The captain retorted, 'I am not at all interested in mistakes people make. It is their own stupid fault. I have no time for losers, and you are a loser, so make sure you're out that cottage before the new family arrive, or I will instruct the builders to throw you out, is that understood?'

'Yes, perfectly,' replied Nigel, 'now can I pass?'

'No! walk round, it's not like you have a job to go to.'

'The Captain' stood directly in Nigel's way.

Nigel not liking confrontation turned around and walked back down the path.

'6 Weeks and move on,' yelled 'the Captain'.

'OK 6 weeks!'

Nigel was normally a placid person but he was still cross as he walked up the drive.

'Hello Nigel, you don't look happy, not like you,' said the lad from the top of the scaffolding.

'I am not, I have just encountered a most rude and obnoxious man, and he made me cross.'

'Let me guess, he wears a cowboy hat, he can be difficult, best keep out his way. I try, too, but going to be difficult. I think Baby, Love are quoting for work on his house.'

Nigel stood a moment, 'I don't normally let people upset me. Best forget about it and have a cup of tea, see you.'

'Yep, don't let him get to you, enjoy the tea, bye.'

Nigel returned to the cottage, put the kettle on and proceeded to make up the fire, whilst it was not too cold at least it was ready if needed.

Hot water in the tea pot, he decided to fill the coal scuttle with coal and a few sticks, and he needed to check what gardening tools were in the old shed.

Scuttle filled, Nigel stood by the shed door. There were some old gardening tools not in the best condition, but if handled correctly they will last a few more weeks.

If I purchased new ones, what am I going to do with them later?

About to head inside, he thought he should check on the paraffin. Opening the toilet door and shaking the container, he thought he was going to need another gallon, that should last until he left.

Finishing his tea, he found it was still light and not too cold, so he decided to walk down to the lake, for half an hour, take in the view and try and release the thoughts of 'the Captain'.

Locking the door, Nigel wandered off. A few vans were still on site outside the house, 'Hello again.' It was the plasterer. 'You do a lot of walking about, suppose it keeps you fit.'

'Not as fit as I was,' Nigel replied. 'How's it going, the weather holding up for you? I saw the plumber the other day, he told me that he's ordering items ready to fit?'

'It's looking promising, most of the heavy stuff is nearly done. We should start to take out the scaffolding tomorrow. We will still need the trestle and board but looking good, sparks and the plumbing team are in next Wednesday. In the meantime, the chippy starts on the second fix. These will all need a couple of weeks.

'We will have to come back and repair bits where the clowns have damaged the walls, but no big deal. Then Rembrandt and the team come in. It shouldn't take them too long, the doors are pre- painted and the windows are plastic double glazed to keep the heat inside.'

'Is that the work finished?' enquired Nigel.

'No, sure enough, the plumbers will fit the toilets, baths and all the other items, then the big boys come in, bespoke kitchen fitters. This house is having the latest fitted kitchen with all the latest gizmos.

'I've heard, the kitchen is having a pioneering heating system, under floor heating no radiators on the walls, all the white goods are behind cupboard doors. There's, what is called, an island in the middle of the kitchen, there's talk of a machine that washes pots and pans. That kitchen is going to be space age.

'Then I believe top retailers and design places are responsible for all the furniture and soft fitting. If the word on the street is correct all the rooms are designed by different people all under the instruction of the architect lass.

'The family that moves in here have got money, all well and good to them. It's put bread on lots of tables around here, I can tell you!

'Nice talking with you, see you,' and off he went.

Nigel thought, one day I am going to get a sentence in with him before he dashes off.

Nigel continued his progress down to the lake.

As he stared into the water, it still seemed devoid of anything bigger than stickle backs. It would be nice to see fish back in here, perhaps some form of aquatic birds. Maybe not, it would only encourage that idiot over there to shoot them or get money off someone else to shoot them.

Nigel stood at the high point of the lake, the view from there was just spectacular.

Best not get to used to it, bit disappointed in myself today. I let my guard down, doing things like that could get me into trouble, and questions could be asked. Watch what you are doing Nigel! he thought.

Best get back to the cottage and make a shopping list for tomorrow and put on the stew for tea.

Passing the Old House he saw the teams were loading the vans ready for home.

'See you tomorrow,' a few shouted.

Nigel took a moment to view the garage from a distance. It was coming on, the team had started to clad the walls with wood.

How do I keep out of the Captain's way until I vacate the cottage? How do I keep out of way of the Captain and Faye thinking about it?

Chapter 9

Hope, Dreams, Love and Truth

Nigel made his way back to the cottage and set about what had now become a routine.

He sat in front of the fireplace eating the stew and drinking a cup of tea.

As I am taking the washing tomorrow to Millie's, think I will have a bath.

First, best clean the pots and pans. Washing up he looked out of the window. It was starting to become dusk and difficult to see down the garden.

Nigel nipped into the sitting room, 7.00 o'clock. Need to wind that up, he thought.

Let's see what the view is like from the end of the lake. Should be able to see the night lights for miles.

Grabbing his coat and scarf, fire guard in place and a lock on the door, off he went.

As he approached the House, a voice rang out, 'Who goes there?'

Forgot about him! 'Hello David, it's Nigel from the cottage, how are you enjoying the job?'

'It's OK. I have to earn a wage for my wife and her mother, she's old.'

'Your wife's old, David?'

'No, not the wife', he paused a moment 'you're pulling my leg.'

'Yes, David, just a little joke.'

Dave continued, 'It's not a very good job, and I will get the sack when the new family move in.'

'Who said you're going to be sacked? Anyway you only get sacked if you have done something wrong and you keep repeating the same mistake. What have you done wrong?' Nigel asked.

'It's when the new family come in, they won't need me, they can look after the House themselves, and that man in the hat said this is all I am fit for.'

'Did he David? Let's sit on the step and talk.'

'I am supposed to keep walking round.'

'Never mind about that,' Nigel rebuffed.

'Tell me about you, the real David, what your dreams and hopes are, you have to have some?' asked Nigel.

'Not really,' sighed David.

'Now, David, we are going to keep sitting on this cold step until you think about hopes and dreams.'

David thought for a moment.

'You see I am big and fat, always have been even at school. Teachers said I wouldn't amount to much. I am 28 years old, and I walk round someone's garden, guarding it. People think because I am over 6 foot 2" I can fight. Kids at school would pick fights, but I hate fighting, Nigel, it's silly.'

'That's good, that's positive. How about your wife, and I don't mean, does she like fighting?' asked Nigel.

'She is lovely, really nice. We got married 3 years ago. We both worked at the factory. We had to take the bus, then the work stopped, and factory had to close. We all got the sack.'

'How long did you work at the factory, David?'

'Since leaving school.'

Nigel looked at David, 'OK and when you had to leave work did you get any money apart from your wages?'

'Yes, we got a bonus for working there for so long, both of us.'

'That's called redundancy, David. That's not getting the sack, no one sacked you. You were made redundant, not the same thing at all.'

David thought a moment, 'I still didn't have a job, no money and we couldn't afford the rent, so Mary's Mum said we could live with her. Don't think she thought it would be this long.'

'How long ago was it you left the factory, David, and what have you been doing since you left?'

'It was not long after we got married. Nearly 3 years, and I haven't had a proper job until this one. The Council let me work on the flower beds in the park and around the old people's bungalows, during the summer. I didn't get paid, it's called voluntary.

'I used to make the hanging baskets that go on the lamp posts. They lent me some step ladders so I could water them. I didn't get paid, but a man from the Government said I would have to stop. If I didn't the Government would stop the dole.'

'OK. What about Mary, is she looking for work?'

'Yes, Nigel, but nothing, she really wanted to be a teacher, but you need money to train, it's really hard.'

'So, you are good with plants and flowers, what's Mary good at?' asked Nigel.

'Cooking and baking. She's really good at it.'

Nigel patted David's stomach, 'I can see that, David, you eat all the pies.'

David came out with a huge smile, 'We are not having pies at the moment. We have to pick from the hedges. The Pub has an apple tree. He lets us take the apples, we have to wait for the summer fruits before we have more pies, it's free.

'When we were both working, we could afford to buy meats and different veg. Mary isn't like me., she's clever, she goes down to the library and takes out books, but now she just looks at the pictures, we don't have the money.'

Nigel looked at David, then pointed towards the house, 'Does it make you cross that you don't have any money, and here we are sitting on the steps of this great big house?'

'No! it's not the family's fault. They have money and lots of nice stuff. I wouldn't want to live in here. The house is very big. I would love to have just a small house for Mary and myself, and a job each. Perhaps me growing plants and Mary cooking?'

'You see, David, you do have hopes and dreams. You hang on to them.'

Nigel stood and rubbed his back side, 'That's made my bum go numb,' pointing at the step.

Nigel spoke softly, 'I like watching people, David, and I watched you talk about your wife. You really love Mary, don't you?'

'Don't be silly,' replied David.

'Tell her you Love her, tell her every day You Love her, because one day it will be too late, see you David.'

David did not look up and Nigel wandered off back to the cottage.

Nigel unlocked the door and screwed in the screw to prevent the latch being lifted. Now, he thought, a bath was on the cards.

He peered into the sitting room. The fire still had flames, a small Scotch sounded much better than the bath.

Nigel sat by the fire, drink in hand, his mind wandered to the events of the last year, but this isn't the time to be reminded of that!

Nigel took himself off to bed, I wonder if David will tell Mary, hope so.

Nigel spoke out loud, 'I Love You.'

Perhaps the Scotch was larger than first thought. Nigel didn't stir at all in the night, but now the toilet beckoned, so best look sharp.

Breakfast was the same as the last five days and becoming a little boring, but needs must be met.

Duty for the day were, call in at the butchers' and get a couple of sausages for week-end breakfast. I also need meat and veg.

First need to see Paul for some cash, then to Millie, then shopping, including some plants off the Market. Let's see what I can grow before I leave.

Nigel opened the back door. What a change! The sun was out and warmth in the air.

What a great looking morning! I am getting used to this, or is it just better than before?

Breakfast pots washed, coat on, collect the wheelie trolley and lock the back door, I wonder if I can get the trolley in the car.

Nigel set off down the lane, he stopped and thought for a moment, Paul's, then Millie's.

If you're going to Millie's perhaps you should take the washing?

About turn to collect the laundry, that done, off he went again.

'Morning, Nigel', said the young lad.

'Morning. Sorry, we have spoken so many times, I don't know your name.'

'Alex.'

'Morning, Alex. I had a look at your work from the steps of the house, it's looking really good, unusual don't you think?'

'I think it's futuristic. You see this beautiful wood on the outside and when the doors are open you see the brickwork inside.

'It's having big wooden doors - a pair for each bay, these will be contrasting colours and have big ornamental hingers to set it off. That lass is one hell of a designer, you don't think she's moving into the Old House do you?'

'You can see yourself living in there with a Lady with an eye for beauty?' asked Nigel.

'Don't you think I look like a Greek God?' Alex said, smiling.

'More like a Greek Urn,' Nigel replied.

'Cheeky!'

Nigel continued down the drive.

Alex had a point. That garage is inspiring, think I will stick my nose in the Pub to see what's happening.

Nigel strolled around the back. The car park was still a mess, but the brickwork was going up, he could tell the new outline of the building now.

There were vast amounts of white plastic lying on the lawn, guess that's the conservatory to the restaurant. There were all sorts of pipes protruding out the ground, black ones, brown ones and a smaller blue one.

Just as he stood trying to work out why we have different ones, a familiar voice called,'Morning, Nigel'.

'Morning, Love,' a second voice spoke.

'Morning, Nigel.' It was the plasterer.

'Yes, good morning, I see you will be dot and dabbing and wet on this job?' Nigel replied trying to sound like he knew what it meant.

'Don't forget the skimming. That's important, see you, Love. Bye Nigel,' and off the plasterer went with a raise of his hand.

Nigel stood and stared, he's done it to me again, just when I thought I knew something about plastering.

'Are you OK, Nigel?' Nigel didn't reply for a while,

'Yes, OK thanks, how's this job going?'

'It's going good, the conservatory people will be in, Monday. We are working the weekend. Once that's up, we can complete the brick work, then on goes the roof, then pandemonium, sparks, plumbers, plasters, and the new kitchen. We are not fitting that, it comes as a package.

'Then the Sparky and plumber come back in for second fix, then the tilers, bar fitters, pandemonium again for the next 4 ~ 5 weeks, then the cottage. So please bear that in mind, Nigel, by the time we have finished snagging it is going to be about 6 weeks. Sorry!'

'Yes, I have been reminded I have to move,' said Nigel.

'So have I, by the man in the hat and he is asking for us to do work on his house and grounds.'

Nigel thought, I have seen the house, it does look nice. 'And grounds?' enquired Nigel. 'I have seen the back of the stables.'

'You wouldn't see it from the road,' said Love, 'or from the back of the stable.

'About three years ago part of the woods were cleared and a pheasant run put in. The new work is, extending the house and constructing new runs for other game birds. Can't upset him and you have to leave anyway.'

Nigel took a moment. 'Look Love! I totally understand, and it only goes to remind me I have to sort out a few things, perhaps we should have a beer together when this places opens, no hard feelings.'

'Love, have you got a minute?' a voice shouted.

'Coming. See you, Nigel. Wait a minute, who's paying?' asked Love.

'That's nice, I am going to be forced out of my home again, you and Baby have lucrative contracts coming up, and you're asking me who's buying the beer,' joked Nigel.

'I will spin you for it,' shouted Love as he walked away.

Nigel continued his journey to the vicarage and knocked on the door. It was opened by Mrs Bright.

'Morning Mrs Bright.'

'The vicar is in here,' pointing him to the study.

'Morning, Nigel. I have your cash I have put it in an envelope,' Paul said, as he closed the study door.

The two chatted away for about ½ an hour.

'I am surprised Mrs Bright hasn't come in with the tea.'

'It's OK, Paul, I need to be on my way. Do you fancy a Chips supper tomorrow?' asked Nigel.

'Yes, see you about 6.'

Nigel and his wheelie trolley continued down the high street over the bridge and onto Millie and Arthur's.

Arthur was tinkering in the small front garden. He looked up at Nigel, then around at the trolley, 'Good heavens, I thought Millie was doing the washing here, didn't know you were taking the machine with you. Come in lad.'

'Morning, Millie.'

'Morning, Nigel.'

'I brought the washing hope it's OK, not too much, I will pay you now.'

Nigel reached into his pocket and opened the envelope and removed some money.

Millie stood back and folded her arms.

'I said I would do your washing Nigel, I will do this load. I don't want you to pay but I will do no more.'

'What's the matter with you?' asked Arthur.

'Nothing.'

'Yes, there is, what is it?'

'He stands there with an envelope from the church and on Sunday we will be putting money in on the Church plate. What's the point in him giving me Church money for me to give it back. He asked the vicar for cash.'

'Is this true, Nigel?' asked Arthur.

Nigel thought for a moment, 'Yes, it is true I asked Paul for cash. Yes, I required cash, but I have money, enough money for my needs. What I don't have is cash, so I asked for a friend to send Paul "Crossed Postal Orders".

'I don't have any form of identification, and I will be moving soon, so Paul kindly cashed them for me, about a quarter of what was sent. It is better that he keeps the rest safe in the vicarage.

'I collected my cash this morning and I can pay for my washing and do my shopping now.

'I hope this explains the cash in the envelope and if you wish I will wait whilst Millie rings the vicar or perhaps Mrs Bright, and she can ask the vicar.'

There was stunned silence. Millie looked straight at Nigel, 'I will ring Mrs Bright and the vicar,' and off she went into the front room closing the door behind her.

'Best make a cupper, Nigel, a strong one.'

'Thanks, Arthur. I did not get one at the vicarage, I can see why now.'

The men were well down their cups of tea when Millie returned, 'I can only apologize, I have been foolish in listening to tickle-tackle. I am so sorry, Nigel, and if you no longer wish me to do your washing I understand.'

'That's OK, Millie, and you did right to check, I appreciate your honesty. It's happened to me before but that time no one checked its validity.'

'No rush on the washing, when do you think I can collect?'

'Weather forecast's good over the week-end. How about Monday?'

'I will collect Tuesday, just in case, now I can pay you.' Nigel handed over the washing and the money, thanked Arthur for the tea and set off into the village.

There seemed more stalls than last week, the weather had definitely helped.

First stop, butchers' for breakfast items, there was only a small queue and Nigel waited.

The butcher looked over towards Nigel.

'Right, ladies, best get your orders in before I am sold out. If the chap wants the trolley filling, I may not have any meat left for next week.'

The ladies turned round, some politely laughed others just smiled.

'Ignore him, he's a good butcher, but people skills? No!' The lady in front explained to Nigel.

When it was Nigel's turn, he was more precise with his order than before, the weather warming up and he did not have a fridge so needed to think about storage.

Meat purchased with pound notes in order to get change for the phone, off to the fruit and veg stall, various items purchased, including 10 cooking apples, and more change.

Then he noticed a new stall selling small plants, which looked ready for transplanting in the garden. The stallholder explained to Nigel that some of the plants were early varieties and would thrive.

So, armed with beetroot, cabbage, carrots and potatoes and more change.

Nigel now needed bed sheets and pillowcases. That was going to prove a little more problematic. It would seem no one sold such items. Need to review that, thought Nigel.

Next stop, the general store, flour, cornflower, salt, lard, castor sugar, milk, matches, soap, bread, eggs, and a few other essential items including 4 cans of beer.

Despite its size, Nigel's trolley was looking slightly full. So were his pockets now, full of change ready for the public phone.

Nigel crossed the road and parked up the trolley by the side of a box.

He entered the box with pockets full of change. He seemed to be on the call for some time and luckily the call ended before the money ran out.

Nigel set off with his trolley.

The climb up the drive was even more difficult dragging the weight of the wheelie up.

Nigel decanted the shopping whilst the kettle boiled, plants placed outside, in the old washroom.

Slugs! Should have done something about that when in the village. Problem for another day, thought Nigel.

Tea in hand, he leant on the open-door frame viewing the garden and wondering where to start.

He only needed a plot about 4-ft. x 4-ft.

Nigel spun round and placed the empty cup on the draining board. What time is it? Checking on the clock in the sitting room, 12.35. He guessed he should have wound the clock before he went out.

Finding the car keys, he set off to view the clock in the car.

Not been started for some time, let's run it for 10 minutes. With the car running he checked the time. 12 minutes past 2, he quickly nipped back in, reset the hands, wound it up and returned to the car.

Taking a step back, he noted how dirty it was, the dust and bits of the trees had left it dull.

It's not much of a car but I used to clean this every Saturday, not the car's fault what's happened.

Looks like I will be going back into the village for a few more bits of shopping. That's Ok, I can drop the beer in at Paul's, he can put them in the fridge ready for the Fish and Chips supper.

Nigel, you're a genius! he thought.

Turning off the engine and locking the door, returning to the cottage to grab his coat, he stood for a moment and thought, I could have a look at the Captain's grounds. It's a bit sneaky. No, go have a look.

Nigel decided to proceed part way down the lane, and as he approached the farm, he left the path and travelled though the woodland, less chance of being seen.

It didn't take long before his progress was halted by a 6-foot-high wooden fence. He heard a horse neighing.

Nigel chose to follow the fence along to the left. He was too small to see over but one panel had warped slightly away from its post, and through the gap he could see pheasants in a massive cage. It's true he does have grounds.

Thinking it was better to go back to the cottage before he was seen, he continued walking in the woods before thinking it was OK to re-join the path.

I wonder how many birds were in that cage, and he is having other pens for more game birds. There are going to be lots more birds in the wild to see and enjoy, the downside is people are going to try to shoot them.

Nigel wanted to see the lights over the valley at evening time.

So, he decided to have the bath he should have had last night, then have tea, then go look at the lights.

Turning the corner by the cottage, he checked on the gas levels, still showing very nearly full so should easily last a few more weeks.

Nigel had purchased a pie from the butchers' and decided to have a baked potato and baked beans for supper.

He closed the back door and put in the screw, he lit the oven and selected a large potato, pricking it first before putting it in the oven.

With dinner on the way, he ran the hot water and enjoyed the refreshing bath.

The bathroom was not too bad temperaturewise, which was a good job as the heater had run out of fuel.

Bath soon over and feeling good he dressed and returned downstairs. He checked the potato - looking good! Time to slip in the pie, checking the time. It recommended 30 minutes.

The final task, opening the tin of beans, saving half for tomorrow's breakfast, then make a pot of tea.

Soon Nigel was enjoying evening dinner. Perhaps I should have made a fire, it is something nice to see and feel whilst eating, but too late now he thought.

Nigel selected a number of items purchased earlier that day, and put them into 2 bags.

It wasn't totally dark, but Nigel thought by the time he got to the lake the light would have faded.

Collecting his 2 bags he set off, he waited for the 'Who goes there?' but it wasn't forthcoming.

Nigel needed to see David so he sat on the step and looked across the grounds. He could just see the Pub. The lights were bright coming from the inside. Bye, Bye vans were still there.

Nigel thought that the chaps were working hard to complete the job and get the Pub up and running again, earning money, but more importantly be a part of the village community again.

Nigel didn't have to wait long before he heard footsteps.

'Evening, David, how are you this evening?' asked Nigel.

'Hello, Nigel. Good, thank you, but the man with the hat has not been yet.'

Nigel asked, 'Does he come every night?'

'No, sometimes in the week, but not Saturday or Sunday.'

'Do you work every night, David, or do you get a night off?'

'Every night. The boss said if I was willing to work, then it's every night. What's in the bags?'

'Glad you asked, I need a favour, not from you but Mary. Do you think she would make me an apple pie? I've not had a homemade one for about 18 months, I would only like one for me. If you have items left over, I don't want them back, ask Mary to perhaps make one for you and the family.

'I think I have everything, but if I have missed something, tell me tomorrow and I can give you some money to get it next week. Do you think she'd mind baking for me?'

'Apple pie!' David thought a moment, 'Mary will not get into trouble, with the man from the government, will she?'

'No, David, making someone a pie will not get you into trouble.'

'Great, I will ask her.'

'No rush, David, I will be going to the chippy tomorrow. So sometime next week, when she has the time, will be good. I am off to the lake to see the view over the valley in the dark, see you later.'

'See you later,' replied David.

The light was fading and steady was the order of the day. Nigel arrived at the spot he thought gave the best advantage point. He was not disappointed, the contrast of the dark with the odd rays of light from scattered houses and a few streetlights.

Cars could be seen winding their way along country roads. Another village could be seen miles in the distance, this only added to the beauty of the area.

Nigel stood gazing into the distance, thinking how lucky he was, but things could change in a few weeks, pity!

The lights in the Pub started to dim as the builders loaded the vans to call it a day and go home.

Nigel started the walk back up the hill towards the Old House waiting by the steps for the arrival of David, just to say, 'Good night.'

David came from around the corner.

Just thought I would say, 'Good night, David. Hope it's not going to rain.'

'Thanks, Nigel, have a great evening, see you tomorrow.'

Nigel wandered back to the cottage, but not ready to settle in bed just yet he decided to have a small Scotch. He needed to think about the future.

Mmm, cancel that thought. He had not made a fire and did not fancy sitting in the dark or sitting with the light on. Bedtime normal routine followed and culminated in his few words,

'I Love You.'

Chapter 10

With the Help of a Digger

The following morning Nigel was up early. He had purchased sausages for breakfast. He washed and dressed. Downstairs, kettle on, he started to cook breakfast. He had to think about future meals as the weather was getting warmer and the fresh meat could go off. Today's was still OK.

Breakfast over, coat on, he headed off to the village, canned beers in hand.

Nigel stopped to admire the garage, the contrast between the inner walls and the outside was truly inspiring, even without the doors on.

As he passed the Pub, some workmen had started, but no sign of Baby, Love.

That didn't stop a wag shouting, 'Bit early for a beer.'

Then Nigel realised he should have put the cans in a bag. Trying to cover them with his coat Nigel continued to the vicarage.

Nigel knocked on the door to have Paul answer, 'Morning, Paul, how are you this bright and sunny morning?'

'Good, Nigel, bit early for drinking, don't you think?'

'It's for tonight with the chip supper. Thought you could put them in your fridge.'

'Good idea, Nigel. I will do that forthwith, come in.'

Nigel went into the study and sat down. Paul soon entered and took a seat, 'So what's your plan for today then, Nigel?'

Nigel replied, 'I have to go to the hardware shop for a bucket and sponge. I intend to wash the car, and perhaps start it. It's not moved for a few weeks, can't let the battery go flat.

'I purchased some plants, vegetables actually, off the market yesterday. I'm going to transplant them later, and if you're still up for it, a chippy supper.'

'Chips sounds good. Say about 6?' asked Paul.

'See you later then, Paul.'

With that Nigel made his way to the hardware shop. As he entered the shop, a cheerful 'Morning, can I help you?' rang out.

'Morning,' replied Nigel to the invisible person.

'I would like a bucket and sponge, suitable for washing a car, and a small garden trowel, and a gallon of paraffin, please.'

'Plastic?' came a query.

'No thanks, I will take a metal trowel,' replied Nigel.

'Bucket, plastic bucket?' asked the invisible shop keeper.

'Plastic will be good.'

Soon the shop keeper appeared with the required goods.

'Oh, it is you, nice to see you again.'

Items purchased, Nigel started to make his way home. He intended to go via the river path, which led to the back of the Pub.

Nigel stopped by the Bank, and stood staring aimlessly at the old building. Must have been a most impressive building in its day. Moving along, he watched the water flow under the bridge.

Fishing. Last time I went fishing was in the canal behind the allotments. Someone gave me some old fishing tackle. I bet the junk shop would have some rods and stuff. Then I need a fishing ticket.

Nigel's thoughts remained with his Dad, down the allotment. He must have been there thinking for a while before gaining composure and returning to the present.

He went back to the hardware shop.

'Morning, can I help? Hello again, forget something?'

'Yes,' said Nigel, 'a fishing ticket, please.'

'I could sell you a ticket. I can sell you a day ticket, a week's ticket, or a season ticket, but it wouldn't be right as it's closed season. You're not allowed to fish, you need to come back in a couple of months.'

'OK, thanks for the information,' said Nigel. The shop keeper continued, 'Apart from the fishing ticket you will need a rod licence, one for each rod.'

'Do I buy that here?' asked Nigel.

'No, you get that from the Post Office. It's a national licence. You can use it anywhere in England and Wales,' the shop keeper replied.

With that the door opened. 'Hello Captain, I was just telling this chap about rod licence and fishing tickets.'

The Captain looked straight at Nigel, 'You can buy a rod licence if you wish. But there's no way you will be fishing my water. You will be long gone before the season starts, long gone, I will see to that.'

Nigel turned to the shopkeeper, 'Thanks for the information, I will keep it in mind, good day.'

Nigel made his way to the door without even glancing at the Captain.

That was lucky. I could have purchased the rods first then gone for a ticket, the chap in the junk shop would have sold me more than I required, and I couldn't use any of it, that would have darkened my reputation.

"You outsiders are not all daft."

Nigel resumed his walk back to the cottage, via the river.

He was surprised on how calm he felt after yet another encounter with the Captain.

Nigel took time on his walk back to enjoy what nature had to offer. The kingfisher was still darting up and down, the moorhen was falling out with everything on the water as always.

Nigel eventually reached the back of the Pub, the conservatory frame was in place, people were working on the roof, workmen were all over the place.

To Nigel it seemed to have some structure about it, still no sign of Baby, Love. First time Nigel had noticed them not on site. Perhaps busy looking at the next job?

Nigel carefully crossed the car park as it still needed a surface covering. Crossing the road he started the climb.

Outside the garage was a large lorry with an HI-AB. As Nigel got closer, he could see that the doors to the garage were being offloaded and laid on the ground. Carefully moving away from the truck he made his way around the side watching the machine's movements.

Safely passed, he headed for the cottage. From the front of the house he could see Love and Alex approaching. Nigel stood and waited for them to get closer.

'Morning,' said Nigel, 'thought you were having a well-deserved day off, Love.'

'Morning, Nigel. It would be nice, but we have been lucky enough to get work, need to make it happen.'

Alex jumped in saying, 'Especially when you had the architect on the phone to you at 8.00 o'clock on a Saturday Morning.'

'Yes, thanks Alex!' Love replied.

'We have to extend a trench for the gas supply. There isn't main gas to the Old House so liquid gas will be stored in an extremely large tank. This was to be sited a minimum of 100 yards from the House for safety, now for some reason it has to be moved another 200 yards away, not a major issue.

'We know we have to dig a 2- cubic yard hole just by the outer kitchen wall for the new underfloor heating system. It will just take a few days longer and a few more lorry loads of soil to take away, not a problem really!'

Nigel thought for a moment. 'Why will you have to take the soil away? Can't you put it back in the trench when the gas pipes in and why does an underfloor heating system need a hole outside?'

'Alex will explain, Nigel. I need to get back to the Pub, see you.'

'Well, Nigel,' started Alex, 'the gas tank can't be near any dwelling in case it exploded. So, I guess, as the tank is so big having it farther away from the Old House makes sense. I suppose if that went up, the estate would have the makings of a third lake.

'I went to the library to look up under "floor heating". It's something new here. It's been used for years in America. I think the architect is looking at heating one room. You dig a big hole and put in zig zag pipe work.

'We bring two pipes out of the hole and add a high pressure pump to the system, then connect both pipes to the underfloor system and fill in part of the hole with protective heat transferring material to protect the pipe work. Then you can put some of the soil back in. The earth is warm, you pump the water round, free heating. I don't think it will scald your feed but adding a few degrees at low level can only be good, yes?'

'Very good, Alex. Why can't you put the soil back in the trench after you have laid the gas pipe?'

'Once the pipe is in, we need to cover it with gravel. This helps in the settling process and helps to stop the pipe from fracturing. Again we can put some soil back but not all.

'Then when I've done that, I have to dig.'

'Can I stop you there, Alex? I think I can hear the phone ringing.'

'OK Nigel,' replied Alex.

And the two men parted. A few second later Alex shouted, 'I didn't know you had a phone.'

'I don't,' shouted Nigel.

'Cheeky!' whispered Alex.

Nigel opened the back door and put on the kettle and went upstairs to find some old clothes that he could use for washing the car in and digging the garden.

He was limited in his choice as he had to leave in a hurry and really not thinking about car washing or gardening clothes. And some clothes were at Millie's.

He picked what he thought he could utilise as old suitable clothes and changed into them.

Off to make the tea and decide on car or garden first.

Car! Filling the bucket with warm water and a squirt of washing up liquid, sponge in hand, Nigel set about removing the grime that had found its way onto the paint work of his car.

It wasn't a new car by any measure, but it had been reliable over the last couple of years. It had taken Mum and Dad on day trips, helped with the weekly shopping, took him and fellow walkers to start points for rambling, helped Dad to visit Hospital to see Mum and of course, allowed him to travel here.

As Nigel worked away, he thought that this was going to take a couple of go's to get it cleaned.

It's your own fault, Nigel, you should have cleaned it more often. As this thought was still running around his brain, a second bucketful was required.

Nigel continued the cleaning process, and his mind moved back and forth from past days to the present day, and what the future would hold, and of course, the time at home and work.

He thought that work was never the same when Mr Parker retired. His replacement Mr Bird was no true replacement. From the first moment Nigel clapped eyes on him and watched his mannerisms, he knew the writing was on the wall for his own career.

Mr Bird was bringing in new systems, reliant on computer programmes, money would be controlled by machine, the planning of the work and purchasing of parts all done by machine.

Nigel knew this was the way forward and could see the potential, but Bird was all wind and gusto. The neatness and accuracy of Mr Parker's work was undone in about 6 months, cash flow could not always be reconciled.

Nigel's bookkeeping was becoming less and less important. Every time Nigel tried to tell Mr Bird about the discrepancies, he would dismiss Nigel's comments.

Then at the beginning of last year Nigel's Mother was taken ill and spent time in hospital. Nigel and his Dad would go and visit every day for weeks, until his Mum came home. The hospital could do no more and Mother would like to be at home.

Nigel promised to take Mum out, maybe to the country house or the seaside, perhaps just watch the horses in the fields, but he never did.

Work allowed Nigel to take time off, without pay. His Dad was also granted time off work, again without pay.

Mother was never well enough to go out again, and before the spring Nigel's Mum passed away peacefully.

Nigel realised that he was possibly rubbing the car's paint work too hard as he tried to hold back the tears. Best to think more about the future and what it may bring.

Moving out of the cottage was the first step, and keeping a low profile, the less people that knew why he was here, the better. They would find out soon enough when the rest of the team arrived.

Don't suppose butting heads with the Captain's going to help, thought Nigel. It's hard to avoid that chap, and as for Faye, not too sure about her. Paul's good, and Baby, Love and builders all seem OK, nevertheless he needed to stay low.

Nigel finished washing the car the best he could. Nothing to wipe off the soap suds. It will do for now. Need to add a wiping cloth to the shopping list.

Nigel retired to the kitchen and started another brew.

Whilst the water came to the boil, he went down to the shed, and rummaged about for gardening tools, finding a spade and fork. Both were rusty, but they would do the job.

Tea made, he stood by what was once a path. Nigel decided where to place the veg patch; it, like the rest of the garden was overgrown, but he didn't need a big area.

Nigel set about clearing the brambles and rubble out of the way. Part way, though, and needing a bit of a rest, best check on the time.

4.35! Need to get a move on, need to be at Paul's by 6.00 for chippy tea.

Nigel put the tools back in the shed and got washed and changed.

A steady walk to Paul's should see him arriving on time.

Nigel locked the back door as had now become a habit and off he set. As he turned the corner he could see Alex and another builder fixing the garage doors. Two were already in place.

'What do you think then, Nigel, big heavy solid doors. Look fantastic, don't they?' asked Alex.

'I have to give it to you, Alex. They do look big doors. You possibly need to be some sort of body builder to open and close them,' replied Nigel.

'Have a go, Nigel.'

'No, thanks.'

'Go on, Nigel, just have a go at opening one of them,' said Alex.

Nigel thought for a moment.

'OK, I don't mind looking foolish,' said Nigel.

Nigel walked up to one of the doors, grabbed the big round handle took a deep breath and pulled.

He almost landed on his back. The door was lightweight, but looked heavy and solid.

'It's a new textured plastic, it looks like the real thing. Not real wood, but lightweight and you don't have to paint it. It's great, isn't it?' said Alex.

'It's good, very good, not sure Rembrandt would agree,' said Nigel.

'What?' Alex replied in an inquisitive way.

'See you,' Nigel said as he walked off.

'What's he on about?' asked the other builder to Alex.

'No idea, let's get another door on.'

As he reached the bottom of the drive he looked back and smiled. The lads were lifting another door into place.

He could also see Faye on horseback and thought himself lucky to not have to speak with her.

There was not a lot of activity at the Pub, but it being Saturday evening, time to give the team a break!

Perhaps they are having a chippy tea tonight?

Nigel thought for a moment, best get a move on before all those hungry chaps scoff all the fish and chips.

Nigel knocked on the vicarage door. Paul answered, coat on, ready to go.

'Evening, Nigel, glad you're on time. My stomach's rumbling. I am ready for this supper.'

'Me too,' replied Nigel.

Both men joined the small queue of people.

Nigel ordered his fish, chips and peas in a tray; Paul ordered chips, battered sausage and curry sauce.

Both men scurried back to the vicarage like two little boys that had been out taking apples from someone's orchard and running off with their swag.

Two cans of beer opened, the friends sat quietly devouring supper, that, both agreed, was well worth waiting for.

'If you're not in a rush, Nigel, how about a board game or cards?'

Nigel thought for a moment, 'Do you have a chess set? If so, do you fancy that?'

'I do, on both counts. You're not one of those Grand Masters of Chess, are you?' asked Paul.

'No, I only ever played against my Dad. Mum was a whiz at draughts, but chess was Dad's. Not played for a long time.' 'Why's that? Or is that delving into personal stuff?' asked Paul.

'No, I don't mind. You see, Mum died 14 months ago. She had been in hospital for a while but despite their best efforts we lost her. Dad was never the same. He basically lost interest in life. I tried to help gee him up. A friend, Mr Parker, and I would take him out in the car, but he always wanted to go back home. Mr Parker would call for him to go down to the allotment. Dad used to go but just sat there.

'Work had to finish him as he never went, which I guess was fair! I think that could have been the tipping point. I am not blaming the Council, they always tried to do their best for him.

'Then one Saturday, I came in from washing the car and went to make a cup of tea for us both. Dad came to the kitchen door, and said 'I loved your mother, and I never really told her, never told her enough.'

'I tried to comfort him, "She knew Dad".'

'He then went and sat in his chair. 'Do you want a biscuit with your tea, Dad?' But I didn't get a reply. I went into the room and Dad had passed away in his chair.

'I guess, if they could, they should have put on the Death Certificate, "Died of a broken heart".

'That will be a year soon.'

Silence filled the room. Needing to move on and wishing he had not asked, Paul spoke,'I think the chess board may be under the stairs.' Sure enough, he emerged board and pieces in hand.

Both men set up the game, Paul fetching the last two cans of beer.

'OK, Nigel, let battle commence.'

The game was evenly matched and took well over 2 hours.

'Checkmate,' said Paul.

'Good play, I enjoyed that. Best be making my way back now, thanks,' said Nigel.

'If you fancy another game next week, we can do the same "Chips and Chess".'

'I will check on my very heavy social diary and write it in,' joked Nigel. With that he started on his way home.

Has he made his way up the drive. He could just about see that the doors to the garage were in place. Even in the limited light available they did look really good. He made a mental note to have a look in the morning.

'Who goes there?' came this jovial voice.

'Evening, David, how are you?'

'Very good, Mary made you a pie. She had some leftovers. You did say we could make another pie, didn't you?'

'Yes, David, and I hope you enjoy eating it.'

'Yours is over here.'

The two walked over to the Old House. By the side of the steps was a bag.

'This is yours, Nigel,' handing over the bag.

Nigel peered inside.

'That looks great, what's in the bottle?' asked Nigel.

'That homemade custard. She had to put it in a milk bottle and put greaseproof paper over the top with an elastic band. Hope that's OK.'

'Thank you, David. I will have that for tea tomorrow, thank your wife for me.'

Nigel gave David a wave and set off to the cottage, holding the bag as if his life depended on it.

Nigel opened the back door and placed the bag into the old bread bin, hoping it was cool enough to keep it fresh till tomorrow. There were still 2 sausages in the tin from the butchers'.

The weather was not really cold, so he needed to consider future purchases of fresh meat - either buy daily or go back to porridge for breakfast or get a fridge.

Screwing the wood screw in, Nigel decided, bed.

I will have a Scotch another night. Washed and in bed Nigel said out loud, 'I Love You.'

Nigel heard the clock chime 8 and decided to get washed. Putting on his old clothes that he had worn the day before, now down for breakfast.

After putting on the kettle, he opened the back door to view the weather, overcast and drizzling, but not cold, which made him rethink about the sausages.

Removing them from the old tin, giving them a good sniff, they're OK, get them in the pan.

Breakfast eaten, second brew on the go.

Nigel thought it best to do the washing up now, instead of later.

Whilst the water was in the sink, he decided to fill the heaters. Any spillage on his hands could be washed off.

With both heaters outside, he retrieved the full and part full paraffin containers, and filled both tanks.

Heaters returned to their rightful place, flame guard left shut, he could not be bothered with that for now.

Hands washed in the leftover soapy water and tea in hand, Nigel leant against the back door frame. Task for today, planting.

It had been hard going the day before. The ground was well overgrown and hard and compact.

Nigel stood in front of the part dug patch, 'Now look here, no messing today, I mean business.'

As he walked over to the shed he thought to himself, I told that patch of ground not to mess with me today!

Looking around the shed, he saw the spade and fork were gone.

I am sure I put them in here, yesterday. I did, I know I did.

Well, I wonder what's happened to them?

Nigel could feel his blood boil, he went inside, and grabbed his coat, he needed fresh air.

Almost slamming the back door behind him, he started to march off down the drive, only to be met by Alex in a yellow digger.

'Morning, Nigel.'

'Morning!' snapped Nigel.

Alex stopped the machine.

'Not our normal self this morning. What's the problem?'

'Sorry, I am OK.'

'Spit it out, Nigel.'

'I got a few veg plants from the market yesterday and started to turn over a small piece of ground to transplant them. I hadn't finished digging yesterday so came back to it this morning, and as if by magic the spade and fork had disappeared out of the shed.'

'Come on, let's go back and have a look.'

Alex jumped back in the cab, started it up, and shouted at Nigel, 'Come on!'

Alex moved off, Nigel's head down, he sadly followed. By the time Nigel got back Alex had somehow managed to squeeze the machine between the car and the gas cage.

Within seconds the front bucket lifted the front end up, the two rear jacks lifted the back end of the machine.

Alex swung the back arm out and ripped into the undergrowth, and unceremoniously dumped it in a heap, the next few strokes saw the teeth cut up about 8 ~ 10 inches depth of soil.

'How about that?' asked Alex.

Nigel stood with his mouth open, not believing what he had seen.

'Alex, that was brilliant, perfect, great job!'

Alex lifted the two jacking legs, lifted the front bucket and carefully pulled back on to the lane.

Alex turned off the machine.

'Are you OK with that?'

'Thanks, Alex, it makes me feel so much better, thanks.'

Alex stood still for a moment.

'Ay Nigel, is that your phone ringing?'

Nigel had to burst out laughing as Alex pulled away toward the house.

Nigel stood by the clean exposed earth, 'See, I told you, I meant business.'

Fortunately, Nigel still had the trowel and set about cleaning up the remaining roots and bits and bobs from the cleared space. Somehow the hours slipped by, possibly helped by numerous cups of tea.

Chapter 11

A Cross Rider

Nigel temporarily forgot about recent events. The kindness shown by Alex, and David and his wife, the vicar, Baby, Love and Millie, all good people that have without a second thought helped me.

These people are the heart of the village, a heart, I was told, was fading fast. I can only hope that when I move out of here, they still feel the same.

Nigel continued to work on the cleared plot, deciding to plant out tomorrow. Not used to working a garden, it had been a long time since helping on the allotment, Nigel knew that he would be stiff in the morning, so have a walk to the lake and a hot bath, and then homemade pie and custard.

Nigel put his tools inside and double checked the door was locked, still in his old clothes walked toward the Old House.

He could see the digger cutting a trench from the house towards the lake. He only had about 100 yards left to do, the trench was about 2 ft. deep, and the soil was laid in a row by the side.

Nigel made his way to the machine. Alex turned the engine off.

'That's better, 5 minutes peace and quiet,' said Alex.

'What's this for, I thought you said the earth can't go back in the hole, it looks likes it's ready for putting back in?' enquired Nigel.

'I am cutting a trench from the house down to the lake. The rainwater that falls on the house will first go into a filter tank, then into a pipe then down to a second filter then into the lake.'

'It is hoped that the two filters will help purify the water, making it better for the fish. Both tanks will have a stained wooden top, easy to remove making it a doddle for cleaning the filters.

'We are putting in a flexi pipe, not likely to rupture and it's only rainwater.

'I understand that the bomb crater will become a lake. We can use some of the soil from the gas pipe trench to help shore up the lower side of the crater.

'Obviously, it's not going be as big as that one, this one will flow into the second lake when we get round to digging it out. The overflow water will be piped into the brook that goes under the road.'

'When are you starting the hot water thingy and the gas pipe?' asked Nigel.

'Hoping tomorrow, we are still on schedule, despite the extra 200 yards dig. We are having to work 6 and 7 days a week, but it's better than being on the dole, and if your boss can do it so can I.

'What do you think of the finished garages then, Nigel?'

'I will be honest, Alex. From the outside it looks brilliant. The stained wood and the doors with the fake hingers, are great. But once the doors are open you see the brick work with the mortar. It is stunning. If it was mine, I would upgrade from a push bike to a second-hand moped to store in it.'

'Cheeky,' said Alex.

As he climbed back in the cab and restarted working, Nigel decided to cancel the remainder of the walk. The sound of the machine working would spoil the moment down by the lake.

Instead of taking the normal way back he walked parallel with the road. This meant that he could see most of the Old House from the front. A view he had not taken a lot of notice before. With the new white window, newly painted boards and facers and the super glossed door it did look impressive, but not overpowering. He thought it added to the village, did not dominate it.

Nigel started to walk across the lawn figuring it was easier than going straight up. The skies had cleared and there was a nip in the air, so Nigel thought a small fire was in order, not only for the warmth but to give that homely feel whilst eating his homemade pie.

Back at the cottage Nigel collected the coal scuttle and walked down to the coal house, collecting some coal and the last few small sticks. He thought perhaps tomorrow he should chop a few more, tomorrow's job!

Back in the cottage, order of service - light heater in bathroom, make and light fire in sitting room, hot bath, supper.

Nigel managed to set both heater dampers first time, that's a result!

Downstairs he soon set a small fire in the grate, guard in place and ready to go back upstairs.

He took a moment, let's put the screw in place just in case someone should try the door.

That done, Nigel went off for a hot bath. With the combination of a busy day and the hot water, there was a possibility Nigel thought, that he could have fallen asleep, as the water now seemed a little cool.

Washed, dried and dressed, he went down and lit the oven, ready for the pie and put on the kettle.

Walking back into the sitting room he found the fire had almost gone out, perhaps I did nod off after all.

Fire restocked with coal, pie in the oven, tea brewing, and the custard in a pan on a low light, Nigel drank the first brew and decided to make a second. By the time I've done that, supper will be ready, he told himself.

Soon Nigel was sitting in front of the fire with a big slice of pie, topped with steaming custard.

He finally finished the supper, forcing the last few crumbs down. What a tasty pie! And the custard was the best, he had to sit back in the chair thinking he could explode.

He must have sat motionless for about half an hour before daring to move, then only taking himself to the kitchen for a small Scotch, he returned to the sitting room, and placing another lump of coal sat watching the flames dance about.

He sat thinking about plans for tomorrow, going to have to be porridge for breakfast. Still have honey left, then dig out any remaining roots, transplant the veg.

Chop some sticks that should take me to the afternoon, then have a walk to the lake and perhaps have a look at the progress at the Pub.

Well, thought Nigel, that's enough planning for tonight, time for bed. Finishing the last of the small glass of Scotch, fire guard in place, time Nigel slowly made his way upstairs. Still full of pie and custard he retired to bed, 'I Love You.'

The next morning parts of Nigel ached so much that he stooped whilst walking, each step down the stair was an effort, the day before had used muscles that had not been used for a while and it felt like every bone in his body hurt. ....

Breakfast took a little longer to make than normal and getting out of the chair after eating was an effort. Nigel knew he had to continue in the garden. He hoped that things would ease.

Opening the back door, he looked down on the old tin.

Didn't think that very well, I still have pie left but I ate all the custard, add to tomorrow's shopping list - cream!

I don't understand how my appetite has changed, I've never eaten so much.

Nigel retrieved the trowel off the shelf, he gingerly knelt on the floor digging at the last few remaining roots and unwanted bits.

Collecting the plant from the outhouse, Nigel started to arrange them on the garden in rows. That will do. He set about transplanting, remembering what his dad had said: plenty of water first, then dig them in, pressing down around the roots.

Taking a trip to the shed in case he had missed seeing a watering can, he noted the step ladders. I will need them in a few weeks.

If I take them in and anyone sees them, a question could be asked - why do I need steps?

If I leave them here then the magic fairies could take them like they did with the spade and fork.

There are all sorts of stuff in here. I will put the steps right at the back of the shed and put whatever I can find in front of them. If someone takes them, I will have to buy some new ones or ask Baby, Love.

Nigel managed to get the steps against the back wall. There was a set of drawers, half a roll of chicken wire.

Chicken wire!

I am going to need that, the bunnies and other animals will feast on my plants.

Using what was in the shed - old tins of paint, picture frame, rotting wooden boxes were all piled up against the steps and the back wall.

Nigel stood back to admire his work. That's OK, the steps look like they have not been used for years, and I got the chicken wire, still no watering can.

Bucket, stupid! You got a bucket. Bucket filled, Nigel returned to the garden.

Thinking about his next move, best if I check how much wire I have. Is it enough to go round?

With a rearrangement of the plants, he had just the right amount. Now he needed stakes to hold up the wire.

I have abundance of wood, I can pick up fallen branches and trim them with the axe, not sure how to fasten the two together, cross that bridge later.

He opened up the coal house door and looked for the axe, moving a few bits of coal and wood, that too had disappeared.

Nigel thought for a moment, time for a cup of tea and a new plan.

Walking back to the cottage, he stopped; I am not hurting as I did earlier. That's a good thing to think about, let's be positive, he told himself.

Do I really need an axe? I can now buy canes and string from the Iron Mongers', no need to hunt wood and spend time cutting it up. Thank you, magic fairies, you did me a favour!

Add to shopping list, canes and string.

Nigel picked up the plants at first, decided to put them in the outhouse, then decided in the kitchen could be better. Bucket and wire put in the shed, time for tea.

Checking on the time, early afternoon, he planned to have a look on the progress by Alex.

Ensuring the door was locked he set off towards the Old House.

Nigel made his way over to the lake. Sure enough there was a trench leading from the house to the top part edge of the lake, with a hole approximately 6 foot square and about the same depth.

This was the spot that Nigel liked to use the most to look over the valley. Best not do that for a while until the top's on, he thought.

Nigel could hear the machine working but could not see it.

He started to follow the straight mount of earth up the hill. The machine went silent. As he continued up the hill part of the machine came in view. Continuing up the hill, he saw Faye and her horse were by the side of the machine.

Nigel moved towards them.

Alex had been digging the trench but unlike the rainwater gully the soil was in a pile, presumably for collecting by the lorries later or use for the lower part of the bomb crater as it couldn't go back in the hole.

Nigel turned towards Faye and Alex, and was about 100 yards away, when Faye sharply pulled on the horse bit and with a kick galloped off.

Alex was sitting sideways to the machine's controls.

'Good day, Alex,' said Nigel.

'It was,' answered Alex.

'You wouldn't believe that woman, Nigel, I go to football matches, I play rugby, I go out drinking with the lads - I am not proud of it, but the language can get coarse. But what that woman has just come out with because I've dug this trench and that trench over there and she can't ride across it, the air was blue, Nigel, I'm shocked!

'I tried to explain it's only for a few days. I can't believe what she came out with. I hope the new owners of this house let her ride across here. If they don't, I don't want to be around when they tell her.'

Alex spung round on the seat and re-started the engine.

Nigel thought best to leave him for now, but he still wanted to see the progress on the Pub.

He decided to go down the old path towards what should be the lane where the brook runs alongside. Sure enough, only a short distance, Nigel came to the open gate and turned left toward the main road. Crossing over onto the pavement he strolled down towards the Pub.

Looking down the road Nigel could see the teams were beavering away.

The front of the building was not all that different from when they started work on it. The car park was all churned up, the sign was still missing a few bits, but it was still recognisable as The Cooper's.

It was not until Nigel walked around the side towards the rear that the true transformation could be appreciated.

The conservatory was in place, albeit, without all the glass. The extension to the far side which was going to be the new kitchen was up, there was a large hole in the roof.

There were large steel tubes on the floor, Nigel guessed that would be the extraction units that would be fitted to the roof.

Inside were flood lights on tripods filling the entire area with bright light.

'Good day, Nigel, come to give a hand?'

'Thought about it, Love, but don't wish to show your lads up, they seem to be muddling by. Are you still on target, time wise?' asked Nigel.

'Think so,' said Love, 'we are coming to a crucial stage, the last few weeks can be tricky. Alex is up at the Old House digging out for the gas tank.

'Gas people are planning on installing the tank a week today. That means we have to lay the slab, latest Wednesday, whilst the tank is not that heavy. I would like the tank to settle before it's pumped full of liquid gas. The pipeline is now longer, and we have more joints. I would like to check them out before we back fill.

'We could fill in the water drainage pipe in the next few days, but Baby and I have decided to leave it open until the gas is fully installed before back filling. After all, it's not going to affect anyone, leaving it open.'

'Absolutely, who's going to mind? You've got a few weeks before the new people move in.'

'We can back fill it all when we bring the machine back on site,' said Love.

'I think that's a great idea. After all it's not affecting anyone, good idea,' agreed Nigel.

Nigel could hardly contain his smile at the thought of Faye ranting about access for the next few weeks.

Chapter 12

Vultures will Circle

Nigel made his way towards the river. The landlord was sitting on an old beer barrel.

'Good afternoon,' Nigel said cheerfully, still thinking about Faye.

'Oh, Hello.'

Nigel could see by his demeanour, he was not happy, 'Is there a problem? Would you like to talk about it, or should I continue on down the river?' asked Nigel.

'You've hit the nail on the head there - down the river.I think that's what's happened to me and the Pub. Look at all that work, the bar, lounge, restaurant, not to mention the kitchen, plus fixtures and fittings, the job's costing a King's ransom.'

Nigel thought for a moment. 'It looks like it could be a pretty penny, that's for sure! You told me you have a contract, that's watertight, what's the problem?'

'I still have to pay the money back, plus 15% of the profit for five years,' answered the landlord.

Nigel walked off and collected another tatty beer barrel and dragged it up to the landlord.

'I don't wish to know your business, so let's just look at this a different way.

'On the day the vicar and I came into the Pub, there were about eight customers. Each perhaps had 3 pints, that's 24 pints. Let's push the boat out and guess a couple of bags of crisps. Now you work out how much profit you made; don't tell me, I don't wish to know.

'Out of that you have 2 wages, yours and the good lady's, the upkeep of the Pub, rates, heating, lighting and all that. How long would you have survived?

'Now if you went under, then you could sell the Pub, not as a going concern, no one comes in! Who's going to buy a rundown Pub whilst in a recession?

'Now take it one stage on.

'You don't have a business to sell, and the vultures will circle for the money you owe, running costs such as rates, electric, gas, insurance, etc. they won't show you any mercy I can assure you of that.

'Now, let's have a look at the new Cooper's.

'It will be bright and airy and inviting; the drinkers will return. There's a lounge area for those wishing to drink cocktails and wine and chat in a peaceful environment. You could perhaps sell teas, coffees or soft drinks out of licensing hours.

'The restaurant, at a guess, has 30 covers. Let's say Chef has only one sitting at lunch and one in the evening, at only 50% capacity. Each meal I suggest will be 5 times the cost of a beer. That's equal to 150 pints, the overheads will be more, more gas and electricity. You have to employ and train 2 or 3 young people. Profit should be about the same, other than that everything else remains similar.

'So, on a pint-by-pint basis, you go from 24 to 150 that's an increase of 625%. I am sure the repayments are annual, but if not, you have 5 years to build a business that is running at 25% capacity.

'Do you think an increase in sales is possible? I think so, don't you?

'I know I am talking pints here but think of the potential- a fantastic village Pub, that's inviting, offers a place to unwind, has teas and coffees, cocktails, a selection of fine wines, food, real food made by a chef and not out of a packet or box.

'You can also open up this area we are sitting in, have outside tables and chairs. Get Baby, Love to make them.

'When the Sun shines people can have a drink in the open air, sit by the river, perhaps enjoy snacks and sandwiches.

'Even if this lot costs a 6-figure sum, paying it back is not going to be a problem, surely. What do you think? Hope that helps, but hey, what do I know about the Pub and restaurant trade?'

With that Nigel stood up, 'Do you own the river side? If so, get the investors to build overnight mooring. Must be a few boaters that pass by and fancy a drink or a meal? Bye.'

Nigel dusted off the debris from his clothes after sitting on a dirty barrel and continued his walk down the riverbank.

He thought to himself, I am getting like that plasterer. I didn't give that poor bloke a chance to talk.

Nigel soon reached the steps leading to the road above. Before he could ascend, a lady and her dog were coming down.

'Hello,' said Nigel.

'Hello, thank you. Not got your wheelie trolley today, then?' replied the lady.

'No, not today,' he replied.

He thought that wheelie trolley must be the talk of the village.

Entering the Iron Mongers', he received the usual bright and cheerful, 'Hello, can I help?'

'Hello, yes, I would like garden canes and string, please.'

'Still hoping to go fishing then, are we? Got the cane for a rod and string for the line, what are you going to use as a hook?' said the shop keeper laughing.

'Sorry about the other day. The Captain can be brutal sometimes. I have to bite my tongue, with the way he speaks to people, but I have to be half decent to him, as the tickets sale helps to pay my way.'

'I thought it was only me he didn't like,' said Nigel.

'I think you could be at the top of his list of not liked people, but according to him, you're moving on in a few weeks.'

'Yes,' replied Nigel, 'I have to move on.'

'Do you know where you're going?' asked the shop keeper.

'I am thinking about camping in that wheelie trolley you sold me, there's enough room.'

The shop owner walked off to collect Nigel's cane and string whilst laughing out loud.

The shop keeper was still laughing when Nigel left the shop.

'What's he laughing at?' asked a voice.

Nigel turned around, 'Hello Paul, my wheelie bag. He's laughing about that, and he sold it to me.'

'You do know it's an oversized one. It was used as a display feature, I don't think it was ever meant to be sold. Then you came along! Let's go and have some tea.

'Mrs Bright's not helping today so we can have a cup without worrying about people ear wigging.'

'Tea sounds good, but I need to buy some cream from the general store. Can you hold these for me a moment whilst I nip in?'

Nigel handed over the garden canes to Paul and disappeared into the shop, moments later re-appearing with his cream and a tin of assorted biscuits.

'We can have these with tea, what do you think?' asked Nigel.

'Good idea,' was the reply. Both men strolled down the road to the vicarage and spent a most pleasant afternoon, tea, biscuits and idle chat.

Nigel waved Paul a "goodbye".

As he walked back down the road, Nigel glanced over to the fund-raising thermometer. It didn't seem to have moved up very much, the weather was warming up. Paul had said that a few more people were attending church, but I guess the congregation still did not fancy spending on the Church to keep warm.

Nigel trundled up the drive. He could hear Alex's machine working in the distance, and wondered if he had forgotten about Faye yet and her outburst.

Nigel put away his shopping. It was still early evening so he decided to take a walk to the lake. As he passed the front of the house Alex's machine fell silent, which gave way to the birds singing, many were landing on the soil from the trench searching the soil for worms.

Nigel couldn't stand in his favoured spot by the lake, as it was now a big hole ready to take the filtration system, which hopefully would greatly improve the water quality and encourage more life back to the lake.

He just sat on a large rock that had been unearthed and started to daydream, his thoughts drifting back to his old hometown and the little house he once lived in, and how things had so dramatically changed.

If it had not been for the help of Mr Parker and Raymond, how different it could have been.

He thought about what he had said to the landlord, 'the vultures will circle' how true that was.

Devising a plan and taking money from Mr Parker and Raymond really helped.

Life became routine for Nigel over the next few weeks, taking and collecting the washing to Millie's, chatting to David in the evening, fish and chips and a game of chess with Paul on a Saturday. Tending vegetables in the cottage garden, chatting with the builders over the Pub, making his regular Friday phone calls.

Nigel spent time watching the Old House get its gas installed, and the rainwater filter system finished and two polished wooden tops in place - one at the top close to the house and one by the lake to hide the filter boxes underneath. He viewed the kitchen floor being assembled and the tiles laid. The ultra-modern kitchen had been fitted and looked spectacular with the modern fitting and island, it now only needed the electrical appliances installing.

Less and less people came. It was looking like the tradesmen had finished on the Old House other than snagging.

According to Baby the outstanding items to be completed were the furnishings, which had been contracted out. Each room would have a different designer.

The Pub was close to being finished, the New Chef had arrived to ensure the kitchen was planned to his liking, new bar and restaurant staff had been employed and were sent off on a training course.

The outside of the Pub had new lettering and lighting. The car park had been resurfaced and marked out, including bays to help the elderly and those who found walking difficult.

The lawns had been cut and beds made ready for flowers. But of course, this only meant one thing, that Nigel would soon have to move out of the cottage.

One Wednesday evening Nigel was sitting on the step, chatting to David, when Baby, Love drove up the drive.

'Evening, Nigel. There isn't any other way we can do this, and it saddens me, but we all knew it had to come, so, sorry Nigel, we would like you to leave the cottage by week Sunday, sorry!'

'Gentlemen, please do not be sorry. As you rightly point out we all knew that this day would come and I thank you for giving me notice. I promise you both, by a week Sunday afternoon, I will have moved out and the cottage will be yours.'

The two boys drove off back down the drive, and Nigel sat back down on the step. A few moments passed. Nigel turned to speak with David. He looked into his eyes which were full of sadness.

'Don't worry, David. Things will be OK.'

'I am really going to miss you. I've enjoyed our talks. I guess I will be getting sacked soon.'

'David! We have had this conversation before. You will not be sacked. It is unfortunate, but you will be made redundant, not sacked.'

David thought, for a moment, 'Still not have a wage will I? But I have a wife I love, and she loves me. I tell her, and she tells me, that's good, isn't it?'

'It's the only thing that matters, David. You will be OK. See you tomorrow, good night.'

Nigel walked back to the cottage. Supper made, he sat by a small fire, which really, he didn't need, but the flame gave comfort whilst eating. Returning the pots to the kitchen, he thought it was time perhaps for a larger Scotch and to plan what happens next. Nigel retired to bed as every night, 'I Love You.'

Chapter 13

Errand Boy

It was not the best night sleep, and Nigel decided to stay by the cottage all day. He didn't feel like going out and talking with people.

After a half-hearted attempt to eat breakfast, he made his way outside to view the results of his labour. Some of the veg. looked OK whilst others seemed to be struggling, not that mattered too much. I won't get to eat them, but I have enjoyed growing something, reminds me of Dad and the allotment, he thought.

As he stood viewing the veg. patch the silence was broken by the sound of lorries coming up the drive.

Well, something to look at, I suppose, so still with tea in hand, Nigel walked to the end of the lane to see one of Bye, Bye vans coming up the drive followed by two lorries, not normal lorries but furniture ones, posh looking with crests on the side.

Love got out of his van and proceeded to open the Old House door.

Nigel continued to walk slowly towards the lorries. Four men were getting out of each lorry, each dressed in smart brown coat.

Going to the rear of the vehicle, they dropped the tail gate, which made a slope. The top half of the door was pushed up out of the way. This revealed brand new furniture all neatly wrapped in plastic.

'Morning, Nigel, told you they are having posh stuff. There will be more vans arriving today,' said Love.

Nigel looked around and behind Love, towards the house, 'If you don't protect that paint work on the door, Rembrandt's going to have your guts for garters, not to mention the architect lass.'

Love spun round. 'Wait, wait, he shouted. 'You need bedsheets on the door, don't mark the door!'

One of the delivery men wearing a bowler hat, gave Love a stern look, 'Sir, we do not use bed sheets, we have bespoke, heavy duty covers for the sole purpose of protecting the customer's property.'

Love turned to Nigel and without saying a word, he had that "told me" look on his face.

The two men parted without any more being said.

Nigel returned to the cottage, feeling somewhat chirpier than before. The delivery man had already made Nigel's day. It was the pick-me-up Nigel needed, so instead of moping around the garden feeling sorry for himself he got his coat and decided to take a walk.

Ensuring the back door was locked, he set off towards the house. There seemed a lot of activity, lots of men in brown overalls, but the vans were still loaded with furniture. As Nigel approached the house, the delivery man in the bowler hat spoke, 'Good Morning.'

'Morning,' replied Nigel.

The man continued, 'Are you one of the designers? They are supposed to meet us on site to direct the furnishings to the correct rooms and position as they so desire.'

'Sorry, cannot help,' said Nigel.

'Who's fixing the curtain rods and tire backs? We can't proceed placing high quality furniture in rooms if workmen are going to make a mess, drilling walls.'

'No,' said Nigel, 'leave them alone, standing on the furniture to reach up.'

It was definitely at this point Nigel became aware that the man in the bowler hat did not have any sense of humour whatsoever.

'I know where the builders will be, I will go and ask them if they can help.'

Just as Nigel turned round, there stood the Captain.

'Good morning, my man,' he said addressing the man in the bowler hat.

'Good morning, Sir. I was just explaining to this chap that we require the services of a man to fit the curtain rods and tire backs.'

'No problem, I can help.'

Turning to Nigel the Captain barked, 'You, make yourself useful and go to The Cooper's and instruct one of the Bye's to come up here immediately.'

Nigel looked at him.

'Yes Sir, no problem, Sir, can I have 2d's for some sweets if I run?'

Nigel made his way down the drive to the Pub. As he walked down, he thought, what a day, first I am feeling sorry for myself, then I am happy, now I am cross. Funny old day and it not even mid-morning.

As he reached the bottom, Alex and a mate turned in, and pretended to try and run Nigel over, sounding his van horn and waving.

Nigel made a playful fist as if in anger.

Nigel arrived at the Pub. What a transformation! The outside looked clean, fresh, inviting.

The car park with its black coat looked as flat as a bowling green. The white painted lines looked like they were asking you to park here.

The front door had been varnished and shone in the light; the brass fittings looked majestic against the wood, it truly looked spectacular.

Nigel needed to find someone, so walked around the rear to find Baby or Love.

'Hello again, Love, I have a message from, No! I have an instruction from the Captain, you are to prevail your services to the delivery men with assistance in fixing curtain rods and tire backs, and if you go now I can have 2d's for sweeties.'

Love looked at Nigel, 'I do like you, Nigel, I really do, but you worry me sometimes. 2d's for Sweeties? You now need at least 10p, catch up Nigel.

'Anyway, Alex should be up there with a helper to do the necessary work.

'What do you think of the old place then, Nigel? It looks like it all came together, the Chef's in the kitchen putting things in the right place for him. Can't have things too high, he's not all that tall, but who cares as long as he can cook?

'I understand, starting next week, they are opening Thursday lunch, Friday evening and Saturday evening and opening day Sunday Lunch - all the events are by invitation only with limited numbers, and it's free.

'It is all to do with what someone called a "learning curve". It's part of a training programme. As the food is free, the landlord and landlady are looking at customer feedback. The big do is on Sunday lunch, on that day both food and drink are free. That's the day when Chef is going to be really under pressure. They're going to be serving hot buffet, with meats cut to your liking, thick or thin, on warm bread. There will be salad, homemade pork pies, sausage rolls, all sorts of new food. I'm thinking of booking the next day off. Anyway it will give you another day to move out, are you invited, Nigel?'

'No,' said Nigel.

'Oh yes you are,' shouted the landlord. Without your help, I could have thrown myself in the river. Not really but you know what I mean.

'Some good ideas of yours, Nigel. We are going ahead with the tables outside. I just need to get the builders to do a better job on the outside tables than they did with the steps outside the Post Office.'

'Funny,' replied Love. 'If you need help throwing yourself in the river give me a shout.'

'How's this job gone then, Love? I could see from time to time the pressure was showing. It was a big undertaking this and the Old House,' asked Nigel.

'It's true, Baby and I were not going to give in. The chap that came to our rescue and the little chap in the bowler and pinstriped suit, showed true faith in us, how could we have let them down?

'Look at the amount of people that had managed to continue to feed the family and pay bills.

'The economy is looking better. I think we have ridden the storm, we still have work. Sorry to say this, the cottage needs lots of work, then I found out why we had to move the gas tank.

'We have to rebuild the house at the end of what was the kitchen garden, the one near the green house, the one the tree fell on.

'Oh yes! And we have to replace the broken and missing glass panes. There's also talk about digging out the bomb crater, to make a second pond, guess the new owner likes fishing.

'The Captain needs work doing, I need to juggle that a little. The architect lass is getting a bit pushy with completing the Old House and in fairness she's right. The Captain can wait a few weeks.'

'Well,' said Nigel, 'it also depends on who you are more scared of, the lass or the Captain.'

'The lass, without a doubt,' he replied.

'Right, Nigel. When would you like to come to a learning curve meal?' asked the landlady.

'If possible, I would like Sunday lunch please.'

'Sunday lunch it is, about 12.15. OK, I need to stagger people, I have a party of 6 in at 1.00 although I understand they are coming in for drinks at 12.00, is that OK?'

'Very OK, thank you, but can I ask if I can bring Paul, the vicar, in with me?'

Love jumps in, 'Sounds like trouble to me. Baby and I are in on that day so if you need bouncers let us know.'

'Thanks,' said the landlady, 'I, am sure it won't come to that, any way if it does, I will get the lass to sort it.'

'The lass is coming to have a look around; they're staying in the Old House. Could be the lass that's bought the old place, after all she's put a lot of work into it.

'See you and the vicar, week Sunday then, Nigel.'

'Everyone's a comedian around here, see you, Nigel,' said Love.

Nigel decided to walk back to the cottage. As he crossed the road he looked back on the Pub. Baby, Love and the team have done a great job on that Pub. I guess the lass needs a pat on the back too.

As Nigel approached the end of the drive, he could see more vans, cars and people. There was a real hive of activity, furniture was being unloaded from the vans and placed on special thick plastic sheets. He could also see what looked like designer type people, each poring over it all, seemingly checking it was all OK before going into the house.

It seemed almost everything was out on the front, settees, chairs, lamps, tables, dining chairs, sideboards, bookcases - all sort of items, Nigel had never seen before. He looked inside a van and he could see what looked like pictures still in the wrapping, rugs and larger carpets, cushions, mirrors, boxes marked "Fragile, take care", so much stuff, looked like there was enough to fill two houses.

Nigel stood, mouth open, yet another van came up the drive, The Electrical Company.

'Hi mate, brought the electrical equipment, where is it going?' shouted the lad.

'What sort is it?' asked Nigel.

'Mostly kitchen items, fridge, washing machine, dish washer, food processors, food mixers, coffee machine, kettle, electronic scales, that sort of stuff. We also have TVs, Radios, a video recorder, too. Where's the kitchen?'

Nigel pointed, 'Around the side. You best get that way, the kitchen's around the back.'

'Thanks, grateful,' shouted the lad.

'You!' shouted the Captain. 'Get back to the builders, these two lads can't cope with all this, I need more people.'

Faye looked from around the door.

'And tell them to bring pans and brushes to clean up after themselves.'

'Good idea, Faye,' said the Captain.

'Well, what are you waiting for, man? You've lived here free for goodness knows how long, earn your keep.'

Nigel was frozen to the spot, fuming with anger. The Captain and Faye have truly overstepped the mark.

Then the lad from the electrical equipment van, appeared.

'Sorry to be a pain, can you get someone to open the kitchen door? No one's answering, we need to install all the equipment in the kitchen units, it's what's called, integral.'

Nigel just stood and stared.

'Are you OK, mate? I only need the door opening.'

Nigel took a pace back, addressing the lad, 'If you would like to ask this gentleman,' pointing at the Captain, 'I am sure he will find a slave or servant to help, as for me I have to run an errand like a good little boy.'

Nigel tried to walk off with dignity, but the inner rage was still burning, it was still there when he reached the back of the Pub.

'Are you, OK?' asked the landlady.

'No, I am not. Are you allowed to sell Scotch at this time of the day?'

'No, sorry Nigel, but I can give you a Scotch.' The landlady went behind the bar and returned with the drink and the landlord.

She handed the drink over, and Nigel swallowed it in one go.

'Better now?' she enquired.

'Almost. Thank you very much, I am not a drinker but just every now and then, someone gets to you and that person, and his sidekick made my blood boil.'

'Oh, let me guess,' said the landlord.

Both the landlord and landlady said in unison, 'the Captain and Faye.'

The landlady continued, 'I will change your and the vicar's booking, Nigel, as those two will be here on that Sunday.'

'No, please don't. I have run away before, and I am done running, but thank you, anyway.'

Now I need to find Baby or Love. Alex is struggling with the work and the furniture people need to start putting the stuff in, and until Alex has completed a room it's not going to happen.'

'Hang on, Nigel, he has gone back to the yard, I will ring him, hang on.'

With that the landlord disappeared into the back.

Nigel took time to have a look around, he had mostly seen it from outside or full of builders.

To the right of the front door was an area with leather chairs and settees, a low-level table, and a grandfather clock. To the left of the door, high round tables, some with high stools, some without any, guess you have to stand at them.

Above the fireplace most of the wall had been plastered, however, there was an area that showed the brick work underneath. Looked like the plaster had fallen off, looked good, a real nice feature!

The bar was now in two halves with an island in the middle, one side could serve the bar and the other side served the restaurant area.

'OK, Nigel, I've spoken with Baby. He is sending lads up now to help. Do you have a moment? I need to talk with you.'

Both men started to walk down to the river.

'Your idea about berths for boats, we do get boats up and down the river, perhaps next year. This summer is on its way, and I think the time spent getting the outside service honed, see how we all cope, do you think we should wait?'

'I think, wait,' said Nigel. 'You may need to dredge the river just by the edge to allow boats access. That's going to take a machine. Then you need to push piles in for the walkway. All that's not going to help thc grassed area with a machine driving on it, and not sure what the river authorities will say, so no, wait till next year.'

Nigel turned and looked back at the Pub, 'That's a fine place you've got there. It looks fantastic, you and the wife will make it special. The village will be proud. Have you tried Chef's food yet?'

'Not yet, Nigel, he is still sorting out equipment. He is getting suppliers in with fresh food samples, seems a bit fiery if the food's not fresh or up to standard. We have heard him, not one for mincing his words. Not a very big chap, but I am not getting on the wrong side of him. I guess the proof is in the pudding or in this case, pudding, starter and main.

'Thanks for the help the other day,' said the landlord.

'No problem, thanks for the drink. I am going to try and sneak back to the cottage without them pair seeing me.'

Walking back up the drive he passed by Baby's and a few other vans.

'Hi Nigel, are you better now?'

'Yes thanks, hope you brought pans and brushes to clean up after you. The Captain and his sidekick will insist.'

'Don't you worry about it, Nigel, those two are putty in my hands,' replied Baby.

Baby and the rest of the team of vans pulled off with Baby waving out the window.

That Scotch was a bit big; I think I need to walk it off, thought Nigel. I will head off down the lane towards the farm.

Chapter 14

Is it Time for Change?

Having passed the Cottage, he noticed to the right, down the hill, something sticking out of the brambles. On closer inspection, he could see it was his spade. Clearly someone had thrown it down the slope hoping it could not be seen.

Nigel descended the slope to reclaim it, being careful to avoid the slippery fallen tree branches and the thorns from the bramble.

The spade had almost gone past the wild bushes, luckily it was perched towards the back, so Nigel had to circle around to retrieve it. Reaching at full stretch he was able to pull it free.

About to start the climb back to the lane, he could hear voices, so crouching low he hid himself out of sight of the lane. As the voices got closer Nigel could tell - a male and female.

That's Faye and the Captain, he thought, really would hate to be seen, I am going to seem a right chump.

As the voices were directly overhead, Faye was heard to say, 'The spade must have fallen even farther down. It got logged in the bramble. Good, he won't find it now. The axe went a lot farther.'

'Are we going back to the Old House tomorrow?' asked Faye.

'Yes,' said the Captain, the lower floors haven't been finished, due to the incompetence of the builders, let alone the upper floor. Don't you worry. I will make damn sure the new people know how we sorted it.'

With that the two walked off and Nigel could not hear what was said after that.

Nigel gave it a few minutes to make sure they had left, and it was safe to come out. Standing up he looked down the slope, how far did that axe go?

I wonder what happened to the fork, he thought.

Making his way back up the hill, now with the aid of the spade he made his way back to the cottage. However, he could make out that the vans were still at the Old House, so he decided to have a look. Most of the furniture was inside, however some items remained in the vans.

'Hello, Nigel.'

'Hello, Alex,' replied Nigel.

'How's it going?'

'Good, thanks. After a slow start we are getting on top of it. You see we had to wait for the delivery as the curtains are all different lengths with different rails and such, so we could not fit the rails until we were sure what went where. There's now only a couple upstairs to do tomorrow, and we are all sorted!'

'Good job, Faye and the Captain sorted it all for you,' said Nigel.

'I kept out of that woman's way, and if you don't mind taking some advice, Nigel, I wouldn't mention anything to Baby, he is not happy. The pair of them gave him a bit of a roasting and he couldn't say much as we are working at the Captain's house in a few weeks.'

With that Baby came out of the Old House looking somewhat battered.

'Hello Baby, putty in your hands, ha?'

Not another word was spoken as Baby jumped into the van and drove off.

'What's it looking like in there, Alex?' asked Nigel.

'It's really posh, come and have a look. I am sure the new owners won't mind. There's been more people in that house over that last 8 months or so, one more's not going to matter.'

'Best not, Alex, I am covered in dirt. I had to rescue the spade. See you, tomorrow.'

'Rescue the spade, from what?' asked Alex.

'See you tomorrow, my friend,' shouted Nigel.

Nigel returned to the cottage. Deciding to put the spade in the kitchen for safe keeping, he started to prepare supper which tonight was tinned corn beef with potatoes and fresh carrots.

Once peeled, and the peelings put on a small pile outside, a sort of compost heap, Nigel looked long and hard at this small heap of part rotting veg. Why bother, I am not going to be here. Same with growing the veg, why bother, the whole thing is pointless.

Wait a moment why are we having the conversation, particularly with myself. You're doing it to keep sane, what would you do without this patch and the cottage?

You need to be thankful. Stopping at home was clearly heading for total destruction, now pull yourself together.

I will, Nigel, thank you. I feel so much better now, Nigel. Good now, go finish supper!

That evening was the same as most other evenings, but clearly this could not last, 10 more nights and done!

The next step will be out into a totally different life.

Change was not Nigel's style. Comfort, routine, his own company. This was all about to change and if Nigel did not embrace the change now, the time to get out will be gone. Once the gun had gone off absolutely no turning back.

Nigel thought long and hard about plans, turning back was still sort of an option or had he gone too far.

He decided to keep busy and stop thinking so much.

He sorted his washing for Millie, and made a shopping list, including as yet undecided ingredients for a pie. Nigel took a moment, I wonder if Mary needed any more items, flour or eggs. Grabbing his coat and ensuring as usual the door was locked, he went off to find David.

One van still remained, however apart from a few bits it was almost empty.

'Evening,' came a voice.

'Evening, have you almost finished for the day,' Nigel asked the man in the bowler.

'Yes, back tomorrow, with two more vans this time for upstairs, beds, wardrobes, chest of drawers, rugs, pillows, sheets, and the normal paraphernalia.

'Wardrobes are interesting. You would think they would go for modern fitted ones, but no, different from that kitchen. I've never seen a kitchen as modern, it looks like it came right out of a magazine. Most of the downstairs is OK. We had a couple of designers in attendance making sure everything is in the right place, they seem happy.'

'Do you mean the chap in the hat and the woman with him?' asked Nigel.

'No sir, they are not designers, and I have to keep professional, so let's say no more. I hope to see you tomorrow. There are still a couple of people inside. The night watchman said he will lock up when he goes there. Bye.'

'Yes, good night,' replied Nigel.

Nigel sat on the steps as the man and the rest of the remaining crew closed the van and drove away.

Soon the lights, one by one, were turned off and the last two people left.

'Goodnight,' said Nigel, but didn't get a reply.

David followed them and locked the door, giving it a good push to ensure it was closed.

'Evening, David.'

'Hello, Nigel. Nigel, you should see inside, would you like to see inside? I can put the lights on, and you can look through the windows.'

'No, you're OK. Thanks, lots more to look after now, David, nearly half full of furniture, the rest is coming tomorrow, I understand.'

'Yes,' said David.

'Then on Monday and Tuesday the cleaners are coming, the man in the black hat and brown coat said that moving lots of soft furnishings will create dust so two days of cleaning, then on Wednesday the lady that Love calls lass is coming.

Thursday and Friday, Baby, Love have to sort whatever the lady needs doing, then I look after the place until Saturday morning. People are moving on Saturday, I will be made redundant not sacked is that right, Nigel?'

Nigel thought for a moment.

'Yes David, could very well be.

Mary should make a special pie for that last Friday. Your wife always makes special pies, fit for a King, speaking of which, what does she need, how are you for flour and eggs and things?'

'Don't know, Nigel.'

'What's Mary doing tomorrow? We could go shopping and she can tell me what is needed, and we can get it together. Can we meet up about 10.00 in the morning, what do you think?'

'That should be OK,' replied David.

'Mary goes to the library on a Tuesday.'

'I've not met Mary. How will I recognise her?' Nigel asked.

'You just bring the big bag on wheels, and she'll know you. Everyone knows you and that bag, Nigel.'

'OK see her tomorrow 10.00 by the Post Office, good night.'

'Have a good evening, Nigel.'

As Nigel wandered off back to the Cottage. Great, absolutely great, I need to keep a low profile and he points out, "You just bring the big bag on wheels, and she'll know you, everyone knows you and that bag, Nigel." Great!

Nigel reached the cottage and decided a cup of tea was in order. He had had one Scotch already today.

Fixing the screw in place to stop the latch lifting, Nigel just stood in the kitchen drinking his tea and reflecting on the day. Full of different emotions and feelings, finishing his tea and taking himself off upstairs he washed and got into bed.

'I Love You.'

Considering the day before, Nigel was grateful for a goodnight's sleep. He wasn't sure of the time, he had missed the chiming of the clock.

Washed and dressed, he wandered downstairs. First the kettle, then check the time: 3.18.

I need to sort a routine for winding that clock up. Grabbing his car keys Nigel let himself out to check on the time in the car: 8.17. Dashing back inside he set the clock and wound it up.

That's OK, thought Nigel. Not meeting Mary until 10.00. Cereal for breakfast with sterilised milk, little point in getting a fridge now, have to make do!

Pots washed, all three of them, Nigel was a little early, so decided to see what was being delivered today at the Old House.

Locking the door and pulling the wheelie trolley, his mind went back to the night before.

'You just bring the big bag on wheels, and she'll know you, everyone knows you and that bag, Nigel.'

As he turned the corner a voice boomed out, 'Leaving, are we? Now you can see how decent people live, nice house, pay their way, not sponge off other people.'

'A very good morning to you Captain, good morning, Faye, what a beautiful way to start the day.And for your information, I will, as I said, be out of here a week, Sunday, possibly PM. Now please don't doddle. I know how much the teams at the Old House are looking forward to your expertise and organisational skills. I'm sure the help and sacrifices you have both made will be appreciated by the new owners, have a nice day.'

Nigel stood motionless so encouraging the pair to move off.

'A week Sunday, you're a scrounger,' the Captain barked.

They both walked off with Faye giving Nigel a look that could melt rock.

Nigel stood a moment to allow time for them to make a reasonable distance between himself and those two.

What a fantastic start to the day! he thought.

I was going to see what was happening at the Old House, not going to do that now. I'm sure I can kill time for 30 minutes somewhere.

Nigel kept well over to the left, keeping as much distance between him and the house, just in case.

Safely halfway down the drive a Bye, Bye van came up. It was Baby.

'Sorry about yesterday, Nigel, that damn Captain and Faye got to me. Work could come our way, so I had to bite my lip.'

'That's OK Baby, how are you today?' asked Nigel.

'OK today, a new day.'

'That's good,' replied Nigel.

'Oh, by the way, they're already up at the house waiting for you, see you.'

Nigel slowly walked off but looked back into the side mirror to see Baby beating the steering wheel with his hands.

Smiling, he continued down the drive. Still with time to spare, as he walked past the Pub a Fire office's small red van was outside.

Nigel thought, what's that all about? Check on that later.

As he entered the village by the sign post he had a desire to inspect the thermometer outside the Church. The weather was much warmer, and people were attending church so surely the collection towards buying heating had gone up.

Heating
Fund

Closer inspection didn't tell that trail, no new red paint had been added to indicate a gentle rise to the goal, perhaps Paul hasn't had time to paint it yet.

Nigel made his way through the gate and followed the path to the cemetery; he knew what he was looking for.

Nigel spoke out in a whisper, 'I made a promise and I intend to keep it.'

He took several minutes to compose himself before turning round and heading off to the rendezvous with Mary.

Passing the Church door, he saw Paul coming out of the Church.

'Morning, Nigel, not stealing headstones are you?' pointing at Nigel's trolley.

'Morning, Paul, this bag could be the death of me, everyone picks on it.'

Paul answered, 'Well, if you do die, then you could save money and use it as a coffin. Where are you off to, shopping?'

'Yes, taking my washing to Millie's and meeting up with a young lady, which will get tongues wagging. Are we still on tomorrow night?' replied Nigel.

'Yes, 6.00, see you tomorrow.'

With that the two men parted and Nigel made his way over to the Post Office to wait for Mary.

Chapter 15

Meeting Mary

There was a well-dressed lady standing outside the phone boxes, the pair made eye to eye contact.

'I presume you are Nigel, there couldn't be two bags like that,' said Mary.

'Yes, I am Nigel, so you must be Mary, the finest cook in the village. Pleased to meet you.' As the two shook hands, 'Well, that should start the rumours,' said Nigel.

'Don't think so, Nigel, people here are nice. It's just that not a lot happens so people try and find an interest. You were number one for a while, but I would guess now perhaps you are third place behind the new people coming in the Old House and the Coopers reopening.'

'What's the word on the new people, who are they?' asked Nigel.

'No one knows yet, but David said some of the furniture arrived yesterday and more's coming today. David said the kitchen looks like one in my books I borrow from the library. We haven't seen inside the Coopers', guess that's not going to be possible, until both David and I get work. I did apply to work in the bar or restaurant, but not this time, perhaps next. Nigel, how can I help you anyway?'

'Well,' Nigel started.

'Let's cut to the chase. I am more than grateful for the pies you make me, they are really nice, but I am aware that cost can be difficult. So I need to pay my way, you must be short of all sorts of ingredients.

'David did not know what you needed, so the best thing is for you and I to meet up and go shopping, and whatever you need, we buy. It is not charitable. The pies would cost lots more and not taste so good.

I am on to a winner in only paying for stuff. You have the skill to make it into something special, so let's go shopping and get what you need, OK?'

Shopping with Mary proved to be an education, going from market stall to stall, picking only the best produce, then into the general store looking for bargains and refusing to pay over the odds.

' I think that's all, Nigel, thank you.'

'Do we need the butchers?' asked Nigel.

'The meat's good from him but he knows how to charge, and we can't afford it.'

'Well,' said Nigel, 'How about you make a meat pie, and I don't have to buy one from him. It will taste much better and we can get enough for all.'

'Well, thanks' Nigel.'

'You're welcome, come on, Mary!'

Leaving the butchers', Nigel turned to Mary, 'That must be the first time the Bag and I have come out of the butchers without being ridiculed.'

'Told you,' said Mary, 'you have moved down the chain, you're up against stiff competition with the Pub and the Old House. You will need to pull something out the bag to get back up to the number one spot, and let's be honest here, Nigel, you have the bag to do it.'

With that Nigel offered to take the shopping back to Mary's and David's, as he was sure that she lived close to Millie's and he needed to drop off the washing.

Mary guided Nigel to her house which was indeed only three doors away from Millie's and Arthur's.

'I need to go there,' pointing to Millie's place, 'that lady helps me with my washing,' said Nigel.

'That information isn't going to escalate you to the top spot, Nigel, we all know about your washing.'

Nigel could feel himself going red with embarrassment.

'I don't think anyone outside the village knows, so nothing to be worried about,' Mary said, laughing.

Both shopping and washing dropped off, back to the village for his own shopping items - butchers', market stalls, general store - all done and the usual pocket full of change.

Nigel stopped off at the public phone box, the call took his last coin and he only finished as the pips went.

Phew! that was close Nigel thought, need to detail the plans by next week.

Nigel's next stop was Paul's, to drop off the 4 cans of beer for tomorrow night's Chippy supper and chess match.

Nigel knocked on the vicarage door, only to be opened by Mrs Bright.

'Hello, Mrs Bright, how are you? Can I leave these with you?'

Handing over the beer, 'It's for Paul and me, to go with tomorrow's supper.'

'Yes, OK,' she said sheepishly. 'The vicar's at the Church, he said if you've came to drop off the beer, can you call in to see him?'

'Will do, thank you,' replied Nigel.

Nigel made his way across to the Church, twice in one day he thought.

Opening the large heavy wooden door, and not seeing anyone, Nigel shouted, 'Hello, Paul, anyone, there?'

'Over here,' Paul popped his head around a door, 'Here, over here.'

'Mrs Bright said you wanted to see me.'

'Yes,' said Paul.

'Only because I saw you this morning around the Church and you looked a bit sad. Obviously, I am aware that you will be leaving next week and wanted to make sure you're OK, don't know if you have anywhere to go. I can offer you a room for a few weeks if that helps.'

Nigel took a moment, 'Thanks Paul, that's really kind and I am touched by your kindness, but I have made up my mind, and I have just come off the phone. I am OK, thank you.

'Perhaps, you asking me here could have been fortuitous.

'You can do something for me. How would you like a guest speaker after service a week Sunday? I can then tell people the reason I came to the village. I think people would be interested. Now, whether you tell them it's me or a surprise speaker, it's up to you, could bring in a few more pounds for the heating fund?

I would only need about 30 minutes and then you and I have been invited to The Cooper's for lunch and drinks, well what do you think?'

'Do I get to know why you're here first?' asked Paul.

'No, that would spoil the surprise.However you and I will have a chat, between the talk and the Pub. I can answer all your questions then.'

'Still not 100% sure, Nigel, using the church as a meeting place.'

'Well,' said Nigel, 'we could use the hall next door, but the heating is not working and the red mark on that thermostat not getting higher!'

Paul took what seemed an age to decide.

'OK straight after service a week Sunday, and I will tell them you're the speaker, how's that?'

'Good, and by the way it's nothing sinister, but it should be, I am the third on the list.'

'What do you mean?' asked Paul.

'Never mind, see you tomorrow, 6.00 o'clock.'

With that Nigel collected his wheelie trolley and made his way to the door.

'One more thing, do you have a duplicating machine. I may have need of a few copies of something.'

Paul thought for a moment, 'Yes I do, not very warm in here! 20p a copy.'

'See you tomorrow,' shouted Nigel.

Nigel made his way back on the road and headed home.

The Fire van had gone from outside the Pub, but he still wanted to know why it was there. Tomorrow's job.

Starting the dreaded climb up the drive, he thought it looked like every van for miles had parked up, it almost gave Nigel a spring in his step.

Soon he and the wheelie trolley were by the side of the Old House watching the comings and goings.

There were vans from yesterday, now unloading beds and mattresses.

Carpet fitting vans, one with house plants. There was a highly decorated van down the side of the Old House, unloading what looked like cooking pots and pans.

There was a van with large boxes marked "Aquatic Filters" and a Telecoms van.

Nigel looked up. There was a man on the roof attaching an aerial to the chimney.

One of the young lads stopped unloading the van, placed his hands in his pocket, looked at Nigel then at the wheelie bag, 'Hi mate, we are missing a fourposter bed, have you got it in there?'

Time for a brew, thought Nigel.

Just as he was about to turn round, out came Baby, with a red face that looked like it was going to explode.

'Hi Baby, I am making a pot of tea, fancy a brew?' Nigel asked.

'I am on my way,' Baby replied.

Soon the kettle was boiling, and Baby had regained his usual colour, 'I could offer you a biscuit, but I don't have any, sorry,' said Nigel.

'This will do nicely. If that chap doesn't get out that house, I may just do something very naughty with his hat.'

'That's bad, I suppose the female's in tow as well,' asked Nigel.

'Nigel, I am sick and tired of the two of them. They're sticking their noses into things they have no idea about, all you ever get out of them, '*Oh, the right people are now coming to the village'. 'It has to be right for the new family.' 'These are our sort of people.'*

'Nigel, the place is full of qualified design people. They spend goodness knows how long designing and acquiring the right furniture, ensuring it is all in the right place, and those two seem to know better. Thanks for the tea.'

Both men went outside with Baby returning back to the Old House.

Nigel stood and watched him disappear out of sight.

He was about to go back in, when the farmer and his tractor came down the lane.

Nigel waved him down, the farmer stopped and turned off the engine.

'Hello, nice to see you're still around, but I heard you are leaving a week, Sunday,' said the farmer.

'Yes, moving out the cottage. But never mind about that.'

'You could help me and lots of other people. Your next-door neighbour and his sidekick are in the Old House sticking their nose into other people's business.'

'Someone is going to put his hat down the toilet, and there could be a strong possibility his head will still be in it. What could happen that would get them out the house, any ideas?'

Mr Snow, thought for a moment, 'Aye the thought of the Captain's head down the toilet is a thought to behold, but I guess someone would be in big trouble.' The farmer took time, 'I don't like lying, but some years ago there was a fox in the pheasant pen, so, tell him the farmer's seen a fox in the pen which is true.'

He stood up in the cab, 'Just looking for the captain, now. Can't see him, if you see him can you tell him about the fox?'

'With pleasure,' replied Nigel.

With that the farmer started the tractor and continued down the drive.

Nigel made haste to the house. He looked for the man in the bowler. Catching one of the lads in a brown coat, Nigel asked him to go find either the man in the bowler or the man in the cowboy hat.

Moments later the Captain stood at the top of the steps.

'Go away now, don't wait until week Sunday.'

'Never mind about that,' replied Nigel. 'As much as I don't like you, I dislike even more the fact of a fox tearing the pheasants apart. The farmer's been looking for you, he's seen a fox in the pen.'

The Captain shouted loudly back into the house, 'Faye! Faye! Come on. We need to get back. Faye, come on, woman!'

Faye came dashing out, the Captain grabbed her arm and almost dragged her down the steps, pulling her along as they passed Nigel.

Nigel spoke, 'Don't mention it, no it's OK really, only too glad to help.'

They had not left the tarmac road that led to the green lane, when the biggest cheer went up from inside the house, one would have thought that 10,000 football fans team had just scored.

Both the runners stopped and looked back. Nigel looked at them and shrugged his shoulders.

Baby, the man in the bowler, and a couple of other people came out. 'What happened there?' one asked.

'Sorry, can't say,' informed Nigel.

'I may have to use it again,' with that Nigel started to walk back to the cottage, with a bit of a swagger.

Whistles and cheers and applause rang out as a sign of approval for whatever he did.

Returning to the cottage, he retrieved the spade from the kitchen and started to turn over the soil between the plants so discouraging the weeds. The plants were starting to look a little dry, still no watering can, so the bucket will have to do.

Nigel went to the shed. There's a surprise it is still here but more importantly so were the steps. He was going to need them next week.

The plants drowned as it was difficult to water with a bucket. Everything put away Nigel, checked on the time: 3.10.

Chapter 16

A Place to Sit

Nigel took a look at his car, as this has to move next week. Best check, it starts. Collecting the keys, Nigel jumped into the driving seat, turned the key. 'Yes,' he said as the car sprang to life.

He decided to sit and wait until the temperature gauge reached normal then turned it off.

As he sat waiting he started to think about the thermometer outside the Church, how come the cash is not coming in? Paul explained that the Church had been very cold and the congregation had been slim, but the indicator had not moved for weeks.

Times have been hard with sky high interest rates and lack of work, but things are now improving. Suppose if people have money problems, then putting food on the table comes before heating the Church.

I suppose money issues got me sitting in this car, having fled home, but in a different way. It's only been about 8 weeks, possibly more, and it's not been too bad, he thought.

A few cold nights, being short of cash at one point made meals a bit boring, not having a TV or radio has not been an issue for him, should have purchased a fridge from the junk shop, bit late now.

Nigel checked the gauge everything seemed OK, made a mental note to try again in the week, before Sunday.

Turning off the engine and returning the keys, still with time on his hands Nigel decided to look at the progress in the house. Grabbing the coat he walked back to the Old House. The aerial man was no longer on the roof, so Nigel hoped he had climbed down and not fallen off.

Looking down the drive, he saw an open backed van coming up. The driver wound down his window. 'Hi, mate, I've a couple of heavy garden benches, where do you want them?'

Just as Nigel was going to speak, Baby came out of the house,'Hello, they look like the benches we were told were coming today. You have two different sizes, don't you?'

'Yes mate, do you know where they are going? Not far I hope. They're really heavy, made of oak', said the driver.

'OK,' said Baby. 'The big one goes down by the lake, the smaller one is closer to the house. I think they are to help soften the impact of the wooden top, that sits over the filters that clean the rainwater.'

Nigel looked at the benches on the back of the van. Not much to see as the benches were wrapped in thick black plastic. Both had large signs with the instruction: "Do not remove this protective cover."

'How far away are these wooden platforms?' asked the driver. 'These things are heavy.'

Baby thought for a moment, 'What we can do is, bring the van round across the front of the house. You will see where we have cut a ditch for the pipework feeding the lake. Stay close to that, you will see the wooden deck. Park up there, keep close to the cutting. Try not to leave great divots. We have to make good the grass before next week. I will see you down there. I need to check which one is going where.'

With that, the driver moved off, carefully manoeuvring between the cars and vans parked outside the front of the house, heading off down the hill following the earth trail and disappearing out of sight.

Baby and Alex and a third person emerged from the front door and walked off after the van.

'Hello again,' said the man in the bowler hat, 'thanks for the help earlier. At first I thought those two owned the house, it was only after remarks like: *"The people moving in here are true professionals like ourselves,"* and *"we must introduce the family to our fine circle of associates."* - 'What a pair of ...! Well, I think we know what.'

'Yes, we know,' said Nigel, 'Are you about finished, seems a big job?'

'This one's not so bad. You see we normally arrange and execute the packing of the family home. In this case everything is new, it's all part of a commercial arrangement, not sure of the details.

'Don't get me wrong, it would still cost a pretty penny, it is offset by no profit. The owners of the Old House will allow top rate magazines to photograph inside when finished, and I understand from one of the designers, even allow people to come and have a look for themselves. That would be people with real money, not like you and I, perhaps even Royalty. Who knows?'

'People treading around your home, bit weird, you could be in the bath, or in bed,' replied Nigel.

'Perhaps an appointment would be in order, don't you think?' enquired the man.

The chap then walked off in a bit of a huff, only joking, thought Nigel.

He still didn't answer the question. Perhaps they will be working the weekend to finish. Didn't David say the cleaners are coming in next week? And Baby just said that the grass must be sorted.

The lass is here Wednesday or Thursday. Need to find out which day, and keep out of the way, don't need her asking questions at this stage of the plan.

Nigel then made his way to view the placing of the benches. Not too close, Nigel, could find yourself taking a leg. The driver said it was heavy, keep your distance!

One of the two benches was in place and the van making its way back up the hill with two lads following. Nigel guessed that Baby had got a lift.

Making sure no one was about he made his way over. The bench looked OK, positioned in the middle of the platform. If you were to sit on it, you would be overlooking the valley, not that he could, the thick black plastic cover was still on.

I wonder when that comes off, thought Nigel.

Taking a look all around himself, Nigel approached the bench. Another quick look around, grabbing one end to lift it, heave, again heave. That bench isn't going anywhere, the driver was correct, it's heavy!

After all that work Nigel decided to stroll up the hill, following the tracks from the van, the driver had done. OK, difficult to see where the van had been. Unlike the big brown score down the grass from the laying of the pipe.

The second seat, now in place, this time facing the house, and not overlooking the valley. The bench still supporting the black plastic wrapping.

Nigel thought, now this one is smaller than the other, I wonder.

No, forget it, I will be seen from the house. I will wait until they have all gone then have a go at lifting it.

Time to go back and get a bath and supper. As he passed the front door he saw the number of vans and cars had reduced in numbers with only four or five remaining.

Reaching the back door, he decided to put in the screw as he was going upstairs. Bath run, bath salts added, Nigel enjoyed a nice long soak, without falling asleep.

Dressed and downstairs, time for supper, as he was able to purchase fresh sausages - sausage and mashed potatoes and half a tin of baked beans.

Everything almost ready to serve, Nigel had to go through the torment of mashing the potatoes with a fork. This is the last time, tomorrow I am going to buy a spud masher, this sound goes through me, LAR, LAR.

Nigel sat in his chair, thinking if he was to stay longer than a week Sunday, could he have eaten outside, like they do on the Continent? That could be nice. Perhaps not sausages and mash; lobster, Beef Wellington, authentic Italian food he had seen in magazines but not tried, so possibly he may not like it. So bangers, mash and baked beans is just fine.

Nigel sat for a time thinking about the future and what it may bring, now feeling momentarily unsure. The die was cast, he was under starter's orders. The starting pistol was raised, no turning back.

Nigel took a deep breath. Check the back door, time for bed, climbing into bed, he needed to get back out just to check the loft hatch. This is no time to lose the bread bin.

Not being able to reach he just needed to check for any movement or finger marks. All looked untouched, back to bed,

'I Love You.'

Hearing the clock chime 8, Nigel decided to get up and wash and sort breakfast. Something simple this morning. Nigel thought two boiled eggs, with soldiers and a large pot of tea.

Breakfast over. Slightly hard eggs made dipping the soldiers impossible, need more practice cooking eggs Nigel decided.

Pouring the last of the tea from the pot, he took a stroll outside to check on the veg. plants. All looked OK despite his trying to drown them.

Vehicles could be heard coming up the drive, so Nigel needed to check on what was happening, so a quick wash of the few pots, coat on and door locked, time to investigate.

He set off towards the Old House. However, a quick look at the shed to ensure the steps were still there. Yes, still tucked at the back, good!

Resuming his trip, he could see a van that looked like a small tanker and a couple of cars.

A driver was still sitting in the van, he winded down the window, addressing Nigel, 'Morning, do you know where the liquid gas tank is?'

'Yes,' said Nigel, 'can I ask what you need it for?'

'We are here to pressure test it before the builders back fill.'

'I only asked,' said Nigel, 'I presume you will need the vans there.'

'Yes,' said the driver, 'this machine will pressure test the tank and the pipework, so it needs to be close by.'

Nigel explained they needed to go around to the gate, giving directions and agreeing to meet them. They set off as instructed. The vans arrived before Nigel could get there, so the instruction must have been OK.

As the vans waited by the gate, Nigel was able to wave and catch their attention and beckon them in. The vans turned in and travelled up the track, and parked alongside the tank.

The operation team started to set about the work.

'Thanks for the help,' shouted one of the men.

Nigel continued to get closer.

'What happens now?' asked Nigel.

'We will pressurise the tank and the pipework up to the shut off valve, which should be just outside the house as it enters the building. We pump twice the pressure than delivered by the gas so we can be sure it's all safe to fill. Once we have passed it off, we allow the back filling, then test at 1½ times pressure, then the gas can be loaded to the tank ready for use. That will be completed later, but not by this team.

'A quick look at the trench, the builders had installed the best quality, hoping we should be OK.'

No sooner had the driver finished talking, a digger pulled inside the gate with Alex at the wheel.

'That's all the team on site. We can now get stuck in. We could be finished by this afternoon, fingers crossed,' said the driver.

With that and a wave to Alex, Nigel started to walk back to the Old House. Passing the front door, Nigel could see down past his cottage to see two figures and a dog walking toward the house.

Strange, thought Nigel, I have been here for weeks and weeks, the only other dog I have seen was the Captain's. Nigel slowed his pace, so had to accidently get within talking distancc, 'Morning, Ladies.'

Each one greeted Nigel.

'Good morning,' one went on to say, 'nice day for walking the dog, don't you think?'

'Possibly,' said Nigel 'never owned a dog. Not something we could afford when I was young, and I suppose, it's never crossed my mind. I've not seen many dogs to be honest, perhaps not that popular in the village, are they?'

One of the two ladies replied, 'There are a few. My friend and I thought we would take a different route today, give the doggy something new to sniff. You don't think the new people will mind, do you?'

Nigel thought for a moment.

'Don't really know, I understand that they are not coming for at least a week. There's lots of people milling about. I am sure the dog will enjoy all the new scents. Bye.'

'Sorry,' said one lady, 'before you go, do you live here? Do you know about the inside of the house? Someone said that the kitchen was to die for, I just wondered where it might be.'

Nigel pointed down by the side of the house, 'Turn left, you will see a white stable door, that's the kitchen. I am sure the dog must be thirsty, perhaps someone will allow you to get the dog a drink.'

The two ladies looked at each other with a big grin.

'Yes, good idea,' said one and without a second to waste off they dashed.

Nigel watched as the ladies vanished around the corner. That dog is going to get a drink if it wants one or not, they are just being nosey, good for them!

Off down the drive, crossing the road, he stood in front of the Pub.

I wondered what that Fire vehicle was doing here yesterday.

Come on, Nigel! Why not get yourself a dog and ask if he could have a drink? And you thought those ladies were nosey.

Deciding to continue into the village Nigel popped into the Iron Mongers'.

'Morning,' came the usual chirpy sound.

'Morning, I would like a potato masher, please,' said Nigel.

'Sorry, the wife spoken for,' said the shop keeper giggling.

'Plastic or metal? Metal tends to be the best.'

'Metal, please,' replied Nigel.

Shopping done, Nigel decided to walk back along the river. He wasn't in any hurry. After all he didn't need to be at Paul's until 6.00 that evening. Anyway, thc river seemed to be teeming with life.

He sat on the bank and soaked in some of the antics by the waterfowl, swans and kingfishers. A couple of ducks.

Over the weeks the river seemed to be much clearer, small fish could be seen under the overhanging tree branches. This is a place and an environment to be cherished, to be kept and looked after for generations to come. One can only hope, thought Nigel.

Sitting by the water he lost himself flitting in and out of thoughts of home, and its people, Mum and Dad, Mr Parker, Raymond. Times spent down the allotment, walks with friends in the Works Rambling club, all seemed so distant now, like most people he had regrets, apart from the obvious, his loss of parents. The complications at work, came a close second in the regret stakes.

Whilst he had girlfriends, none really worked out, which could have been a good thing because of the way he had to leave his hometown. Time elapsed, his memories drifted away with the river's current.

Chapter 17

A Place to Drink

Nigel decided it was time to get up and walk back to the cottage, first passing by the Pub. As he reached the rear of the Pub, vehicles were unloading barrels of beer and crates and all sorts of other items.

'Morning. I think it's still morning but on a day like this who cares?' said the landlord.

'Someone's happy,' replied Nigel.

'Yes Nigel, this is the first delivery in weeks and weeks, and I am glad to see it. We have real ales, traditional beers, we have Lager, stouts, Ciders all on draft. We have all sorts of mixer drinks, the new wine fridge came a couple of days ago, it has a glass door.

'I am told it encourages diners to view and buy. We have a rack dedicated to red wine, again all on view. We even had a case of Champagne, we may possibly have that for some time, maybe a bit rich for around here but let's give it a go.

'We have different glasses for different drinks, the team are back off their training course full of enthusiasm. They're inside sorting the tables and bar. The place is alive, Nigel, it's going to be fantastic!'

'Good, I take it from your demeanour you're one happy Pub person?' asked Nigel.

'There is more, Nigel, the suppliers we used to deal with would have charged us twice the cost of this new one. It had all been done by the investors. He rang me last week and suggested a stocking policy. If I don't sell it, it can go back free of charge, not much of this will be going back. Perhaps the champagne?'

'That's a good selling point, cheap beer,' said Nigel.

'You keep that to yourself; the drinks will be reasonably priced. Thank you!

'The fresh food is coming in Wednesday, Chef sorting that. I am going to leave it with him. Strikes me as one not big on negotiations if you catch by drift.

'Anyway, it's his kitchen. The trainee seems to enjoy working in there, so fingers crossed, we will see on Thursday. The big one will be the Sunday lunch with the buffet, I know it's all invited guests but still nailbiting.

'One of the big possible stumbling blocks could have been all the certification, food standards, fire assessment and various other certification but all went through without issue. The fire officer commented on the high standard included in the design, that architect is something else. Well, Nigel, you will excuse me if I attend to the staff and help with all this stock.'

Nigel noted how the landlord swaggered with pride, good for him. Reasonably priced not going to make a great deal of difference to me, not going to save a lot on three pints; four, and I will need a taxi. That's not saving, it's spending.

Nigel started to head back. Looking down the garden, he noticed that the tables had still not been made, perhaps later, he thought, still time.

Nigel decided to walk down the road, then cross over to the lane, then enter by the gate, to see how the gas man and Alex were getting on.

Entering the gate, the gas van was slowly driving towards him, 'All done, passed with flying colours, the tanks will be filled in the next couple of days,' said the driver.

'OK great, I will let someone know.'

Good, thought Nigel, continuing his walk towards the house.

He expected to see Alex, but he must have finished and gone. The ground was all level. There was a pile of soil and stones, guess that's what's leftover. Presume someone will collect or take it down to the bomb crater.

As he walked up toward the house Nigel could see the line of brown soil, where the pipe had been laid.

Alex had done a good job, once the lawn turf had been laid and taken root, no one's going to know it's there. Apart from the two wooden tops that covered the filter, and with the benches on them, it sort of looked right.

There was now only a couple of vans outside the front door. The place looked a bit quiet after days of frenzied activity.

Time for a brew, thought Nigel heading to the cottage. From the side of the Old House came an elderly couple with a small dog.

'Hello, lovely day.'

'Yes', said Nigel.

The couple started to engage Nigel in conversation.

'Nice house, been a bit of a wreck, but looking grand. Now, is it yours?'

But before Nigel could answer, 'Hope you don't mind we had to treat the doggy to a drink, asked the nice man if he could oblige. Very helpful, did you say it was yours?'

The man continued, 'the kitchen is very futuristic. The man was telling us that it's heated under the floor, not the whole house, just the kitchen. It's very nice, have you been inside? The back door is like a stable it opens in two halves. Really nice, well, must be going, it's chippy tea night. Bye, nice talking with you.'

With that the two walked off down the drive.

Yes, thought Nigel, nice talking with you!

Don't suppose your son's a plasterer. Never got a word in. They're off for a chippy tea, what time is it?

Entering the cottage Nigel went to view the clock. Crumbs it's 4.45. Need a quick bath then off to Paul's.

Nigel was bathed, changed and out the door at 5.30. Should be at Paul's for 6.00. Checking the door was locked, off he set. As he turned left heading down the drive a voice shouted from the Old House, 'Hi Mate, do you live here?'

'No, I live at the cottage. Well, at least until week tomorrow, why?'

The man continued to shout, 'Just wondering if an animal shelter purchased the house - more dogs came here than Battersea.' With that the chap returned inside.

Oh dear! thought Nigel best get a move on before anyone else asks questions.

Nigel made his way to Paul's, a quick tap on the door and the vicar was eager to go.

'Hello Nigel, had a good day, saw you down by the river earlier, you seemed miles away.'

'Just thinking Paul, just thinking.'

Soon back in the vicarage, meals unwrapped and beer poured, the two sat silent until the last of the chips was finished.

'Are you still on for the explanation of why you're here next Sunday? Nigel, I am going to announce it tomorrow, see what reaction we get.'

'Yes, still on, Paul, then off to the Pub for the buffet. I am sure I am going to need a pint.

'Went by the Cooper's today and they're delivering all the beer and wines, even champagne. The landlord seemed very pleased. He has all the necessary permits and documents, so good luck to him for next week.'

The two men sat down to their game.

'Checkmate' calls Paul, 'suppose we have only one more evening session before you move on, going to miss these.'

'Suppose you are, if you win most of them,' answered Nigel.

As the two men parted, Nigel addressed Paul, 'I will nip in on Wednesday, to see what reaction you've had. If it's poor we could cancel, let's see. Thanks for the support, see you Wednesday.'

'Yes OK, see you Wednesday about 11.00?'

With that, Nigel started his walk home. Passing the Pub, he saw the curtains were closed but the lights were still on. Guess the team had a lot to put away and tidy up.

Up the drive as he rounded the corner, 'I know who goes there, I don't have to ask. Hello, Nigel.'

'Hello David, how are you?'

'Very good, look what Mary made.'

David produced a meat and potato pie beautifully decorated around the edges and a pastry with a rose in the centre.

'David, have you brought the wrong pie, isn't that one yours and Mary's?'

'No, said David 'we have the biggest one, this one's yours.'

'Thank Mary for me, it looks great, thank you. See you tomorrow.'

'See you Nigel, have a good night.'

Nigel put the screw in the door, and thought for a moment about a Scotch. He had had two beers and a large helping of fish and chips, best not. Off to bed, 'I Love You.'

The next morning Nigel woke to the sound of dogs barking, not heard that before. Quickly washed and dressed, Nigel opened the back door to be greeted by a little grey-haired dog, which on seeing Nigel gave a bark, then shot off around the side of the cottage.

Nigel poked his head round.

'Sorry about that. She's very brave, gives a bark and then runs off like the clappers.'

'That's OK, don't normally get dogs around here, seems to have become a popular walk these last few days.'

'Oh, has it?' queried the owner, already knowing the reason.

Nigel retired back to the kitchen and brewed the tea. Not sure why, but I am ready for a fry up.

Sausages and a slice of bacon almost cooked, eggs gently cooking, Friday night beans boiling, time to enjoy. And enjoy he did, but feeling a little full afterward.

Think a short walk should help. The sun is really trying so no need for a coat. I will have a walk to the lake and take in the view, thought Nigel. The pots and pans can wait.

Door locked, off he set, peeking round the corner. Any dogs and their owners? No, all clear, nothing outside the Old House this morning. Well it is Sunday, good for a day off.

But as he turned by the house a gang of men were working on the ground, laying turf.

'Morning,' shouted Nigel.

'Morning,' replied a few of the crew.

Nigel continued to the lake, the sun dancing on the water. He sat on the grass by the edge, not wishing to disturb the covering on the seat and the sign clearly said, "Do not remove this protective cover."

Nigel occasionally turned around to view the progress of the new lawn which was getting closer until finally reaching the wooden floor.

'This is some bench, this is a proper seat, look at the workmanship, viewing only the legs, that's proper wood,' remarked one of the lawn team.

'I would like to see under it, but we are instructed not to damage them. I need to ask you to move or get wet. We have a bowser of water up there. We need to wet the grass in. Don't want you to get soaked.'

'No problem,' replied Nigel.

The crew had a large rose on a hose and ensured the newly laid lawn was well and truly wet, before waving to Nigel and driving off.

Nigel continued to sit staring at the view, lost in a daydream.

The rest of Nigel's day was just lazing about, tending the veg and brewing tea. The dog population had returned to its normal level, nil. Nothing was happening at the Old House, things were really quiet.

Perhaps I should do something, thought Nigel.

I know! As no one is about I will go and have a look around the outside of the Old House.

Best to lock the door, he had come this far and did not need anyone finding the tin box in the attic.

He strolled along the lane and stood at the front of the house; it was an impressive building with all the work that been undertaken. It looked really nice.

He proceeded around the far side of the Old House, he wanted to see more of the derelict house behind the greenhouse.

Walking around the back, he noticed that a tree had indeed fallen across it, demolishing half of it and someone had then turned it into a storage shed.

Just has he looked up a silver flash caught his eye. Following it along he saw two new wires had been strung to the old telegraph poles - one set of wires led to the Old House, whilst in the other direction they disappeared off towards the Lane.

They must be the phone wires. I must have missed that installation. Come on, Nigel! You're slipping, he thought.

He started to amble back to the cottage. Could have an early supper and then sit with David for a while. Now with a bit of a spring in his step he was back at the cottage.

Nigel took out the pie, there's enough here for four. I am never going to eat all this even in three sittings. Can't waste it, I will cut it in half and do my best.

Whilst it was cooking, he washed the pots and pans from the morning. Soon the aroma of the pie filled the kitchen, he plated it up and with a cup of tea, sat in his chair and set about supper.

Leaving only a few morsels he sat in the chair feeling very full, he couldn't even drink the tea. Need to get out he told himself, need fresh air.

Taking his coat and ensuring the door was locked he slowly walked toward the Old House.

'Who goes there?' came a chuckling voice from behind a tree.

'Evening, David.'

'How did you know it was me?' asked David.

'Just a good guess, I suppose,' replied Nigel.

'Are you OK, Nigel? You're walking funny, have you got tummy ache?'

Nigel stood a moment.

'Yes, I have tummy ache, I have eaten to much pie and I am over full.'

'That happens to me. Mary said I eat too much.'

David leant over and whispered to Nigel, 'But she puts the food on the plate, not me!'

'I can't use that excuse. I put the food on the plate. Let's walk, David.' The two men strolled toward the steps of the house.

'I need to walk round, Nigel, you wait here.'

'Good idea, David. I will do that.'

Nigel with some effort took a place on the step.

Seconds later the Captain and Faye turned the corner.

'Well, what have we here?' the Captain asked.

'Are you practising for your next role, you're short of a begging sign and a tin to collect the money?'

Nigel took a moment, 'Why do you find it necessary to insult people all the time? Can't you leave it be, given I move out of the cottage next Sunday?'

Faye jumped in. 'The Captain's correct, people like you only take, your sort are not welcome here.'

'What is my sort?' asked Nigel.

'The sort who take what's not theirs, live off other people, not willing to do an honest day's work or pay their dues. You even asked the vicar for money, yes, we heard about that too,' replied the Captain.

'Well that just about sums it up. Guess you two can't wait until next Sunday,' answered Nigel.

'I can assure you if Faye and I were not expected to attend the Gala Buffet at the Cooper's, I would personally help you on your way, until then I am counting the days.'

And with that final comment, they both strolled off down the farm lane.

Chapter 18

A Very Dark Place

David appeared from around the corner.

'Sorry, Nigel. I heard, but I didn't want to get involved. They don't like me, and I need this job if only for another week.'

'Don't worry David. If you hadn't guessed, they don't like me either,' said Nigel.

David looked at Nigel for a moment.

'Why didn't you tell them you didn't ask the vicar for money? It was a mistake, you only asked him to cash you a Postal Order.'

'How do you know that, David?'

'Millie told Mary and other people that she had done you wrong and was sorry.'

'If you don't mind, David, I think I will turn in now. That lovely pie of Mary's has now gone down. See you tomorrow. Good night, David.'

'Good night, Nigel, chin up!'

Nigel, with a heavy heart and an even heavier stomach, climbed into bed. 'I Love You.'

Nigel had a poor night's sleep, meeting the Captain and Faye played on his mind.

Nigel put on his trousers and without washing took himself off downstairs. He filled the kettle and started to make himself a pot of tea.

Removing the screw from the door he walked into the back garden. Rain was falling steadily. He looked at the small veg patch, and fell to his knees, tears formed, and gently rolled down his cheeks. It would seem that every bad thing that had happened in the last year, culminated in this moment.

Nigel decided he needed time to mend, he could not turn the clock back; and it was now too late to change what was about to happen. With that he went inside, closed the door, put the screw in place, ensuring it was extra tight.

Over 48 hours passed before the door was reopened, every emotion flowed out of the cottage.

2 days of sadness and pain, anger, ill feelings, wishes, hope, dreams, but the biggest burden to be expelled was self-pity.

Nigel felt he had suffered enough, much of his own making, so be it. Time to move on, and that's what he intended to do.

His plan for today was quick bath, try some breakfast and off to see Paul, then off to collect his washing which should have been collected yesterday.

Bath done, honey on toast, pot of tea, door locked and off to see Paul. As Nigel walked around the corner, several small vans were parked up. Some of the vans' doors were open, a man was up a very long ladder cleaning the windows.

Forgot the place is being cleaned the next two days. The architect is coming today and tomorrow.

Need to be out of sight.

Nigel made haste down the drive, crossing the road and heading towards the village, looking at The Cooper's. The same cleaning firm's vans were outside the Pub, cleaning there as well.

'Morning, Nigel, the vicar was looking for you yesterday,' shouted the landlady.

'I am off there now, thanks', Nigel shouted back.

As he approached the vicarage, Paul came running out, 'Where have you been? I've been looking for you, have I got news for you, come on in this is exciting!

'Mrs Bright, Nigel's here, come in, come in, sit down.

Mrs Bright, he's here.'

'I heard you the first time, I will be there in a moment,' she shouted.

'Everything OK, Paul?' asked Nigel.

'It's better than alright, Nigel, it's tikitiboo!'

Mrs Bright brought in a tray of tea. Nigel noticed three plates, full of Chocolate biscuits.

'I know how much you like Chocolate digestive, Nigel. I brought them especially for you,' said Mrs Bright.

'Do you mind if Mrs Bright sits in on our conversation, Nigel?'

'Not sure, Paul. What are we chatting about?'

'Sorry, Nigel not told you. I announced on Sunday that you are giving a chat about why you're here, and asked people to let me know if they're thinking of coming, so we can print the correct numbers of duplication. Nigel, the numbers are fantastic. The Church is going to be full. The rumours have started already, speculations on what you are talking about.'

'What are you talking about? Have a cup of tea, one sugar. Here, Nigel, take three biscuits,' said Mrs B.

'Thank you, if the rumour has started, what's the thinking?' asked Nigel.

Mrs Bright moved in closer, now sitting on the edge of the chair.

'Well, someone said, you are from the Inland Revenue, checking on people not paying taxes.Then some think you're casing the joint, ready for a robbery, but the big money's on you trying to build new houses across the river and you're here to sound us out.'

'OK Mrs Bright, show me the evidence to substantiate these thoughts.'

'I can,' she said.

'Don't think you are a tax man. You're nice, and you take washing to Millie's, so, no, not a tax man.

'You could be a stake out man. You keep yourself to yourself, you've been seen looking at the Bank, but more importantly "the Post Office". Every Friday at the same time you use the public phone.

We've heard you talking about shotguns, changing names. You talk about maps and stones and you are leaving Sunday. Now is that a possibility?

'Now mine and the vicar's money's on building a new estate, which we will strongly oppose.'

'Go on, Mrs Bright. What is the thinking behind the last hare-brained idea?' said Nigel.

'See, already denying it! This is what the village is thinking, get out of this if you can.

'Some big cheese puts up the money, puts you in the cottage to worm your way into village life, then do up the Old House. All the rooms have been fashioned by designers, that's so you can bring round the people having a new house built to see fine furniture, and hopefully buy some. That kitchen's beautiful, isn't it?

'And more, everyone knows a village needs a good Pub so they pay to have that done up, helps to sell houses, and you're often seen looking out over the valley. But, this one is the nail in your coffin, Nigel, got you banged to rights.

'Last Autumn a gang of people were measuring the land around here and over the top behind the Old House. Then going down by the Captain's place, then following the river. They had one of those measuring things on a wheel and plans of the country side, and one of those light things that works out how big hills are.

'What do you say about that? have a biscuit!'

'Thank you! Not sure what to tell you both, other than do-not put your shirt on any of those ideas. And I will tell you why!

'Tax man - I was thinking about sending in armed Police to arrest Millie on tax evasion, but a couple of pounds a week didn't seem to warrant the expense.

'Now, I am interested in people ear wigging my conversation whilst I am making phone calls.

'Let's agree, I spoke about guns and plans and whatever. I am moving out Sunday. If I and others are to rob the Post Office on Friday, I am hardly likely to hang about to tell everyone on Sunday how we did it, and I suppose, I am to run off with the swag in my wheelie trolley, no sorry! Not robbing the Post Office or Bank, or anyone else.

'This one could be tricky, Mrs Bright, to deny, but I will have a go. One more biscuit, perhaps, Mrs B. thank you.

'So, a gang measured the land using a Measuring wheel, sometimes called a perambulator. If houses are to be built over the other side of the river, why measure this side? Why would anyone wish to determine the height of land using a Theodolite again on this side?

'Posh furniture! The rooms look a lot bigger than any normal house. I guess the kitchen at the Old House is much bigger than any kitchen I have seen.'

Mrs Bright jumps in to say, 'It is. Mrs Frank and I took her dog for a walk and the dog needed a drink.'

'As I was saying, the rooms, not that I have been inside, look much bigger, so no good in a normal home, and my final closing statement to the jury is, the Pub is on the wrong side of the river, and if someone is going to pay to "do up", as you say, a Pub, then the one up the road would be much better.

'Sorry, one final thing. The view from up by the lake is beautiful and is worth spending time appreciating it.

There it is, Your Honour, I rest my case, I may as well have the last biscuit.'

'Well, what are you doing here?' asked Mrs Bright.

'Come along Sunday, and find out like everyone else. Are you OK, Paul, you look a little perplexed?' asked Nigel.

'You've eaten all the Chocolate biscuits.'

'So, I have. Thank you, very nice. Must go, need to collect my washing. Not really, we are going to storm Millie's and Arthur's house, drug barons you know,' said Nigel tapping his nose.

Nigel arranged to see Paul, Saturday, for chippy tea, and perhaps early Sunday morning to do the printing. He bid his goodbyes.

Walking towards Millie's. Listening to telephone calls? Half the village going into the Old House's kitchen pretending to water the dog, *come on*!

Arriving at Millie's, Nigel knocked on the door.

'Open up, it's the Law,' he shouted.

Arthur opened the door, 'What are you doing, you daft devil? Come in.'

Nigel briefly explained the discussion at the vicarage, and how ludicrous it all was.

'Couldn't agree more,' said Millie.

'You said they were building houses,' rebuffed Arthur.

'Shut up and go in the front room,' ordered Millie.

'Guess, that's it then, Nigel. No more washing. Thanks for the opportunity, it has helped.'

'No, thank you. See you Sunday in Church then in The Cooper's,' said Nigel.

'Church yes. Cooper's, no, we can't afford that.'

'You have to, Millie, all the regulars have to go. It's bad luck not to come along. The landlord's relying on people to give an honest opinion on his ales and food. It's a buffet, you have to come. It's all been paid for. It will only go to waste.

'David and Mary are invited, mostly for their knowledge of food. Don't know who else, but you have to come.'

'OK, I think Mrs Frank is invited, the five of us can all go together,' replied Millie.

'Five of you, sounds like trouble to me, best bring the Wheelie Bag. Arthur can bring you home if you get tipsy. Tell Mrs Frank, sorry no dogs, she will have to leave it at home. I am sure she will understand,' informed Nigel.

'Mrs Frank does not have a dog. What made you think she did?' asked Millie.

'Oh, sorry my mistake. See you Sunday.'

Washing under arm, due the fact he forgot the wheelie bag, he set off for home. Being Wednesday, it was the village's half day closing, some of the traders were closing including the butcher.

As Nigel walked by, the butcher grabbed Nigel's attention, 'Hi, could you blag the Post Office on a Monday. Friday's a good day for me, can't have police about. It's not good for trade, have a think about it will you?' he said laughing.

As he was continuing to walk along, out came the man from the Iron Mongers'.

'Knew that bag would come in handy, you can get some cash in that.'

'We've done that one,' said Nigel continuing, 'Anyway you sold it to me, makes you an accessory to robbery, think about that!'

Nigel continued along the road, stopping only to put his clean underwear under the towels, did not need everyone seeing them. It's enough people around here seem to hear everything, not even sure I should walk past the Post Office.

Holding tightly to the bundle of clothes, Nigel soon reached the Pub, strangely quiet, nothing parked outside, little in the way of lighting to be seen.

Chapter 19

The Architect Visits

Standing at the foot of the drive ready to do battle yet again, marching on up the hill, he was still impressed by the garage, that ramshackle building had been turned into something special.

Outside the house was two of Bye, Bye, small vans and a very nice-looking car, what was remarkable thought Nigel, those vans were sparkling clean.

Whoops, the architect! that's the reason for the clean vans, she was coming today and tomorrow to sign off the house and the Pub.

Nigel almost ran the rest of the way back to the cottage, head down, thought Nigel.

Washing away, and a new brew in hand, possibly a good time to check the car starts, been a while!

Sure enough, the faithful little car fired up. Nigel left it running whilst chancing a look around the corner.

Nigel braved a sneaky look around the corner toward the house, just to see the car heading down the drive and Baby, Love and Alex standing by the steps.

Nigel walked towards the Old House.

'Good afternoon, gentlemen, and how's your day going?' Nigel said cheerfully.

'Well, it could have been a lot worse. A lot worse,' said Love.

'There are a few bits of plaster that's been knocked off, so that needs sorting. Then the painter will have to come back. She then turned on a tap and the pipes started to knock, that's got to be done. She even changed her shoes and checked on the lawn, noting that the new grass was a slightly different shade to the original, but she thought that would blend with time.

'She checked the benches to ensure no one had tampered with them. She would like a copy of the gas safety certificate and electrical test, and a few other small things, overall OK.

'The big let-down was some clown somehow invited the local dog community to walk round the back. Its smelt like an outside privy. If I find out who sent them, I will make them clean it up.

'Yes, Love, good idea. Let's hope you don't find out, I mean I hope you find out. So you have to bring the plasterer back in again. Suppose he will dot and dab, perhaps decide to wet, what do you think?'

'Yes, Nigel. Need to get on, work to be done,' said Baby and the pair jumped into one of the vans and drove away.

'All right, Alex?' enquired Nigel.

'Yes, good, thanks. She's some classy lady. She wears lovely clothes, and smells nice, a real nice lady.

'Got to get started on the snagging. The architect said that 5 or 6 people will be arriving Saturday. They are all staying Saturday and Sunday night with the first two parties leaving Monday morning.

'She asked if we could do a bit of shopping fresh milk, tea, just a few bits, for breakfast Sunday morning, so I am off now to get it.'

'Alex, before you go, it's Wednesday, half day closing, best get fresh items Friday, not today,' informed Nigel.

'We could tell Baby, Love the person allowing the dogs round was the Captain. What do you think?' joked Nigel.

'Not a good idea. Baby, Love have allocated men for your Cottage, but the architect sort of insisted that we start the house around the back. You know, the old one that the tree fell on, before starting work for the Captain.

'She politely pointed out that she could put a lot more work Bye, Bye's way than the Captain.

'So, someone's got to tell him and her on the horse we will not be starting for weeks, and before you make any smart comments, Nigel, it's not going to be me, that tells them. Thanks for the advice on the shopping.'

'No problem. Do not forget to add disinfectant. What do you think about the plasterer?' asked Nigel.

'Yes, Nigel, see you,' as Alex turned and went inside.

Nigel made his way back to the cottage and turned off the car engine. Only to hear the Captain and Faye walking up towards him, waiting for them to approach. Taking a deep breath Nigel spoke to the pair, 'Good afternoon, you've just missed a nice, well-dressed lady, your sort of person.

'To show no ill feeling I can inform you that some people will be taking residence on Saturday and Sunday, and I understand the owner is due late Sunday.

'As for myself, I will be attending Church, Sunday morning, then perhaps a quick drink at The Cooper's, just the one, don't agree with drinking and driving, hope that's OK?

'One of the builders is still in the house, I understand that he needs a word about some work you require. As I say' no ill feeling have a nice day.'

The Captain looked stonily at Nigel, 'Just because you are unable to sort your affairs out and you ended up here it's your own fault. I want you gone on Sunday, understand sponger?'

With that both Faye and the Captain walked off.

Nigel stood and thought for a moment, that wasn't very nice, a bit mean, really. Poor Alex is now going to get his ear bent, to be a fly on the wall at this moment!

Fancy someone allowing dogs on the back lawn, what is the world coming to, chuckling away to himself.

Nigel was still smiling to himself whilst making a brew. Pouring his tea Nigel decided to open the front door and stand and drink his tea whilst leaning on the door frame waiting for the Captain to walk by.

He didn't have to wait long, as they both approached, 'Did you see the builder?' asked Nigel.

'Sunday,' snapped the Captain and continued to walk down the lane.

Moments later Nigel saw Alex walking towards the Cottage. He shouted, 'OK Nigel, nice work. Cheeky. See you, tomorrow.'

'Any time Alex. Only too happy to help.'

Nigel closed and bolted the door and returned to the kitchen. He continued to prepare his evening meal and decided to talk with David after finishing his dinner, but he didn't really fancy any, perhaps the packet of biscuits had something to do with it.

Nigel's appetite had not totally returned, and he felt bad about leaving food. He thought a walk over to the lake would help, and on the way back a chat with David would perk him up.

Nigel locked the door and started to walk to the lake. He took a moment and thought about checking on the step ladders but decided, no, he did not want to become more paranoid about them.

Passing the Old House, he did not see David, which was OK, Nigel would spend time with him later.

Perched at his favourite spot by the lake Nigel looked out in awe at the beauty and tranquillity of the surroundings. Why are people so driven by greed and destruction whether it be a person or property?

Nigel didn't have any idea how long he was there, but it was now dark and time to turn back.

As he approached the Old House he could see the silhouette of David's big build.

'I go there,' he shouted.

David laughed, 'I know it's you, silly. I keep walking down the hill to see you are OK, and not ready to jump in. I have been watching you standing there, you have been ages, best have a sit on the step.'

'You didn't think I would jump, did you?'

'Not sure, Nigel, you are not your normal self. I don't like to see you unhappy. You're not worried about robbing the Post Office are you, and it all going wrong?'

Nigel looked up at David only to see a big booming smiling face, 'I will let you into a secret. The vicar and I are going to steal the Fish and Chips van.'

David thought a moment, 'That's OK, Mary and I can't afford fish and chips, so I don't mind. Let's sit down and look at the lovely valley.'

The two men sat and watched the foxes come and go, even the badger took a stroll, the owls could be heard in the distance.

'I am going to miss these times together, Nigel. You have been really kind to Mary and me, not many people have ever done that.'

'Things will change David. This village has a heart and soul buried within it, it only takes the people to bring it to the surface and understand what sacrifices others have made to keep it so beautiful.

'Let's talk about happy things, I hope you are coming to Church, on Sunday. I hear they have a fantastic speaker coming. Then down to the Pub to sample the food and drink. Are you looking forward to the day, David?'

'We are coming to Church, but Mary said we may look a little out of place in the Pub. You see we can never afford to go, so it looks like we are only taking advantage of free food and drink.'

'You must go, the landlord and landlady are expecting you both. You have to test the food, they are relying on you two. Anyway if you don't come, I will get Millie to carry you up there.'

'You're being silly now, Nigel. I like you like this, Happy! I will be sorry to see you leave. My last day is Friday because the new people are coming in on Saturday. Will you come and see me?'

'No David! I will see you in Church and The Cooper's on Sunday. Anyway who said Friday will be your last day, perhaps you will carry on guarding the Old House.'

'No, the man in the cowboy hat said they don't need people like me round the place. I am not their sort of people. If they need a security person, they will look for a professional team.'

'Think I am going to turn in now, David. Don't worry about him, the man's a buffoon. See you tomorrow. Thanks for the chat, good night!'

'Good night!'

Nigel walked back to the cottage. Ensuring the screw was well in, he decided to go to bed.

'I Love you,' he whispered.

Chapter 20

The Taking of New Pictures

Nigel awoke to the sound of the farmer's tractor passing by, which disoriented him for a moment thinking it was Friday and market day.

Now being awake, time to get up, wash, get dressed and go downstairs for breakfast. Little need for a fire as the weather was warming up nicely, so much so, he drank his first brew outside, listening to the birds singing.

Nigel was a little devoid of plans for today, a little down, thinking about moving on Sunday, and the fact that so many people seemed to wish to know why he was in the village at all.

But determined not to return to that dark place he needed to act positively, so locking the door and standing by the edge of the cottage - left, or right?

Over the sound of the birds singing, Nigel could hear vehicles coming up the drive. That's odd, he thought. I understood that everyone had finished apart from the odd bit of plastering and a paint touch up.

That made his mind up for him. This needed investigating. Checking on the front of the Old House, he saw about six or seven vehicles parked up, including two small vans.

As the people exited the cars and vans, some started to unload. The vans were full of black boxes and tripods. Then, someone shouted, 'Morning, do you have the keys?' pointing to the Old House.

'No, I don't live here.' 'Oh!' said the man, 'where do you live?'

'I live in the cottage just around the corner.' 'Do you have the keys to that?'

'Yes,' replied Nigel, 'of course I do!'

'Well, we've had a long drive already this morning and a cup of tea would be nice.'

'Could be a problem I only have two cups,' Nigel informed the man.

'That's alright,' replied the man, 'I only need one, don't worry about this lot. They can sort themselves out. One sugar, please.'

Nigel turned around muttering under his breath, 'Damn cheek! What does he think I am, an on-site café?'

Returning with two cups of tea, he found a few tripods had been set up and some of the black cases were open, revealing what looked like very expensive cameras.

'Here's your tea,' said Nigel.

'How long before someone arrives with the keys? We need to crack on.'

'Not sure, said Nigel, 'perhaps when you have finished the tea I could read the future in the tea leaves, if I'd not used tea bags. Anyway, why are you here?'

'Photo shoot. Going to be here right up until dark. We need the house lit up in the dark to show it off all illuminated. In the meantime, all the up and coming designers will be advising on us taking pictures of their top designs, ready for the major magazines.

Smart thinking, the rooms get the best new designers who are trying to get into the top end market, and best furniture makers showing off their skills, all at rock bottom price. All the new house owners must do is allow people to come in and view for the next few years. Someone's got their head screwed on.

Nigel was now feeling a quick escape was in order before he ended up making bacon butties.

No need to worry. Nigel spotted a Bye, Bye van coming up the drive.

As Love climbed out of the van, 'Sorry I am late. Needed to find my ticket to collect my pictures from the developers, I've recorded "before and after" pictures.'

'No problem', said the photographer, 'this chap's made me a decent cup of tea whilst we waited.'

'That's nice of you Nigel, two sugars, please. Whilst Nigel's doing that, I can let you in,' said Love.

Collecting the cup from the photographer, off he went chuntering under his breath, 'Perhaps I should wear a black and white uniform with a little white hat. Should have turned left and minded my own business.'

Returning with another cup, Nigel handed it over to Love. 'Leave the cup on the step I will collect it later,' instructed Nigel.

'Where are you off now, Nigel, to the village to get some biscuits?' asked Love.

Nigel grinned, and turned towards the cottage. Best lock up whilst I still have some tea left.

Cottage safely locked, he made his way down the drive. He hoped the photographer would take a couple of pictures of the garage with the doors open.

A few steps farther he could see cars turning onto the drive. These could be the designers helping on the photo shoot. Let's hope at least one of them carries a flask of tea, it's going to be a long day.

As he passed the Pub the landlady greeted Nigel with a, 'Good morning, what a great day!'

'Yes, it is proving a be a busy one already. The Old House is having pictures taken. There is an army of designers and people with cameras, lights and tripods all sorts of stuff, best keep out of the way.'

'Don't you fancy being in the picture then, Nigel? It could be a turning point, snapped up by one or two of the major film companies, seeing you in a few years' time, name up in lights, 'The adventure of the man with the wheelie bag'.

'They are coming here tomorrow; the architect lass is using her designs of the Pub to influence breweries to adopt some of her ideas. I need to stop calling it a Pub, it's The Cooper's. We are going to be more than just a Pub, mark my words! See you, Nigel.'

'Yes, see you.'

That's a turnaround. A couple of weeks ago they were ready to throw themselves in the river. Any more remarks about the bag, I may well push them in.

Before he had made a few steps,'Hey Nigel,' shouted the landlady, 'we can't make it to the Church on Sunday, we have to be here. Why don't you tell us now?'

'Nice try!' replied Nigel.

Goodness me, people are interested in why I am here, hope I am not going to disappoint.

Continuing his walk, he found himself staring at the signpost in the middle of the small roundabout with its arms pointing in different directions - but to where?

Looking past the signpost he could see the church gauge indicating the progress of the heating fund.

Progress, if any, was slow. It could be next year before enough money was collected, by which time very few people would come. Two years of cold empty church may be too much for even the most dedicated church goer.

'Morning, Nigel, what a great morning it is!'

'Morning, Alex, yes, it is.'

'What are you staring at, Nigel?'

'Guess I was wondering why there's a signpost with blank signs, and why the Church barometer isn't going up?'

'That's easy! The people around here know where the roads go, and not many people are giving to the Church heating fund as the weather is getting warmer. Simple.'

'See you, off to the Old House, there is a photo shoot happening, and I could get my picture taken!'

'That's possible, Alex. Perhaps a statue of a Greek god standing in the garden?'

'Cheeky!'

Emerging from the Post Office the Captain boomed, 'Are you still here?'

'Good morning, what a nice day.! What a grand day it is!!' replied Nigel.

'Now, I only agreed to pass a message if I bumped into you, what a pity I have!

'Anyway, there's a team of photographers up at the Old House and they're looking for two of 'the right type of people' to showcase the high class of design and manufacturing standard. Someone that will enhance the quality of the decor, and someone suggested you, heaven knows why, and yes, I know 'out Sunday'. '

With that Nigel continued his walk, but he could not help looking back, the Captain had gone into the phone box, hopefully to ring Faye - two of the right type of people!

That was very bad Nigel. Don't add lying to your sins. Sorry, but it did feel good.

It is such a nice day I will buy a newspaper and sit on the park bench.

Paper duly purchased, Nigel settled down to bring himself up to speed with world events, but due to an error Nigel found himself reading the local paper which covered about ten square miles, not really what he was hoping for.

Trying to find something of interest, he noticed a casually dressed gentleman sitting at the other end of the bench.

'Good day, anything of interest in the paper?' the man asked.

'I am sure there will be, but not found it yet,' answered Nigel.

'The paper is aimed at local people,' replied the man, 'who tend to find lots of useful items in it. I guess you're not local then?'

'No!' said Nigel.

'Why are you here? You see, I write articles for the paper, and you could be of interest to our readers.'

Nigel needed to think quickly, 'If you're interested why not come to Church on Sunday?'

'What good will that do me?' replied the Gent becoming somewhat agitated.

'Well, you have surprised me, you write articles for the paper. One of two big events to hit the village in a long time is happening Sunday, and you don't know about it,' with that Nigel stood up, 'See you Sunday. Bye!'

Nigel walked off hoping that would be the end of the matter.

'Wait a minute,' shouted the man, 'what's the other thing that's happening?'

Oh, good grief! thought Nigel.

'It's the grand opening of The Cooper's, after its complete refit. Free food and drink, but by invitation only!'

'How do I get an invitation, I suppose I could use my press pass?'

'No need. Do you know a chap they call the Captain, wears a cowboy hat?'

'Yes, everyone knows him.'

'Go and see him, I am sure he will only be too happy to help. Now tell him you're from the press, no need to say it's local. He likes that sort of thing.

'It is possible he is at the Old House on a shoot - photos, not guns. You do know where the Old House is, I suppose?'

'Thanks,' and off the Gent went heading at a fast pace towards the Old House.

Turning out to be a funny sort of day, thought Nigel.

'Hi Nigel, how's the day going?' asked Paul, appearing from one of the shops.

'Funny sort of day, a team of photographers are at the Old House. One thinks I'm there to make cups of tea. The landlady tried to get me to tell her Sunday's news. I sent the Captain on a wild goose chase, then Alex thinks he some sort of Greek god and I meet the village idiot disguised as a newspaper reporter, so I sent him off to the see the Captain. They will make a good pair. Anyway, what has your day been like so far?'

'Visited some parishioners, drank tea, chattered about this and that, nice part of the job.

'Speaking about newspapers, Mrs Bright said someone from a newspaper rang the vicarage enquiring about Sunday's speaker. I think she was a bit sharp with them, told them to come along to the Church on Sunday and find out for themselves.

'Sorry, I can't stop, Nigel. I need to make sure the sermon on Sunday is a good one. If I do a good job, I could get some return visits. See you Saturday?'

'Yes, good for me,' replied Nigel.

Nigel made his way to the bridge as he decided to walk the river route back to the cottage, but not before stopping to sit on the riverbank and watch the river's wildlife go about their business.

Three days left, it's going to be difficult enough come Sunday. Hope the press stay away, had a belly full of them and the police when I was living at home.

Come on Nigel! you can do this, just get past Sunday.

What am I going to do with that wheelie bag?

That light-hearted thought soon had him concentrating on the activities on and around the river, but needs must and time to head back to the cottage.

Soon, Nigel was at the back of the Pub. As he approached, he could see that each one of the dining tables were laid out. Glasses on the table shone, the knives and forks gleamed against the pure white tablecloths, every table was laid identically, chairs positioned within inches of the table, each cloth had the same amount of overhang. The place looked magnificent!

He could see people inside, best leave them to it.

Crossing the road, he could see cars were parked right down as far as the garage. Never seen that many cars before, even at the height of the building work.

Nigel could see a myriad of people moving about around the Old House and decided to keep low. The last thing he needed right at this moment in time was his picture being taken.

Just as he turned the corner a voice shouted, 'Hi, Nigel.'

'Hello Alex, come round here, out of sight.'

'How's it going, are they almost done?'

'Why are we hiding around the corner?' asked Alex.

'Never mind, what's happening?'

'Well, the chap takes over ½ an hour to take a couple of pictures, sometimes nearly an hour. It is painfully slow and boring.

'Except for when the Captain and Faye arrived.

'Now! That was interesting, thought these two and the photographer were going to come to blows.

'The situation really started to turn ugly when some bloke from the local newspaper kept asking the Captain for a ticket to the Pub on Sunday. When the Captain told him it was nothing to do with him the reporter got really cross, ranting about freedom of the press, accusing the Captain of standing in the way of free and honest reporting of the events. Not sure how that ended.

'I had to go and move a chair by about two inches. Between the designer and the photographer every room must be perfect, and it seemed moving a chair was beneath them, so muggings here had to go do it.

'Still, nice to see it's done correctly and to everyone's satisfaction. Can't wait to see the pictures when they have been developed.

'Why are we hiding around the corner?'

'Never mind,' said Nigel, 'see you later. You better get going. There must be something that needs moving by now.'

'Yes, suppose so!

'Why did the Captain and Faye turn up? And who put the idea in the mind of the reporter that the pair gave out invites to the Sunday bash?'

'It's beyond me Alex. Some people get these ideas out of thin air.'

With that, Nigel continued the few yards back to the cottage. Unlocking the door he needed to check on what he had available for tea.

He had been buying bits and pieces but not been concentrating and failed to construct a menu.

Having scanned the cupboards - beans on toast, and he could cut the mould off the cheese and spread over the beans and grill.

Tomorrow is Market Day. Nigel decided to plan his 3 last meals. Must remind Alex to buy the items the architect asked for.

Food ready, he decided to eat outside, quickly grabbing an old wooden pop bottle case from the shed.

Nigel perched himself on the case using it as a seat. Plate on his knees, he tucked in. Mother would not approve of this, food is meant for the table. It will be OK, a bit like camping when he was a scout.

Food consumed, Nigel looked back at the old cottage.

It's sort of grown on me, the cold weather was a bit uncomfortable but as the weather warmed, it's not so bad.

Completing the washing up, Nigel locked the back door and made his way back to the Old House.

The few cars that were left had been moved farther down the drive, and the photographer had set up his camera on a tripod about 100 yards down the lawn. All the lights at the front of the Old House had been turned on and an array of light and shadows burst from inside.

A voice whispered, 'Who goes there?'

'Good evening, David. Why are you whispering?' asked Nigel.

'He is taking pictures of the house,' David replied.

'Don't think you and I talking normally will affect the photographs in anyway, David. Are you turning the lights out and locking up when he is finished?'

'Yes, I have all the house keys. I have to keep them all night and Mr Bye will pick them up very early in the morning. He has something coming and needs to be here when it arrives.

'Tomorrow night will be my last night, will you come and see me?'

'Of course. Anyway it may not be your last night. Perhaps the new people will need someone to look after the Old House.'

'Perhaps so, but Mary said I must go to the Unemployment office on Monday. They help us with money, not a lot, but we are very grateful. Summer's coming, we can start picking fruit from the hedge rows and ask the landlord if we can take some apples. It all helps to feed the three of us.

'I am sorry you won't be here, Nigel; I like talking with you. You are always very nice and don't make fun of me or try and hurt my feelings. Thank you!'

'I am not always nice, David. Some people are bad and nasty, and you can't always be nice to them, no matter how hard you try.

'I now need to go for a walk, I will see you in a little while.'

With that remark, Nigel walked off head bowed low. He made his way to his favourite spot by the lake, carefully avoiding the photographer's lens.

Nigel sat by the lake recalling times at home and work, as he had done many times before over the past few months. The past is the past, what of the future? Well!

I must move out of the cottage, Sunday.

But, not before Church and I need to come clean with Paul, I owe him that much!

As ever, time rolled by. Nigel was stuck in his own mind, trapped by his own thoughts. It was only when the traces of light from the Old House were extinguished, and he could see the last remaining car leave the drive and head off down the road, that Nigel took a moment to put his thoughts away before heading off toward the Old House looking for David.

As Nigel approached the main door, he could see David struggling.

'Are you OK, David?' Nigel asked.

'No. I can't find the keyhole, and I don't know which key I should use. It's too dark.'

'Well,' said Nigel, 'go back in the house, put a light on so you can see the keyhole, find the right key, put it in the hole, then turn off the light, close the door and turn the key before removing it from the hole.'

David followed Nigel's instruction and within minutes all was locked up, safe and sound.

Soon the nocturnal animals were out hunting or playing in the dim light of the street lamps. David and Nigel sat watching and chatting before Nigel decided it was time for bed.

'See you tomorrow, David.'

'You won't forget, will you?'

'No, I won't forget! Good night.'

Soon Nigel was in bed, for going a drink of Scotch. 'I Love You.'

Chapter 21

The Plants are Doing Well

Nigel awoke to a strange noise outside his bedroom window. Peering through the curtains, he saw a large lorry pulling up outside.

As quickly as he could he got dressed and ran down the stairs. This needed close investigation.

Unbolting the door, Nigel dashed around the side of the cottage, only slowing to a nonchalant pace to give the impression of disinterest.

'Morning, Nigel, hope we didn't get you up,' said Love.

'No, I was just making a cup of tea.'

'Thanks, Nigel, one sugar, please.'

Damn it, caught out again. Perhaps I should stay here in the cottage and open a little café, what with builders and photographers, and people walking borrowed dogs! Could be money in it.

Returning with tea and still chuntering, Nigel politely asked what was happening so early in the morning.

'It's building materials for the cottage, bricks, blocks, slates, and timber. Some of the load is for here and the remainder, and a second load is for the house near the green house. Hence the early start so we can get both drops done,' explained Love.

Nigel walked around the other side of the lorry to look at the load being placed on the brambles and scrub; the bricks and slates did not look new.

'Why are you using old used bricks and slates? Is it cheaper?' Nigel enquired.

'Technically, Nigel, they're called reclaimed. When something gets knocked down, an old warehouse or old house, the reclaimer collects the bricks and other materials, cleans them up removing the mortar and paint, and re-sells.

'These are more expensive than new ones. It was the architect that insisted that the cottage will keep its look. Likewise the other house on the other side.

'Both houses will still look old but be insulated, helping to keep the places warmer in winter.'

'Sounds good, is Alex about? I need to remind him about the architect's shopping list,' said Nigel.

'Yes, he is in the old house tidying up after the photographer yesterday. We've had to get the cleaner in again.

'The architect is coming today with some of the top retailers and manufacturers to show off the designs. After all, some of them have possibly paid a fair few bob and need to see what they have paid for.'

'I suppose so,' said Nigel, 'perhaps I should have a quick tidy up just in case she comes round for a cup of tea, everyone seems to!'

'That's a good idea Nigel, best leave the tea bag in longer, next time, here's your cup, see you!'

Nigel returned to the kitchen leaving the lorry still unloading.

Breakfast eaten and now washed and dressed, Nigel grabbed his wheelie bag and set off to purchase the items for his last few meals at the cottage.

Rounding the corner, Nigel spotted Alex.

'Don't forget you need to get some shopping in for the people coming this week-end.'

'Morning, Nigel. No, not forgotten, thanks!'

Nigel crossed the road. Passing the Pub he noticed a few cars in the car park.

He had seen them the day before, it was the team of photographers. He only now remembered that pictures were being taken for the breweries, highlighting the architect's work and ideas.

As he continued his walk, he thought, she sure knows her stuff, seems to get what she needs, the Old House and the Pub are lovely pieces of design work.

Passing the Post Office, Nigel spotted the two telephone boxes. Now should I use them as normal?

I need to think about that.

Passing the wool shop, he saw things looked much brighter and fresher than on that first day in the village.

The same could not be said for the Iron Mongers' or the junk shop across the road. Their windows looked just the same. Even the woollen fire guard was still under the table and the weather much warmer now.

Entering the butchers', he was asked the question, 'Ready for Sunday then?'

'Suppose the Captain's been telling everyone I'm leaving. Making sure I go.'

'Don't care about that idiot. I mean the talk on Sunday at the Church. Come on give me a snippet of what you're talking about, could be a nice juicy steak involved.'

'As tempting as that is, come along with all the others, then for a few drinks at The Cooper's, could be fun.

'Now, four pork sausages, a black pudding and 6 eggs and a chicken and leek pie, please,' asked Nigel.

'Are you sure they will all fit in the bag?'

'That's more like the butcher I have become accustomed to!' Nigel said, smiling.

Waving bye, Nigel made his way over to the market stalls, far more now than when he first came across it, and the traffic was definitely busy, no wonder the farmer used the track at the cottage on a Friday.

A few pieces of vegetables purchased to go with the pie, then over to the shop for the usual four cans of beer.

I never really thanked Paul for helping with cash. Let's have a bottle of wine to go with the chippy tea, two beers and a glass of wine may help me think clearly, and beat him at chess.

Purchases all bagged up, time to call in at the vicarage to drop off the beer and wine.

After a knock on the door, it was quickly opened, 'Hello Nigel, come in, what a lovely day!' Paul said chirpily.

'Yes, nice. How come you're so cheerful?' Nigel enquired as he handed over the drinks.

'Sunday is sold out. Figuratively speaking, you're the talk of the village, along with the new owners of the Old House and the invitation opening of The Cooper's. The weather's going to be nice so the Pub can invite more people, some can go outside.'

'Yes, will need to stand up. Bye, Bye have not made tables yet.'

'Be fair, Nigel, what with the Pub and the Old House and now the two cottages, and the Captain's work, they're really pushed.'

'How come people know it's both cottages? I only found out this morning when a big lorry dumped off a load of second-hand bricks and roof slates,' asked Nigel.

'Not sure. Mrs Bright told me. Guess one of the Bye's told her, you know what the village is like?'

'Yes, I do,' said Nigel. 'She didn't tell you about Sunday, did she?'

'Nice try, Nigel! What's with the wine?'

'For tomorrow. It could give me an advantage over the game. Must be off, see you tomorrow.'

With that, Nigel made his way over the road towards the Post Office.

I think I will make a call.

Putting his hand in his pocket and inspecting the coins, it seemed a call was going to be out of the question, due to the lack of the correct change. Well, never mind.

Just as he was about to continue back to the cottage, a man and a woman approached him, 'If you need change for the phone we can oblige.'

'Thank you, but I don't really need the phone today, everything is in place. Thanks again.'

Good grief!

I now have people waiting for me to make calls, so they can listen in. Should have gone in and made up a story. Best not, that sort of thing helped to get me here in the first place.

Passing the Pub, he saw the photographer's car was still there along with a few other expensive looking cars.

Best keep a low-profile. Men with cameras can spell trouble!

Nigel made his way over the road and started up the drive. As he approached the top, he could see a couple of cleaning vans.

Nigel turned down the lane heading for the cottage. On the right-hand side was a long row of bricks, blocks, timber, slates, bags of cement. A big heap of sand and lots of other items he did not recognise.

As he turned the corner he could hear voices, 'Please, not that idiot in the hat?'

'Hello, you three,' addressing Baby, Love and Alex.

'Hi Nigel, hope you don't mind we are just working out a few details before starting on Monday.'

'We are OK with the electricity, that comes in overhead, via those wires. We think the water travels in that direction,' pointing towards the Old House, 'no mains gas to worry about, it's the sewage.'

'Don't you know where it is going?' enquired Nigel.

'No, not really! You see these old houses just had a big hole in the ground, it all goes in there and nature takes care of it.

'Now it could be that as you have an outside privy, the hole could be close by.'

'We were just admiring the veg. patch, Nigel,' said Alex. 'Do you feed the plants? They do look healthy. You must feed them something? I bet they taste good too. Should we come round on Sunday and help you harvest them to take with you?'

'No thanks, you're OK. On second thoughts I could give them to the Captain, as a farewell present.'

'Cheeky!' said Alex.

'We had better get going and double check on the Old House and grounds. Hand over's on Sunday and I don't want to upset the architect. Not too worried about The Cooper's, the landlord and landlady have that covered.

'Up here needs to be right. I am guessing the new owner will be coming sometime over the weekend, and if they have employed that lass then they must be perfectionists themselves.'

As the three walked off, Baby shouted, 'See you later then, Nigel.'

'Yes, see you,' shouted Nigel.

Turning round, Nigel stared at the veg patch. No, surely not.

They are growing well!

No, it's too close to the cottage. Who would put a hole there?

With only two nights left, Nigel decided to have an early tea and then go down to the lake and then meet up with David.

Pie in the oven, potatoes washed and on a medium heat, Nigel couldn't resist going out to the veg plot.

No, they're pulling my leg. As Nigel stood close to the plot edge, he jumped in the air, landing flat footed. See that looks OK.

I am sure you get dafter, he said to himself, how stupid can you get?

What if the ground gave way? You would be in a mess, literally!

Tea consumed and pots washed, Nigel set off for the lake. As he passed the Old House, Nigel stood and gazed up. How different it looked now from when he first arrived. Those builders and all the other teams have done a great job. I hope the architect is happy, it looks great, he thought!

He continued his walk and soon stood on his favourite spot and admired the English countryside.

Soon, lost in his thoughts, time drifted away. Thinking back on his life so far, one moment at School, happy times spent with Mum and Dad, days out at the zoo, or seaside or Mum's country house, that was all taken away far too soon.

Trepidation momentarily filled his heart.

What of the future?

That could be answered on Sunday, to the good, or not so good.

In his mind it was difficult to recall, putting faith in people got him to move out of his family home and now standing by the lake, alone.

Sunday will come soon enough.

For now, it was time to meet up with David as promised, walking up the hill Nigel could see lights on, inside the Old House. This was unusual as David didn't normally go inside. As he got closer, he saw parked outside a Bye, Bye builders' van.

'Who goes there?' a voice chuckled.

'Hello, why are the lights on in the house, David?'

It's Mr Baby and Mr Love. They're checking that everything is OK for the Lady coming tomorrow. I must be extra *vig-i-lant* tonight, don't let anyone make the place untidy.'

'Well, David, the place does look very nice.'

'Yes, it does.'

'Guess this will be the last time I will see it this close up. When the new people come tomorrow, they won't want me hanging about. If I'm lucky I will see it from the road. I will miss working here, having a wage makes me feel good.'

'Mary's been saving a little bit of money every week, but I have to go to see the man at the Government on Monday to sign on.'

'What are you doing, Nigel, you have to leave the Cottage on Sunday? I am really, really going to miss you.'

Before Nigel could reply, Baby and Love came out of the Old House.

'Evening gentlemen, what a pleasant evening! I presume you got it out.'

'Got what out?' asked Love.

'That big rat, about the size of a small cat. But you will know that now, having chased it out. Not keen on rats to be honest, don't mind water voles. They're OK. I used to watch the water voles when...'

'A RAT! No one said anything about that, not now, well not anytime.

'A RAT, if she sees that she will have our guts for garters. We have been here months and never seen one, let alone near the house, where has that come from?' continued Love.

'Perhaps they heard you talking about the hole under my veg plot at the cottage and decided to move out.'

'That's funny, Nigel, really funny. Any more of that and you could find yourself in that hole on Sunday.'

'Did you see a rat, Nigel? asked David.

'No, David, just teasing this pair.'

'Let's turn off the lights and lock up and go home. Need to be up bright and early just in case we get a call from the architect,' suggested Baby.

The pair turned off the lights, locked the front door and climbed into the van. 'See you tomorrow, Nigel,' one shouted.

David and Nigel watched as the van went down the drive, out of sight.

'That was a bit naughty, Nigel, you had them worried.'

'Never mind, David. Let's have a seat on the step and look vigilant. I hope you still have hopes and dreams that we spoke about all those weeks ago, David, and you still tell Mary you love her.'

'It's hard to have dreams, Nigel, when you have little money. Do you have dreams, Nigel? You never said. You must have enough money, you have Fish and Chips every week and have washing done for you, and have nice food. You have a car, and use the telephone a lot.'

'It is a fair point you make, David. I did have money, lots of money, more than enough, but not now, most of it has gone, but I still have dreams and hopes for the future.

'Sometimes you need to share these dreams, you have Mary, you should both share those hopes and dreams together.'

'Who shares your hopes and dreams, Nigel?'

'No one now, David, because I have not really shared them with anyone. I only have a promise to keep.'

'You need a lady, like Mary, or a good honest friend to share them,' said David.

'I very nearly did have a lady. Only she turned out to be a bad person.

'I didn't see it at first, and possibly never would if it hadn't been for the help of my old Boss, Mr Parker. He taught me a lot about people. It was only because of him I noted tell tale signs about the woman's true intentions.

'I think that's enough about my past for now, David, it's the future we need to look towards to, speaking of which, I hope you are coming to Church on Sunday and then onto the Cooper's, and I don't want to hear you saying about not having any money to pay. The landlord needs you and Mary there.'

'We are going with Millie and Arthur and Mrs Frank. I heard the ladies talking. Why did you think Mrs Frank had a dog?'

'My mistake, David,' said Nigel.

'People are excited about your talk, the church is going to be busy. Mary said you could be number one, it's a difficult call between you and the Cooper's opening on Sunday with free food and drink.'

'I will ask you on Sunday which one won, David.

'Until then let's enjoy the evening watching animals play and have idle chit chat, and staying vigilant,' suggested Nigel.

The hours passed, until it was time for Nigel to return to the cottage, 'See you Sunday, my good friend.'

'Yes, good night, Nigel, and thank you, sleep tight.'

Nigel put the screw in the door, thought about a Scotch but decided against. Climbing into bed, he thought about his bread bin in the loft and when it would be best to remove it. Guess it needs to be tomorrow, need Paul to print copies.

'I Love You.'

Chapter 22

Old Photographs

Nigel tossed and turned during the night, restless about the bread bin and its contents. Also he needed to talk with Paul. Picking the right time was going to be difficult, had to be done before Sunday.

The light was shining through the window. Little point in waiting for the clock to chime, he had forgotten to wind it up again.

Getting out of bed, washed and dressed, Nigel made his way to the kitchen. He selected two of the sausages and lay them side by side in the frying pan, a gentle flame under the pan. Next, the kettle.

Removing the screw from the door Nigel opened it up to reveal a beautiful morning. The birds were singing, and the rabbits were playing in the undergrowth. Not many mornings here to enjoy, pity. It had not been that bad!

Sitting with breakfast plate on his lap, Nigel needed to sort out the best time to talk with Paul and decided to stay after church on Sunday morning.

He now needed to sort out the bread bin. Plate and cup cleaned, Nigel took himself off to the shed to retrieve the steps. There was a bit of a battle as Nigel had ensured no one could easily use them to access the loft.

Steps out and now placed at the top of the stairs, Nigel gingerly climbed each one. Gently opening the hatch, he raised up one more step. Waiting for a few moments for his eyes to adjust to the dark, he could see the bin, sitting between two joists. Reaching it was going to be tricky.

Shuffling along on his stomach and trying to stretch his legs to remain on the steps, he could just reach the handle on the top of the bin. Positioning himself, he grabbed the handle and pulled. The bin was free, but Nigel had lost his footing on the steps and not too sure where they were.

Moving slowly backward and waving his legs around in the hope of one of them making contact with the steps, sure enough the steps were still in place, and he very carefully lowered himself onto a rung. Stepping down one rung he reached up for the bin. He manoeuvred both himself and the bin to the safety of the bedroom.

Now he needed to replace the hatch and put back the steps. This time, at the front of the shed, will do.

Nigel took a moment, now I have the bin what to do with it? He had limited options, either wheel it around all day, lock it in the car, or ask Paul to mind it.

The decision was to leave it in the boot of the car, it couldn't be seen. Before locking it away, Nigel removed a photo from the bin. This was going to be copied ready for tomorrow.

Bread bin loaded and a quick check to ensure no one had seen him placing the bin in the car, he returned to the cottage, collected the photo. Coat on, door locked, he made his way down the drive.

Despite it being a bright, sunny day, the Pub was ablaze with lights. Inside he could see lots of activity, perhaps getting ready for some important people. Can't be, he thought, I am not going until tomorrow, and off he went, chuckling to himself.

Nigel turned the corner and spied the two empty phone boxes, thinking for a moment, I could phone the speaking clock and have a conversation with it, that should get people talking.

As he was routing about in his pocket for change a voice shouted, 'Morning, Nigel.' It was Paul on the other side of the road.

'Yes, morning. I've brought something for you to copy for tomorrow's talk, it's a photo.'

'OK, Nigel, let's go and print them off now. I'm not even going to ask you about it. I will wait for tomorrow,' answered Paul.

The two men entered the vicarage and made their way to the study.

'How many copies do you need, Nigel?' asked Paul.

'One per pew, perhaps?' Nigel replied.

'Not likely. I've a new heating system to buy, everyone can have a copy, that should be about 120?'

'120 at 10p each,' gasped Nigel.

'120 at 20p each and you know it. Colour's an extra 10p per copy,' Paul said as he pressed the copy button. 'Whilst that's printing money, let's have a cup of tea.'

'Should we leave it running, what happens if someone comes in and sees them? Anyway the pictures are old and in black and white, that's 20p each.'

If you're talking about Mrs Bright she's not here today. I didn't notice it was only black and white. Let's have tea!

The two chatted over tea and biscuits. Then the drone of the copier stopped. Returning to the study, they sensed the heavy smell of copying fumes filled the air.

'That's not a pleasant smell,' said Nigel.

'It's smells like money to me Nigel. That will be £30, please.'

'It's smells like day light robbery, and it's £24.'

'Oh yes, maths was never one of my best subjects,' replied Paul.

'Well, it still is one of mine. If you still have some of the money from the Postal Order take from that. Thanks for the tea, will see you about 6 O'clock?'

Nigel said his goodbyes and proceeded down the high street, 'Morning Nigel, see you tomorrow,' shouted a man across the street.

'Yes,' Nigel replied. Who's he, I wonder?

'Looking forward to tomorrow,' shouted a stranger.

'Yes. Good.'

Nigel continued his walk, only to be stopped by a lady, 'Hello, hoping to get a good seat tomorrow. It's exciting having a speaker. I hear you are leaving the village afterwards, we are going to miss that wheelie bag, bye.'

I can see it now. If I ever become really famous, they will erect a bronze statue of the wheelie bag and place it at the top of the high street. Cheek!

Think I am going to walk back down the river, less people. Nigel walked down the steps and continued his return to the cottage.

He decided not to stop and admire the scenery. He had left the car and its contents for too long. He was also aware that the guests of the Old

House could be in residence and the last thing he needed was to bump into them.

Walking through the Pub car park, he could see inside there was a hive of activity. He was almost compelled to investigate, but the thought of the car made him decide to continue.

As he stood at the bottom of the drive, it seemed that nothing was happening up at the Old House so he marched quickly up the hill, not really noticing the climb for once. Soon, passing the garage, he was around the corner and out of sight of anyone by the Old House.

A quick glance at the car. All seemed well. He wondered if he should have cancelled the evening with Paul and stayed close by. No, he thought, I am becoming paranoid, it will be OK!

Nigel had a couple of hours to spare, time for a brew and then a bath. He decided to walk to Paul's by the lane and past the farm. No chance of bumping into any one from the Old House.

Bath done, nice clean shirt and trousers, ironed to perfection as usual by Millie, Nigel set off to Paul's but not before trying the car door more than once.

The evening felt peaceful, the sound of a light breeze in the trees and the smells of the woodland drifted around. The birds were singing, the occasional glimpse of a rabbit.

Nigel stood and looked all around him. Despite the events of the past, Nigel could feel the tears welling up and the thought of this moment never being repeated.

His eyes were drawn past the canopy of trees to the blue sky with the odd wisp of cloud coming into and going out of view, he thought of his talk tomorrow and how things could have been.

Time to move on, he thought.

He made his way between the farm and the back of the stable block, luckily no sign of the Captain to spoil the evening, following the road to the Church. The thermometer came into view, not a lot of movement on the indicator, but hopefully after tomorrow it will have risen by at least £24.

Crossing over, he saw Paul was waiting on the wall by the vicarage, 'Evening, Nigel.'

'Evening Paul, keen, are we, or just hungry?'

'Looking forward to our chippy tea, Nigel, and can't help feeling sorry this will be our last.'

The two men joined the small queue and ordered their food.

'Looking forward to tomorrow's talk,' said the lady serving. 'Me, too,' said the other lady. 'Me, also,' said the man frying.

Walking back to the vicarage, parcels in hand, 'Is everyone coming tomorrow, Paul?' asked Nigel.

'Don't think the Captain will be there, not your biggest fan, but other than him, yes!'

The two men continued over to the vicarage and sat in silence eating supper, neither of them up for meaningless conversation. When supper was finished, both men sat quietly. This was the time for Nigel to come clean with Paul. But before he could speak, a knock on the front door.

'Won't be a moment,' said Paul. Nigel could hear talking but not what was being said. Paul returned to the room, 'Sorry, Nigel, I must go out. Church business, sorry!'

'No problem, see you tomorrow. Hope everything is OK.' With that Nigel put on his coat and proceeded to the front door, passing a lady in the hall who was very upset.

Nigel closed the door behind him and stood on the street looking around. Eventually making his way over to the Church gate, he stood for a moment, 'Well, lads, tomorrow's the day, I keep my promise.'

Nigel made his way to the cottage, one of those journeys, remembering starting and finishing but not the time in-between.

Screwing the door, he slowly made his way upstairs, and sat on the edge of the bed. Mum and Dad, if you're listening, I may need you to hold my hand tomorrow.

'Love You.'

Surprisingly, the night's sleep was kind to Nigel. He was up, washed and dressed. A cup of tea was all he needed. Breakfast was off the menu, his stomach was turning with nerves and trepidation.

Keys taken off the sideboard, the bread bin was removed from the boot and placed in the wheelie bag. Coat on, Nigel checked the time, a little early, but he could have a talk with the lads, before church.

Slowly walking down the drive, he noted a couple of posh cars parked outside the Old House, little point now in staying low, he thought.

Reaching the bottom of the drive Nigel crossed over. That was easy he thought.

Nigel stood by the roadside, no cars, I know it's Sunday, it's very quiet.

Nigel passed the Pub, the lights were on and people inside, big day for them, he thought.

He was soon at the Church gate, the sound of singing filled the air. What was the size of the congregation, did the Church sound really full?

Something he would soon find out about. He had a little time to spare and walked around the side of the Church and stood talking to old broken head stones.

Sometime later silence fell from inside the church, Nigel knew this was it!

Making his way around to the church door, he saw Paul was waiting. 'Come Nigel, what a great day this is! Come inside, go to the front. I will hand out the photos whilst you get ready.'

Nigel and the wheelie bag made their way to the front, there was a gentle buzz of eager anticipation.

Nigel opened the bag, removed the bread bin, unlocked it, and removed some contents.

Looking down the pews,he saw Paul had handed out the photos and gave Nigel the thumbs up, and mouthed, 'good luck'.

Nigel took a deep breath, he seriously did not expect this sort of turnout. He started, 'Good Morning. I understand that you have all come here to listen to me explain why I am here.

'This will be delivered in two parts, one in this Church and the other at the Cooper's, neither of which you will need to worry about. I hope you will not be disappointed.

'You see early last year my mother passed away, and a few months after that my father died. Like most of you that have lost family members know, eventually a time comes when things need to be cleared out of wardrobes and drawers.

'Some people come across surprising finds, this old bread bin was mine, not sure why it has a hasp and staple. I found all sorts of things inside, things I never knew about, and I hope to share some of my findings with you.

'So sorry, I am not an international spy, not a drug baron, or a criminal wanted by Interpol. I am a normal person, with a story I feel needs to be told, and I hope to tell you the story so people can be finally recognised for who they were and what they gave.

'Paul has kindly printed a picture for you to refer to, later.

'You see we all have names, as you know I am Nigel, here we have Paul, I see Millie, Mary and David, these are given Names, some have titles - Vicar, Lordship, even Sir, others have Nick Names, the most famous two around here, are, although not here - Baby, Love.

'Others have Names thrust upon them which are not nice nor desired, some take Names that they're not entitled to, but more about that, later.

'This story starts around 1916. Five boys meet for the first time outside an army recruitment office, how do I know this? I have a diary, written by one of the five. It explains these boys were scared and afraid so decide to pretend to be friends. This way the army promised to keep them together, known as the "Pals' Brigade".

'Two had heard the call, joined up and made a difference. A third boy ran away from home. His Dad beat him with a leather strap. A note in the diary reads, "If I am going to die then I am going to die fighting back." There were also two brothers from a Children's home, both thought it would be better on a battlefield than stay in a home. These five boys, one just turned 16, joined up.

'The recruitment officer knew these lads were too young, but numbers of men willing to fight needed to be raised. The diary explains the boys have a few weeks of training before being shipped to the front. The diary did not say where the boys were, but by accounts of the action, they may have struck lucky and didn't see the worst of the fighting.

The diary reports that after being offloaded from the truck and marching for hours they came to the deployment station. The five lads were lined up, a hugely built Sergeant walked up and down the line of the boys. 'None of you look like you could make a difference, you lot can stay back here until you are more scared of me than of the enemy, then you will make a difference.'

There are spaces in dates in the diary, but the next set of entries offer an insight into these boys' progress. Penny was assigned to the big guns, Spud was put on latrine duty, Whippet was a runner, Nurse was put in the hospital ward, and the writer of the diary was put onto steam engines and horses.

Not a lot of entries were made, much of the same day to day stuff, the big guns kept firing, and the odd skirmish by both sides.

Then a change. I will read directly. "Today the Sergeant came to see us. Tomorrow, lads, you are going to make a difference. We have a plan that's going to take the Hun by surprise. The guns are to unleash a deadly barrage of fire, then all able-bodied men will line up in three waves.

On the first whistle get ready, on the second whistle over the top and we rush the buggers, then a third whistle, the second wave will have a clear run, we run like hell at them, they won't know what's hit them, the fourth whistle- well, it's sort of all over. By then the first two waves will have made a difference.

You, lads, will be in the first wave, make sure he knows when to go, referring to Penny who was now deaf because of the big guns. [Nigel waits a moment]

Ladies and Gentlemen there is a gap in the dates between the last and the next passage which I will read.

Been in hospital, I think for over a month, the nurses won't get me a mirror, but I know what I look like. Thinking back to the battle, we took them by surprise alright, first the big guns fall silent, whilst we take up positions. If the Hun didn't hear the first whistle, they sure as hell heard the second. We made 50 yards, Whippet 60, then a flash of light and the five of us were taken down like dominoes.

4½ of us really, the shell exploded by the side of Whippet. He took most of the force, we were thrown into a bomb crater. Whippet took most of the blast, only half his body was left. Spud had various wounds, some of them made by his brother's bones flying through the air.

Nurse's right leg took shrapnel, I got it in the neck and face, Penny hardly a mark, we all lay in a bomb crater. The nurses in the hospital had given Nurse extra bandages and morphine. Without that both, he and I, wouldn't have made it. The whistle went again, the second wave ran, they didn't even make it 50 yards, slaughtered.

The signal went out to regroup. Most of waves one and two were dead. If Jerry had come over there wasn't enough of our lads left to repel them. Luckily, they didn't come. [The entries stopped there and resumed days later].

Nurse did his best, the morphine helped. I remember the bullets flying overhead, the noise was never ending. The Germans just kept firing. Luckily wave three ran back and started up the big guns, that made Jerry duck.

Penny wanted to try and get back, the poor sod could not hear the bullets. If they found out we were in that hole they would have chucked a couple of mortars at us. I remember looking across at Spud, he was holding what was left of his brother, like a mother holds her new-born.

Darkness fell. We had been in the hole over 10 hours. The Germans stopped shooting, but every now and then they would send up flares. We decided it was time to leave. We talked about one staying behind trying to keep the snipers down.

Nurse and I decided all four needed to get out, no good talking to Penny, and Spud lay rocking his brother. Somehow Penny knew what we were about to do. He gestured to Nurse to stay. Grabbing me, he dragged me back to the trench, and pushed me over the side. Off, he went back to collect Nurse, he dragged him back, not a shot fired, off again back to collect Spud, who surprisingly came without complaining.

Penny threw Spun down to the waiting medics. I remember a single shot and blood. Penny fell into the trench; I now know where that shot went, and let's say he will not have children. The bullet passed straight through his private parts.

[Nigel paused, clearly requiring a moment to regain composure.] There are other entries, but I will move on. Nigel started to read,

Today, Nurse, Penny and I are being shipped out.

I have seen my face and the Sergeant said it was unfair to subject my face on the Germans. Penny's going home as he is deaf and the Sergeant does not want him captured as the Germans will think we all don't have balls.

Nurse lost part of his leg, he's going home as well. They're trying to empty the Hospital as new lads are coming in and having a hospital full of wounded soldiers could be demoralising.

We were loaded into trucks ready to pull off. Spud stood watching, his eyes blank. We had only been shot and lost bits of our bodies. Spud had lost his mind, he gave a sort of wave, but we don't think he knew why.

The truck was about to move when we heard the Sergeant shout some abuse at our driver. He came around the back and threw some papers at us. He walked straight up to Spud without missing a step, picked him up and threw him into the back of the truck. Take him back, he's not going to make a difference. The Sergeant shouted more abuse at our driver, and we were on our way home.

[Nigel stopped again. With a heavy swallow he asked: with your permission I will restart toward the end of the diary]. We have been at this place convalescing now for around 3 months. It's nice, sits on a hill overlooking the valley.

There's a Pub down the bottom, the locals are nice, but the army have decided to close this hospital and we can all go home. After all, keeping a place like this open costs money, and they say the war is coming to an end soon.

Spud works in the garden, digging potatoes, bit ironic, but he and the gardener will continue growing veg, to help out the villagers.

Penny's not going home, thinks his dad will have a go with the belt again. Anyway, the local farmers offered him a job.

Nurse helps a builder, he's not bad at that sort of thing, he will do alright. As for me, I can't go home. I broke Mum's heart when I left. Seeing me like this will finish her. The pub said I can stay there and do odd jobs for my keep. The locals have a jar on the bar and occasionally drop a farthing in it.

This will be my last entry: I start a new chapter in life, thank you diary for helping me through difficult times,

Regards, Lofty Lancaster.'

So, Ladies and Gentlemen I have nearly finished, you see the diary stops there, but we have a few letters that will bring me to the end of my story, and why I started with Names.

If I may, I will read one or two,

Dear Lofty, I am glad those farthings in the jar helped to bring your Mum here, and you can go home head held high (what's left of it) I never asked before, do you think we made a difference? Your friend, Penny

I will now read a letter some one year later.

Dear Lofty, Thanks for the recent letter and picture. Why is a pretty girl like her marrying you? Even with my bits missing there could be hope for me yet. It is with a heavy heart I have to write that Spud was found in a trench he had dug. They say he was hugging his spade, like he hugged his brother. They say it was minus 10 and he froze to death. Good luck, Your friend, Penny.

Nigel took out his hanky and blew his nose. With your consent I will continue.

Dear Lofty, You're a daddy, never thought you had it in you. I don't! Things are good on the farm. We get help from the ladies of the village, as there is shortage of men. (Don't bother coming back I am OK, thank you). Sorry to write but we have lost Nurse. He had some form of heart attack, they say due to not having all of one leg. You never did tell me if you thought we made a difference. Your friend, Penny.

Nigel held up a piece of paper, I promise this is the last letter

Dear Mr Lofty, It is with deep regret I have to inform you of the passing of Mr Penny, an accident on the farm. The cows stampeded, and despite shouting warnings, Mr Penny was trampled to death, I am sorry for your loss. Regards, Rev. Lee

So, to the nib of why I am here, you see I spoke about Names, and when I discovered these items in the bread bin I needed to come and have a look.

Late in the summer of last year I drove over, and I found the graves, including that of Lofty, who's made a request that his ashes be sent over to be buried with his friends.

The graves are in a poor state but more importantly the information on the stones were incorrect, so I have all the correct documentation to have 3 new headstones and 2 memorial stones made and erected.

The stones will be white marble, with black inscription. All will have the Brigade emblem, in which they served. Each will have a ceramic picture of the five of them on each stone.

They will display their correct Names and friendship names, if you wish to refer to the picture I will read left to right

Alan Tanner (Penny), William Brown (Nurse), Henry Potts (Whippet), Edward Potts (Spud), Richard Lancaster (Lofty).

On each of the stones in gold lettering will be written the following statement.

'They Made a Difference'

So, Ladies and Gentlemen, this is one of the reasons I have come to the village. The second part will be told at the Cooper's. I hope you all come along, the food and drink has all been paid for.

More importantly the landlord and landlady need to put the staff and Chef and themselves to the test. I know it would mean a lot to them if after all the hard work if you could support them.

Paul and I will meet you all there, thank you for listening.

Instantly the congregation stood and applauded Nigel.

Paul handed Nigel a hanky. The two men waited until the last of the congregation had left, 'That was some story Nigel, lots of heartfelt emotion. I am grateful you have taken the time to share with the village. Now to show my appreciation I will take you for a pint,' said Paul.

'You're far too generous there, Paul. First I need to take the wheelie bag back, not taking that to the Pub. Anyway it will be safer in the cottage.

'But I will tell you the rest of the story.'

Chapter 23

Take Even a Penny and you're Finished

Nigel continued his story as they walked.

The two men followed steadily behind the stream of people heading to the Pub.

Nigel started.

'It was a normal Monday morning as I went into work. The only difference was that Mr Bird was not in, and still was absent at 9.30 which was most unusual. I continued with his work the best I could, but unlike, when working with Mr Parker, I was not always privy to all the information. So, when it was time for the daily morning meeting I attended as normally if others were on holiday. When it was time for the financial report, I could not offer all the information the Directors were asking for, which irritated the Company FD.

"Why do you not know the answers to the question, Nigel?" asked the FD.

"Because some of the transactions are not logged as they used to be. It automatically transfers into the computer."

"Oh yes," replied the FD, "I am aware that you dislike the new modern system."

"It is not that I do not like the system, I understand that change is important, but the results of any system new or old, should be the same. I have told you on several occasions that the finance cannot be reconciled."

"Nigel, we are all aware that Mr Parker taught you well, but it's time to move on, come out of your cave and move into the 20th Century."

The FD continued. "I will investigate the current situation and report back in tomorrow's meeting, however, I am hoping that Mr Bird will be back in the morning."

The MD turned to me, "Thank you for trying to offer a report, Nigel, but it's facts we need, and I have faith in you to bring the correct information tomorrow if Mr Bird fails to show up again."

I told him, "Sorry, I do not have access to the information on the computer. I have not been told the password."

The MD continued, "Please try, you may leave now. Thanks again."

'I left the meeting and returned to the office. What the FD said was unfair, I told him on a number of occasions there was something wrong, I could tell. So, I searched the office for something that would help. I did find some computer disks but without being able to operate the computer I was helpless. I had a friend, Raymond. He liked computers and he might be able to help. I took the disk round to him, and by a stroke of luck, his Company and ours ran the same software.

'It was then that I found some Company names I did not recognise. Three had payments made that totalled over £120,000. IP Mega, Row Spar and D.R. Gibson. I asked Raymond to print it out ready for the meeting next day.

'Mr Bird was not at work that day either, which was not surprising. I continued to work mostly away from the office so the FD found it difficult to locate me.

'But I was searching for any evidence of these Companies and anything that proved we actually purchased anything. The people in the Stores did not have any recollection of these companies.

'Time for the meeting had arrived and in I went. I must be honest I was out for revenge on the FD, job or no job.

The meeting started with me, unusual.

"Do you have all facts and figures for us today, Nigel?"

"No, but what I do have will be of interest."

"No, it won't!" said the FD, "We told you to bring in everything."

"I have brought you 120000 things that would keep you busy enough."

"I will not be spoken to like that, Nigel. Out, and I will speak with you later."

It was at that time the MD jumped in, "It's not like you, Nigel, so I guess it's important, what is it?"

"I told you I cannot get access to the computer, but I did find some computer disks and was able to get a friend to read them."

"You took our finances to a third party, that's a dismissable offence," said the FD.

At that moment I had nothing but contempt for him, but I continued, "The disks show three companies IP Mega, Row Spar and D.R. Gibson - the three of them have been paid almost £120000." With that I just sat back and waited.

"Well!" asked the FD.

"Well what?" I replied.

"I have been spending most of the morning checking for these companies, knowing, I would not find them."

"How did you know, Nigel?"

"IP Mega, Row Spar and D.R. Gibson - recognised it straight away.

Have pictures of them on my cave wall. They are all birds, anagrams, Magpie, Sparrow, Songbird. You see Mr Bird had a sense of fun.

Question is, how was he allowed to set up at least three companies and pay them over £120000? Oh! and by the way when I checked his desk drawers most of his personal things had gone."

I advised them to ring the bank and the police. I have to admit the silence was deafening as I left. At that moment in time, I was not sure if I should pack up my desk. I went back to the office and sat and waited.

The wait was short. A lad came running in, "The MD needs to see you, now, Nigel."

OK what for I thought? Still I had enjoyed my time at the factory. Inside the MD's office I was invited to sit.

"Nigel, we are in trouble. We have been on to the bank, there's a possibility that we could be looking at £200000 + it is going to break this company. What can you tell me?"

What could I tell him? I didn't know much, other than what I had said earlier. "You could start with a stock check, guess the company will be short on stock. Check customers have not been asked to make part payment costs upfront. Check monthly payments have gone out, insurance, overhead costs, pensions all those type of things."

I have to be honest Paul; I thought the man was going to cry.

The MD asked me, "Nigel, could he have done this all by himself?"

That's not for me to say, "What he has done, is above me. It's a police matter, they will be able to access the computer. Sorry."

"Nigel, please try and find out how bad it is, let's see what needs to be done. My life's work is within these walls. I will authorise the bank to give you any information you need."

"OK," I told him. "But I will not transact any payments at this moment in time, that must be made clear to the bank, in writing, that's my terms."

"Why?" he asked.

"Never mind, you need to assign only two or three people to authorise payment. At this moment in time, it needs to stay in tight control, three at the most!"

'I spent weeks looking through payments. I had the police looking at records, the Inland Revenue had not been paid, nor the council tax. The Company was close to being bankrupt.

'Then a stroke of luck, in my rush I had not taken the disks back from Raymond, and he had a bit more time to look through them. He found another bank account with about £50000 in it, more importantly still in the Company's name which Mr Bird had set up.

'Great news I thought. I told the FD about the find, big mistake! Within days I was being investigated, with the police asking how come I and a friend suddenly found £50000, if we were not part of the conspiracy to rob the company. We were accused of getting cold feet and now we had been found out trying to pay some of the money back.

'I was arrested and charged, the court released me on bail. That's not the end. People I had called my friends for years disowned me. Someone threw a brick through my car window. My only piece of luck in all this was that Mr Bird's Mum took very poorly, and he came back from Spain to visit, thinking that no one would see him. His mother lived miles away. Well, luckily for me they did spot him, and the police arrested him.

'He did some sort of deal with the Police, and admitted the theft. When asked if I had anything to do with it, he laughed at the thought. According to the Police he called me a Neanderthal, I belonged in a cave. Funny, that was the second time someone said I belonged in a cave! I was released without charge; no more action would be taken against me. Most of the money was returned, but not until the Court case was over, still it allowed the Company to borrow from the bank on a short-term loan.'

'What happened to you?' asked Paul.

'I was invited back, but would you go back? Not one of those so-called friends or work colleagues came to see me during this awful experience. So, I went in one day, collected the cup with my Name on it and left. On the way out I bumped into the MD. "Great, Nigel, to see you back."

"I am not back! No one stood up for me, including you. I am off, but I will leave you with a thought. How come Bird was able to execute the theft, not on his own, and in Bird's statement he said I belonged in a cave. Who else thought that?"

'That was me out of a job, in almost 25 years. I was offered work, by Raymond's Company but I was OK for money for a few months and perhaps needed to rethink things. That's when I discovered the soldiers' story I told about this morning.

'However strange things had not finished with me. About two weeks after I finished work, a man knocked on the door and introduced himself, and called me by my Name and asked to come in. The news he gave me almost floored me, but he agreed to come back, in a couple of days to discuss in more detail, and advised I had a competent friend who could advise me. That friend was going to be Mr Parker

'Now bearing in mind I had visited the village a few days before and that's why I knew the address of the vicarage, I didn't need my friend's advice on what to do, I just needed him to help execute it. Which he did better than I ever thought possible.

'About a month passed and another man knocked on the door. He knew who I was, and asked to come in.

He then proceeded to talk about winning the football pools and said he thought it was me.

"Yes," I said, "but technically not me, stay there I will go and get it."

'Will I get my name in the paper?

'Very possibly, so I went upstairs and retrieved the bread bin. There in the bin was the letter that accompanied a cheque from the Pools' Company. I proudly showed him, he swore at me.

"What's this? £172.13s.6p"

"Yes, my Mum and Dad won £172.13s.6p when I was about 11 years old, it helped them pay for this home. Do you wish to take my picture I asked him?"

'He swore at me again saying he had paid good money for this information, so I suggested he ask for a refund, and he swore at me again, slamming the door behind him. Strange fellow!

'Now here is the really strange thing to happen. As if that was not enough one Saturday I was washing the car and a lady around 60 years old asked if I was Nigel.'

"Yes," I said. She continued, "Well, it is possible that I am your Aunty - Aunty Dot, Dorothy.

I was stunned. I mean, it's not every day a relation you have never heard of comes unannounced.

She continued, "Guess it's a bit of a shock."

"Yes, just a bit."

"I am your Mum's sister; I don't suppose she mentioned me very often?"

"Mum didn't mention you at all. Funny that."

But I didn't know about Mother's side. I did not know much about Dad's. Too late now!

"Well," she continued, "let's go inside. Have a nice cup of tea and I can fill you in."

'She then continued for hours to fill in a part of my family history I knew nothing about, how the girls were split up at about 5 years old. Dot was able to keep in touch with some family whilst Mother was taken miles away. All seemed probable, and even if she was not related, at least, she seemed happy finding me.

'I have to admit, Mr Parker taught me well about watching people and she seemed genuine. Didn't ask for anything apart from more tea. She parted with a handshake and off she went to the train station.

'End of the matter, I thought.

'Not the end, Paul, by a long shot. About two weeks later I received a letter outlining a bit more history, and a couple of photos of two young girls, possibly 4 or 5 years old, supposably Mum and Dot.

I didn't reply, still trying to build bridges with neighbours, which was not going well, "no smoke without fire".

'Saturday morning while I was washing the car, (funnily enough) Dot's back, this time with a lady about my age, pretty, slim, nice hair, lovely autumn dress, with matching bag and shoes, an open coat with fur lining.'

'Didn't really notice her then, Nigel?' said Paul.

Dot continued, "Hello again, Nigel, this is Sofie, she's our *adopted* daughter."

"Hello, Nigel."

'Now Paul, I missed that clue, too busy looking at Sofie.'

'What clue?' enquired Paul.

Why would you introduce someone on the very first meeting as, our adopted daughter?

'Anyway, I will not bore you, let's just say the visits got more frequent, nothing of an intimate nature, however a bond was forming. When they left, I would get a handshake from Dot and a kiss from Sofie.

'Suggestions were made that she could stay over one night, without Dot being around, or I could go up to theirs and all this time she gave the impression that butter wouldn't melt.

'Clue number two, again missed, talk stopped being about Mum and focused more on me. Dreams, ambitions, goals in life, if I had money? Money, Money, Money!

'Between the two of them the conversation turned to money in one form or another. Which bank do I use? Why don't you buy a better car? Sofie would love a holiday abroad, just the two of us. Lovely house, but a bigger one would be a better investment. Why don't we go to a really nice restaurant?

'I am sure they were not listening, I tried to explain. I've been with the same bank since leaving school. They're a good bank. I'm between jobs and I don't have money to throw around. The car was running OK. There's only me, why do I need a bigger house, and I don't know if I like foreign food, and nice restaurants can cost.

'Clue three, which started the alarm bells ringing, remarks like "come on Nigel, you can afford it, and a man with your money, let your hair down and let's have a spending spree, you should get a credit card."

'I finally agreed to have lunch in a posh bar before she and Dot boarded the train home.

'Paul, I can tell you now my luck changed that dinner time. The bar we went into was nice, very pricey, anyway who was in there but Raymond. He was waiting for his girlfriend. I invited him over. This was a mistake in Sofie's view, she was not happy. Raymond could tell and soon made an excuse and returned to the bar. Things seem to return to a more pleasurable atmosphere. It was about time for them to leave but not before the pair went to the toilet and I was left with the bill.

'Paul, I don't spend that amount of money on a week's shopping I nearly fell off my chair! The pair boarded the train, the usual handshake, and this time a long, lingering kiss.

Chapter 24

Help from Friends

'Later that evening there was a knock on the door. On opening I found it was Raymond, and his girlfriend, Sue. Sitting in the living room, they both looked a little sheepish.

"What's wrong?" I asked them.

Raymond explained, "Nigel, over the years you have been a rock to me, and I feel what I am about to say may spoil our friendship. It's with a heavy heart I need to tell you something. I presume the girl at lunch time is a close friend, someone perhaps you like, I mean like a lot."

I asked them, "Why?"

"The young lady and the older lady went to the toilet together, at the same time, purely by coincidence Sue followed them in. When Sue came out, she was laughing, saying that some bloke is on his way to being turned over. They were now sure, that he had a massive amount of cash, and the young lady felt sure she was about to break him. Sorry Nigel, Sue didn't know that bloke was you, until you all went out together. Sorry!"

I explained to them what had happened.

"The older woman had come about 6 weeks ago, claiming to be my Aunty on Mum's side, the younger Woman is her adopted daughter. Convenient not being blood related, should it have got in the way of any closer friendship."

I continued, "I will tell you something else about a week before the so-called Aunty turned up, a press reporter came, claiming he could uncover a Pools winner. Didn't seem so happy when I showed him Mum and Dad's Pools letter from around 20 years ago, showing a win of £172.13s.6p. Seemed a bit upset.

"The question is, what do I do now? Apart from thanking you both for the information. I appreciate it. Thanks."

'Paul, I admit I was in a dilemma.'

'What did you do?' asked Paul.

'Went to bed and slept on it. During the next day, I was hanging out the washing and a neighbour being nosier than friendly, asked about my Aunty.

"How do you know about her? I asked."

"She was around here, what? 6 or 8 weeks ago, asking questions about your late Mum. I've lived here all these years and didn't know your Mum had a sister."

"No, Mrs. M, neither did I. Strange world, bye!"

'So, Paul, I only had one option, to go and see Mr Parker. I told him all the details, and he said he needed to think about what to do next. I remember his parting words, "Don't worry she can't get your money; you don't have any to speak of."

'Which was a bit worrying, I thought I had, still what you never had and all that!

'A few days later I was trying to get into the house whilst balancing the shopping and a neighbour, Mr Marriot, went by.

"What have you been up to this time, Nigel? Bad enough you trying to ruin the factory?"

"What are you talking about?" I asked him.

"That fellow, that's been hanging about asking questions, looks like a Policeman, or investigator."

"Possibly a Press reporter?" I asked.

"Could be!"

"Thanks, Oh, and by the way it was me that found out about the missing money at work and reported it. If I hadn't the company would have gone bust."

"Yes, but how did you know? No smoke without fire, Nigel! Good day."

'Well, Paul, I can categorially say, that was it! Neighbours think I am thief, two women are trying to do, who knows what, not steal my money as according to Mr Parker I don't have any, and to top it off some newspaper reporter asking stupid questions.'

'Come on then, Nigel, don't keep me in suspense, what did you do?' asked Paul.

'Move! Move out of the place I had loved and been raised in. Find a place that would appreciate what I could offer and have people around me that cared about others.'

'Why do you not think here is OK? After all you are moving out this afternoon. Is this village not what you are looking for?'

'Never mind about that, let me get on with my story. Mr Parker came up with a plan, it would need the help of Raymond.

'Firstly, I was to pack and go and live with Helen, Mr Parker's daughter, as she needed help with work. I would be away for about 4 to 6 weeks, and I was not to tell anyone where I was going. Either Mr Parker or Raymond would pick up the mail and check on the house whilst I was away.

She lived in a lovely little house out in the country.

'Now that seemed a good plan. However, how much was that going to cost, as it would appear I have a lack of funds?

'Next part of the plan, I needed to ask for money. Mr Parker insisted, I have to admit Paul, I must have been in a poor state to borrow money, so I told him he needed a better plan.

'He was adamant. Go on ask!

'So, I asked, can you lend me some money? With that Mr Parker put his hand in his pocket and pulled out some change, there you are, that will cover it. Now go and see Raymond. He knows you're coming and ask him for money. Make sure the other people can hear or see you.

'Paul, I had no idea what was happening, but I followed instruction. Luckily Raymond was in an open plan office. He greeted me and asked what I wanted, so I whispered, can you lead me some money? And the idiot almost shouted, you need me to lend you some money, better come this way. Paul, I could have died on the spot. He took me into another office with a big window, so people could see me. He made a big deal of giving me about 50p in change not that anyone could see how much.

"Hope that's enough, Nigel, pay me back when you can."

'Must go busy, you know. With that I left. That office must have been a mile long, it seemed it was. I had to walk past other people who were all staring.

'Next day I packed what suitcases I had and took off to Helen's. I enjoyed it there, but she made me work. It was non-stop for weeks on end, still enjoyable.

'Mr Parker phoned me about a week later to tell me the grapevine was in full bloom, metaphorically speaking. Someone had even asked Raymond if he had lent me money.

'Anyway, work at Helen's was about done, so time to return home. It was only a few weeks from Christmas. Should be at home, after all it looked like it was going to be the last time.

'Paul, I had not got the second case inside the house before one of the neighbours was there, asking me, had I had a nice time, where had I been?

'Yes, thank you, I explained I needed to get in and get the place warm.'

"Well just thought I would let you know that your Aunty and that lovely lady have been a couple of times, said they would write."

'I couldn't get in fast enough. I almost fell over the cases. I spent the next few hours going through the mail, which included three from the ladies, hoping I was OK and they were looking forward to seeing me again and how much they missed me. Even gave me a phone number to ring upon my return.

'Must be honest, Paul. Not keen on starting that all over again, I was secretly hoping they had gone away. Raymond left me a note telling me that the reporter was still hanging around, persistent little fellow. Even been down to the allotment and spoke with a few people including Mr Parker, who informed him that he did not wish to talk about Nigel as he had borrowed money and had yet not paid it back.

'Christmas came and went without me really noticing. Oh yes, I had a small tree, no decs, Mr and Mrs Parker invited me round for Christmas and Boxing Day dinner, which was very nice. On New Year's Eve, I think I was in bed by 10.30.

'Then one Saturday morning a knock on the door. Now I normally wash the car, but the water would have frozen. Anyway a knock on the door, it was the reporter. Now Mr Parker had said if he was to arrive, welcome him in, make a cup of tea, treat him like a long-lost friend, but don't forget to let it slip about the ladies.

"Hello, come on in, it's freezing out there." The reporter seemed stunned. "Come on you're letting the warm air out. You look frozen. How about a nice cup of tea?"

"Not finished with you, something's not right, I am still searching for a Pools winner." You found me. Well, Mum and Dad, £172 and*, don't give me that* he shouted, I have been given 3 possible addresses and yours is one of them.

"Milk and sugar?" I asked him, thought he was going to explode. "You know your informant. Is it possible that he or she is telling lies? I mean, those two women that keep coming around seem to think I could have a bob or two."

"What two women?" he asked.

"Two women! They lie. In fact come to think about it you all seem to have a similar accents. Co-incidence, I suppose. Biscuit?"

"Where are they from?" he asked me.

"The train stations!"

Not big on humour that chap, not that big on the Queen's English either.

"Who are these women?"

"I don't know, they keep going on about money, bit like you. I had their phone number once but threw it away, think it started with 051 or was it 015, not sure."

"Don't you have a phone?"

"No, can't afford one. Really had no need, use the call box if need be. You've not drank your tea."

'Must tell you, Paul, I hope he writes better than he speaks. The editor must have a nightmare with him. He sat there for a while, his eyes moving about. So, I asked him what he was looking for. I would gladly get it, if I had it!

"No matter," he told me.

"If you leave your phone number and some money, I will give you a call next time the ladies are planning to come over. Could be useful? Could be a story in it - three people sold lies and sent on a wild goose chase. Oh no, you would be one of them, silly me!" He put his business card on the table and started towards the door.

'I don't think he liked me, he swore at me again and slammed the door that hard it bounced back open. I was about to ask for some money for the phone but decided best not.'

Paul interjected, 'As much as I am enjoying this story, Nigel, any chance of getting to the end and down to the Pub? It's free beer and food.'

'Not much longer. Anyway it's deemed a private party, not selling alcohol so staying open all day.

We need to walk over to the bench by the lake, come on!'

Chapter 25

Coming Clean

'Now for the final part of the plan, a few days later, I rang the ladies and the reporter, and arranged for them to come over Saturday around 2.00.

'Well Saturday arrived. I was almost packed. I planned on leaving around 1.00 and leave the rest to Raymond and his team. Around 12.30 there was a knock on the door. I hid behind the curtains and peaked around them, it was the reporter, the idiot was early. I did not have to wait long before he went away, however it left little time so I grabbed what I could and loaded the car and left.

'I can only tell you what happened next from a third party.

'Raymond and a couple of his lads waited in the house. Now Raymond's a big lad, well-built. His stepdad owns a storage warehouse and a number of vans, so all that Raymond had to do was wait. Sure enough a knock on the door. Opening it, he spotted the two ladies.

"Come in."

"Who are you?" they asked.

Raymond continued, "The neighbours said you were coming. I understand that you are related to the reprobate that lives here, well he owes me money."

At that a second knock on the door, on opening it, he saw, there stood the reporter.

"Come in," said Raymond, firmly closing the door behind him, "come into the middle room."

Now according to Raymond, you could have cut the atmosphere with a blunt spoon.

"What are you doing here?" asked the reporter.

"What are you doing here?" asked Dot.

"And what the hell are you doing here, Sofie?"

"What's this, some sort of television quiz?" asked Raymond.

"You," pointing towards Dot, "I was told you could be his Aunty, are you prepared to pay his debt?"

"No, I am no relation."

Raymond turned to one of his lads, "Go and find that neighbour who told us about his aunty and bring her here."

"OK!"

"Hang on a moment," said Dot, "it was all a mistake, we are not related, it's a big misunderstanding."

"What about you?" pointing to Sofie. "I was told it would be easy."

"Told by whom?" asked Raymond.

"Him," pointing at the reporter.

"Look!" Raymond said angrily. "*Someone owes me money.* Now pay up or I have the furniture.

Start loading lads!"

"Now, you three, amidst you, you made him scarper. Now if you three had minded your own business I would have had my money. Now I have to move this lot and put it up for auction. All, time and money, now who's going to pay for that?"

"I have freedom of the press on my side," said the reporter.

"Freedom! Rubbish, you work in the butchers'. If I hadn't told you about this chap you wouldn't have had any idea. You're useless, that why I asked Sofie. You're an idiot, told you that report thing wouldn't work." Dot continued, "I was sure this was the address I quickly saw on that piece of paper."

"I told you when I first met him this address did win about £173, about 20 years ago, you stupid woman."

Raymond seemed really angry now, "Someone owes me money", banging his fist on the table

"Look, sorry for the mess but these two put me up to it. Can I leave?" asked Sofie.

"Go on all three of you, you're getting in the way of loading the vans, go on get out!"

Nigel continued, 'And I understand my furniture is still in storage at Raymond's place.'

Paul thought for a moment, 'But you don't have much money. How are you going to pay to get it out after all this time?'

'Come on I need a hand,' approaching the bench Nigel produced a small pen knife, 'here, let's take the cover off.'

'Can't do that. It clearly states do not remove.'

'Never mind about that, do you wish to see under it, Paul?'

'Yes, but what about the new owners? They're not going to be happy, especially if they find out the local vicar did it.'

'Too late. Nigel cut away the thick plastic covering to reveal, a most beautiful oak bench facing the valley, proud of place on the top rail was a ceramic and gold photo of the Soldiers, and an inscription, which read.

'See Lads, you did make a difference.'

Paul stood for a moment, whispered a prayer, made the sign of the cross, bowed his head. You are still not answering the questions,' said Paul as they walked to the cottage.

Neither spoke until they reached the cottage. 'You left the front door open, Nigel,' said Paul.

Nigel released the wheelie bag and went to look. The door was not opened, the door had been removed. As he stood looking at the hole where the door should have been, he could see straight through into the back yard.

Walking by the side of the cottage, he noticed a new chain and padlock on the gas cage. Viewing past the mesh he saw the gas valve had been turned off.

As he turned the corner, both, the front and back door, lay on the ground badly damaged by what looked like being beaten with the spade that lay by the side. Even the veg patch had been damaged and plants torn up.

Nigel went inside. Nothing appeared to be changed. His few possessions were still there, nothing inside had been tampered with. He collected his car keys and returned outside.

'This is the work of very mean people and does not represent the village, Nigel. I am really sorry,' said Paul.

Nigel removed the bread bin from the bag and placed it into the boot of the car. 'I need a kindness; can you please go and open one of the garage doors?

'I am going to hide the car in there. Don't worry about anyone seeing you. Who's going to question a man of the cloth? Anyway nothing in there to steal.

'Watch when you open the door, they are much lighter than they look.'

Nigel climbed into his car. First turn of the key and the car sprang into life. He drove round to see Paul looking very sheepish, not comfortable at all.

Nigel backed the car in making sure he touched the back wall. Not that he needed to, there was plenty of room. Getting out, Nigel checked the door and checked again, definitely locked!

'If you don't mind me saying, Nigel, you are taking this very well. Still not sure about you using the garage,' said Paul.

'Stop worrying. I wouldn't do anything that's going to get you unfrocked or de-clocked, I may need to come and live at the vicarage.'

Nigel glanced across at the Pub. 'Time for that pint you promised me,' said Nigel.

As the two approached the Pub a sign read, 'Private Party, by invite only.'

The two entered the Pub, which was busy. Looking around to the left side of the entrance screen they saw the cosy corner had a small party sitting, enjoying glasses of Champagne, a sign read 'Table Reserved.' On the other side to the right-hand side, standing at the tall tables were Baby, Love and presumably their wives.

Dotted around, Nigel could see, David and Mary, Arthur and Millie, Alex and a few fellow builders, Mr & Mrs Snow from the farm, and the butcher. He also recognised the crew from the fish and chips van, two policemen in uniform, as well as lots of other people he had not seen before.

There was one group of people sitting by the bar instantly recognisable, that being the Captain, still wearing his hat, Faye, and four of his supposably upper class sporting pals.

'I will get the first round in, Nigel,' said Paul.

'Very big of you, Paul, considering it is all free this lunch time.'

'Do you know, Nigel, I think I can be over generous. Sometimes I wonder who's paying for all this?'

Both men walked over to the bar, 'Two pints of bitter, please.'

Paul turned to Nigel, 'I'm surprised to see two policemen here, especially in uniform.'

'They have been instructed to be here,' replied Nigel.

The landlord handed over the drinks, 'Cheers, lads.'

'When are you going to finish your story?' asked Paul.

The Captain spoke up, 'Surprised to see you drinking. Wouldn't have thought you'd agree with drunk driving. The food will be out in a bit. I brought you a plastic sandwich box so you can take some of the free buffet with you. I know how much you like freebies.'

'Let's get this straight from the start, Captain,' said the landlord.

'This has been, and always will be, a friendly Pub. If you don't like it, please drink elsewhere.'

Nigel jumped in, 'Don't worry he may not be drinking in Pubs for some time.'

Nigel walked up to the group and virtually stood in the middle of the six of them.

He looked the Captain clearly in the eyes, 'Did you remove the doors from the cottage and turn off the gas?'

'Yes', snapped the Captain.

Nigel turned to Faye and sternly asked, 'Did you help?'

The four other fellows started to laugh, 'You took the doors off? Brilliant,' one of the party said.

Nigel turned back to Faye, 'Did you help?'

'No, Nigel, I said it was wrong.' Nigel looked straight at her.

'It's time to nail your colours to the mast.'

'What do you mean by that, you silly little man?' said one of the group.

Nigel re-joined Paul, took a swallow of his beer, turn to the vicar, 'Look after that,' pointing to what remained in the glass.

'No trouble, Nigel,' ordered the landlord.

Nigel walked over to the cosy corner, bent down and spoke to a very short man.

The man reached down into a leather bag and removed two neatly folded pieces of paper.

The man then proceeded over to the two policemen and handed over the documents and held a very brief discussion with the Sergeant.

Nigel returned to the bar, finished his drink and asked for two more.

Nigel walked up to the Captain,'You should have been in Church this morning. I explained one of the reasons I am in the village. I hopefully explained actions of brave boys and how important it is to recognise Names. Having said that, I'm going to introduce you to Wig.

'Now Wig is not his true name, so that makes a bit of a mockery of what I have just said. However, his name is extremely difficult to pronounce, and he does not wear a toupee. He's a high Court Lawyer, a very good one, and he's going to address you on my behalf.'

The Captain turned his back on Nigel and continued to talk with his friends.

Faye walked away from the group.

Chapter 26

Wig

Wig pulled up a bar stool, sat himself against the bar and tapped the Captain on the shoulder, the Captain turned round, gave a disapproving look and turned back again.

Wig spoke, 'I'm going to try and educate you on points of Law. Then I intend to offer you the results of my investigation, asked for by this gentleman here,' pointing to Nigel.

Which clearly, was a waste of time as the Captain refused to listen.

'You will do well to take a few minutes to be frivolous, but I strongly advise you to take note of my delivery.

'Sir, as you may or not be aware of the two types of covenant that are attributed to land, and both apply to all the buildings, within its bounds. By this, I mean "The Old House" and its substantial amount of land.

The property had the original owner as being one 'Henry Francis Saile'.

'Saile purchased said land and had erected a number of dwellings, first the Old House, then two cottages and outbuildings, then the Farm, plus buildings for the safe keeping of animals and feed stock, and the roadside house.

'When the greenhouse and associated building were complete, Saile applied for a decree of the court which imposed several conditions, on all the buildings on the Estate. These are called covenants. These conditions still apply to this day.

'There are two different types of covenants - positive and restrictive. The difference is important as you will find out shortly. Positive and restrictive covenants affect land, and its buildings in different ways.

'I will endeavour to explain the Positive Covenant. This requires some type of action, perhaps, the building of a fence, or a new foot path or road. Positive covenants are generally a contract between the original parties to the deed imposing the covenant. The good news, if it were to apply to anyone, and I say 'if' it does not bind future landowners, and appeals can be made to the court.

'Now I will explain the Restrictive Covenant. This limits or prevents the use of land in precise ways to the benefit of other land. I am not going into great detail, but it basically explains the Court ruling which means that the benefit and burden of the covenant relates to land itself and not to the landowner.

'What does this mean? It means and there are a number of restrictions.

'Saile' was, if nothing else, determined to protect his land, and I do have to take off my Wig to him, what a great job he did.

'In simple terms, remember this applies to the land not its owner.' Wig turned to Mr & Mrs Snow, 'Please be assured this does not apply to you as your Covenant stresses the normal activities associated with standard farming practices.

'It does however apply to other buildings on the estate. The ruling is, I will condense them for reasons of time.' Wig continued, 'I will cut it truly short,

'The Covenant states in Law, no dwelling to be used for business purpose, no new building can be erected. No extension to building without permission of the landowner and can only be applied for the purpose of improvement or essential to the running of the estate. No dwelling is permitted to keep or breed non-domestic animals.

'No part of the estate, including its woodlands, lake or lands, can be sold as an individual entirety. All building erected on the estate, all rights to hunting and fishing will remain whole, only the entire estate can be sold or disposed of without exception, by Law.'

The Captain jumped up 'Don't make unsubstantiated claims, everyone knows I have the rights for fishing and shooting, and once more, you stupid little man, I own my house I have the deeds.'

'Sir', replied Wig, 'I cannot refute the fact of my stature. In some quarters I can be referred to as short or even little, however I am far from being stupid, and I refuse to exchange words with you on the subject.

'It suffices that your deed of ownership is worthless, drafted by a Conman. No such registration is logged with the Land Commission nor can it be, as I have explained regarding the Covenant as filed in The Court of Law.

'You, Sir, own very little, almost in its entirety it is owned by the estate and in turn the new owner of the Old House. You Sir, in short, have been a buffoon.

The Captain stood waving his arms.'No! No! this is not right; I purchased the house from the owner of the Old Peoples' home. He sold it to me. This is not right, it's not right!'

He screamed slumping down in his chair head in hands, he returned to his feet, turned to Wig,

'If you know so much who's the family that purchased the Old House?

'You're so clever, what's their Name and when are they moving in? What you are saying is nonsense, I'm sure any reasonable person will understand. This covenant thing is ridiculous, well who are they?'

Wig thumbed though some paperwork, 'Ay, here we are, the Family Name is "Lancaster". I understand that they are moving in today.'

Faye pointed at a couple in the cosy corner, 'You moved into the house today, you must be "The Lancasters". Welcome.'

'No,' came a quick reply from the man at the table, 'we have been invited over for the weekend. It is true that the "Lancasters" own the 'Old House and all its lands, I know them, I went to school with them, but it's not me'.

Faye turned again, 'I saw you going into the Old House pointing at the well-dressed young lady.'

'It's true I too am staying at the Old House. I am the architect, I am responsible for all the design work. I also designed this Pub, hope you like it.' With that comment the place rang with applauds of appreciation.

People were now clearly listening to the conversation.

The Man sitting by the side of the young lady spoke, 'And before you ask, yes, I am staying at the house and I am not a "Lancaster" either. I, like Wig, understand that he is moving in today, but it is getting late.'

Mrs Bye who was at Church earlier, stood up looking a little puzzled, then sat back down. Moments later back on her feet, 'I've got it.'

'Well, I don't want it,' shouted Baby.

'I think I've worked it out,' she continued, 'one of them Soldiers was Private Lancaster, the man that stayed here, he was "Lancaster" Farthing in the jar man.

'We still don't know who the "Lancasters" are, and why are you so interested in those five brave boys, Nigel?' asked Mrs Bye.

'You're leaving the Cottage today. You have never said where you're going. I think it's you, you own the Old House it's you!'

'Somehow you are related to the boy in the picture,' she continued.

People in the Pub started to gather closer to hear and witness the happenings.

Nigel bowed his head, took a moment, 'Yes, it is me, the boy in the picture was my Grandad and yes, I own 'The Old House' and all its land, all the buildings and rights to the land.

'I had to keep it a secret, I needed to understand people, see the kindness in some, and root out those who would try and exploit me. This way I can repay those that are true people, those with hearts that show kindness to others, that kindness still runs in some in this village. There is still work for me to do. I need to address a couple of people. That can be done tomorrow, after I move out of my cottage.'

'Nigel! Did you put up the money for this Pub?' asked the landlord.

'Yes, for what your Grandparents and the villagers did to help Granddad. Mr Parker came over late last year. If anyone knows about people it's him, he could tell that the Pub was in trouble, so I wanted to help.'

'What about our Building Company?' asked Baby.

'Same story,' replied Nigel, 'You needed help as did Nurse. Your family was there for him. I can't help everyone individually, but I can help to put new life and hope back into the village.

'The Pub is a good place to start, part of the contract is to employ local youth, give them hope and a future. Those soldiers did not have any hope, or any future. Those lads almost gave their lives, and the Country turned its back, this village didn't.

'So now the youth that live here and nearby can benefit. With all our help we can give them a positive outlook.

'Likewise, with Baby, Love the builders will take two young people and have made a commitment to give training. They sort of did OK with Alex over there.'

'Cheeky,' shouted Alex.

'Then the Farm and the farmer gave Penny work and a future.

'Then the Old House - this will offer employment and it comes with living accommodation, just need to find a couple of decent builders to do up the cottages.'

The sound of a forced cough came from behind Nigel,

'Hey,' cough, cough...

'Oh! yes the Church and your vicar. I suppose he too plays a part. This man stood by me when this got a little tough. We had an agreement, no Church talk and no asking me questions, and for the last 10 weeks or more, worked a treat, and I thank him for that help.

'I am sorry it's a bit late but we will sit down and talk Church stuff, like repairing the hall so everyone can use it and socialise. We will have new heating installed, I may know a couple of half decent builders that have lost some local work.'

Nigel walked up to the Captain, 'I have tried to forgive you for all the horrible things you have said and called me, all the accusations. Earlier this week I had concluded that you cannot be all bad, but your action today in removing the doors and turning off the gas, was the last unkind action you will perform.

'I told a true story today about brave boys and how their Family Names can be recognised and etched in stone.'

Nigel raised his voice, it was tinged with anger. 'You sit there calling yourself Captain, when allegedly you are a conman and not a very good one, selling time shares that didn't exist.

'Wig along with the Inland Revenue looked into your history. You had fled owing tens of thousands of pounds, you skipped court bail, the police have had a warrant out for you for years. You call yourself Captain. Wig checked with the Ministry of Defence, your Name does not come up anywhere, which also means that you have deceived the villagers, laid false claim to lands and rights and applied for Grants and even for a Gun Licence illegally. Wig continued to check your history and you are still wanted on bail.

I think I can leave it there; Sergeant Darwin has an arrest warrant.'

'What about me?' asked Faye.

'Not sure about you, you've done some nasty acts. Do you live in the same house as him?' asked Nigel.

'Yes, he asked me to sell my house and move in, we were setting up business together.' Faye turned to the Captain, 'Have you spent my money?' she asked.

'Most of it on home improvements, building pens and increasing stocks, marketing in glossy magazines to sell more shooting and fishing.'

'What about our money for the shoot?' asked another. 'Spent most of that too,' he replied.

With that Sergeant Darwin cautioned him and led him from the Pub. 'Not sure what's going to happen with you, Faye. The first time I saw you I could see a glimmer of hope. We can talk next week, have a drink you look like you need one.'

Nigel turned to the people viewing the goings on, 'This isn't how it should be, please continue and eat and drink and make new friends, after all it's what Public Houses are good for.'

Chapter 27

Employment Opportunities

Nigel walked over to Millie and Arthur,

'Sorry about that, but he's not a very nice man. I was glad to see you in Church this Morning. I need to ask you if you can help me. Now you know that I am going to live in the Old House. I am looking for a housekeeper and a gardener. It would come with onsite accommodation but not straight away. Baby, Love need to make some improvements to the cottage, before you can move in. About 4 ~ 6 weeks, could be quicker. I have another ongoing project I need them to look at the same time.

I think you will need help Arthur, I have someone in mind, I will be back.'

With that Nigel found Mary and David, 'Hello, the food should be coming shortly, bet it's not as good as your pies, Mary, but don't tell the chef, I understand he can be a bit fiery.'

'There are some fine foods coming out, Nigel, I've read about this sort of fine dining. Bit posh for a Pub but it will get people talking and perhaps even change dining altogether.'

Nigel thought a moment, 'But perhaps a mix of fine and good basic food, like pies, mostly pies, and beans on toast and bacon butties. What do you think about that?'

Mary quickly came back, 'I would secretly still like to try the posh end, not on my budget or in our kitchen but we can all dream.'

'We can all dream, isn't that right, David? We had this discussion that night on the steps. Will not be doing that anymore, you been sacked, haven't you?' asked Nigel.

David sat up straight. 'No Nigel, I have been made redundant due to lack of work.'

'Oh, then you're available?' asked Nigel.

'Yes, signing on tomorrow, and you're leaving so no more pies, but I will find some work.'

Mary addressed David. 'He's not leaving, David. Nigel owns the Old House. It's his house you've been looking after, silly.'

'Do we still get pies?' David asked.

'David, if you live in a big house like that you don't come to us to make pies,' Mary replied.

'Couldn't agree more,' replied Nigel.

'There's no way I am asking you to cook me pies in your kitchen. However, I would ask you to cook pies, and beans on toast and bacon butties, in the Old House's kitchen. If you're looking for work then I need a cook, not all the time, I would like the cook to train someone, perhaps a young person.

'I also need a gardener to work with Arthur. I am hoping Millie will be the housekeeper. The cook and garden position come with onsite accommodation, but not for a few weeks. Not the work, that can start tomorrow or as soon as possible. It's the onsite accommodation. Baby, Love will have two projects running together, and your house needs a lot of work, a tree fell on it, think about it.'

Nigel stood up to find the Snows, but he was taken aback. The atmosphere was electric, with people chatting and laughing, just what a Pub should be.

Nigel found the farmer and his wife. 'Aah, Mr and Mrs Snow, glad I found you.'

'I suppose this is where we find out how much we owe you. Well I can tell you, we don't have any money, we barely manage,' said Mr Snow

'Sorry, he's been dreading this moment,' added Mrs Snow.

'Well,' said Nigel, 'let's not beat about the bush, here's what I would like. As a starter, could you bring your tractor and a plough, and turn over the Old House's garden plot? You know, the one near the greenhouse, not sure Arthur and David are going to manage it with a spade.

'Then I think you need to clean out the barn and sheds, ready for livestock, which the estate will fund for the first year, how much you buy is up to you. You're keeping them, and I would like 15% return on your profit in that year. If you do OK then we can talk about it this time next year. I think that covers things for a while?'

'Wait a minute, what about the money we owe?' asked Mr Snow.

'Oh that! your Grandad and Dad paid in advance by means of a Penny. See you later.'

Nigel stood up and headed toward the seated area where Wig and the others were sitting, but was stopped by Baby, Love.

'Got a moment, Nigel? Think we need to chat.'

'In a minute, Baby, need a bit of fun.'

Nigel spoke to the architect and pointed across the bar. The lady stood up and only as a lady can, slid over to Alex and spoke, 'Geia sas poio einai to onoma sas'.

Alex looked shocked. 'I don't know what you're saying,' he said,

She asked, 'Are you not Greek, I was told you were Greek, perhaps even a Greek God?'

'No, no I am Alex. I am English, British, I was born in the next village, I live with my Mum.'

'Oh,' she said and gracefully walked back to her seat.

Alex sat there for a few moments mouth open. He looked around the Pub to see people smiling and laughing. He stood up, looked straight at Nigel. 'Cheeky.'

Nigel, still smiling, walked back over to Baby, Love.

'Sorry lads, couldn't tell you. It would have spoilt what you were doing, both here and the House, thinking I was looking over your shoulder all the time.'

'Did you organise all this?' asked Love.

'No, that chap over there knew you were the right people and Wig just sorted it legally. I worked with the architect, Helen, for a few weeks, trying to find the right suppliers, but, mostly getting under her feet I think.'

Mrs Bye looked at Nigel, 'It's your money, what is this all about?'

'You figure it out. You were in Church this morning,' said Nigel.

'Have a beer, Nigel,' Alex thrust a pint in his hand, 'Cheers' and walked back to his table.

Mrs Bye spoke 'Those four lads came back here. That's why they're buried here. One died on the farm, one had a heart attack. The builder, he worked for their Dad, didn't he?'

'Your Grandad, lived here, a Farthing in the jar man.'

'What are you talking about?' asked Love.

'Shut up, I am thinking.' Came a stern reply, 'That leaves just one soldier, you sorted the Old House, and the Pub. You have definitely helped us all.'

'I am off to talk with others. I will be back.'

Nigel walked back to Paul at the bar. Let me introduce some friends. The two walked over to the cosy corner, 'Hello, everyone let me introduce Paul, he's the village vicar. Guess you can work that out by the dog collar. This is Mr Parker, we once worked together. He has helped me with all this. This is Helen his daughter, Helen's the architect. This is Wig, whom you have seen in action. This is Raymond, who has been a great help, and this is his fiancée, Sue. All hitting the champagne, I see.'

'It's all free,' said Helen, 'we are only helping the landlord. He was concerned it may not get drunk, only helping out.'

'You and the vicar will get on OK. He offered to buy the first round, knowing it's free,' informed Nigel. The high level of noise was broken by someone tapping a glass, 'Ladies and Gentlemen, Buffet is now open. The staff will be pleased to carve your meat to order.'

The landlord and landlady came over with another bottle of Champagne, 'Who ordered that?' asked Nigel.

'Sorry, Nigel, our instruction was to bring another bottle when the previous one was empty.'

'Really!' growled Nigel.

'Well, this pint pot's very nearly empty. Guess I better get this filled, ay, Nigel.'

'You know for a vicar you can drink a lot.'

'One of the first things they teach you at College, helps me to blend in,' answered Paul.

'Do you have a moment, Nigel?' asked the landlady. 'Am I to understand that all this is because of you?'

'No, all this is because of the kind-hearted landlady, helping a disfigured man gain respect, and moreover, the kindness, love and compassion of the village and the Farthing jar.

'What reaction are you getting from the locals? The first night was Thursday. How did it go?' asked Nigel.

'Not without hiccups. The staff are great,' she leant over and whispered, 'it's him. [meaning the landlord]. If he doesn't buck up his ideas, then I am going to trade him in for a younger man with money,' giving Nigel a suggestive wink.

Alex had seen and heard the teasing.

'Well, well, and you only living across the road, she could hide the moped in the garage. Have a beer,' thrusting another pint in Nigel's hand.

'Thanks Alex!'

Alex continued, 'Just thought I would let you know. Faye, the woman on the horse has been across to me and apologized for her behaviour, when I was digging the trench, nice gesture. If you need the garage turned into a stable let me know,' laughing as he walked off.

'Hi Nigel, these pints are going down, a treat, could be the price,' said Paul.

Nigel managed to get most of the remaining drink down him.

'Come on, I need to show you something,' said Nigel.

'Does it mean leaving the Pub?' Paul asked.

'OK, no leaving the Pub! Change of plan. We can do it tomorrow, and I can finish the story too. Can you come round in the morning?'

'Sound just fine, let's go and have a look at the food.'

Paul walked over to the cosy corner, 'Nigel and I are eating. Please join us.' 'Good idea. Landlord, one more bottle please,' shouted Wig.

Nigel stared at him. Wig just gave a sarcastic grin, and the group stood in wonder of the spread and range of food.

Chef had been asked to showcase the ability of the catering.

Not knowing what to have they stood debating, what to go for first. The kitchen door opened with Chef bringing out more tasty treats.

'What do you think then, Dad, fit for a High Court Barrister?'

Time moved on, the place was alive, the young staff seemed to be coping well, the landlord and landlady were chatting away with customers. Food kept coming out of the kitchen. Everything was good.

The vicar was at the bar again, yet another little 'pop' as a cork left the Champagne bottle, David was slumped in a chair, Alex was now talking with Helen, presumably in English.

Nigel felt a tug on his arm, it was the butcher.

'We can sort the tab out, next week, Nigel, and yes, I am sure it will include a discount.'

'Good, thank you, didn't know I was having a tab.'

'Yes, Mary just spent the last ½ hour sorting it out, not that I had much of an input, but great to supply the Old House with fresh meat and produce, thanks.'

'Yes, you're welcome,' said Nigel, totally bemused.

'Well,' thought Nigel, Mary was quick off the mark.

As Nigel looked around Mary was waving, beckoning him over.

'Nigel, can Millie and I have a look around the house?'

'Yes, of course. I will find who has the keys.'

'Don't worry about that, Nigel. We've already got them.'

'OK, see you later.'

Nigel was by now feeling a little wobbly, best get some more food. Staring at the spread he did not know what to have.

'This type of food could hit my business, I guess I've already lost two customers, you and the vicar.'

As Nigel turned it was the Fish van man.

'I think your place is safe.'

'Nice one!' replied the fish man.

Nigel continued to chat and mingle with people. Slowly a few folks left but still a good number remained. By now he had given up on pints. Being of slight build, Nigel was now hitting the red wine.

Chapter 28

A Sign of Change

'Morning Nigel, how are you this morning?' said Love.

'What time is it, and why are you in my bedroom? I don't feel well!' whispered Nigel.

'Not surprised, the amount you put away, and the vicar said you don't drink a lot normally,' continued Love.

'Come on, Nigel. Get up, we need to start on the cottage. Anyway, why are you here, thought you were moving into the Old House yesterday.'

A voice from downstairs, shouted, 'She wouldn't let him in, not in that state, in case he was sick.'

'Who?'

Millie said she was a housekeeper not a babysitter, not cleaning his sick up because of drink, so I brought him back here.

'Good thinking, Alex.'

'I need to get up, not well,' repeated Nigel.

'Go on, then. You're still dressed,' said Love.

Nigel spent a lot longer than normal in the bathroom; indeed, the poor chap was not well.

Baby, Love and the team started to knock the place about, thumping, banging, throwing things outside, creating dust, too much for Nigel. He needed fresh air desperately.

He managed to make it downstairs and out to the lane, just in time for Mr Snow to come by with the big, noisy, smelly tractor.

'Morning, Nigel, just off to plough the garden. The wife and I really appreciate your help. Are you OK? You look a bit under the weather.'

'Go away and take the damn thing away from my head,' retorted Nigel.

'Oh, it's that type of under the weather. You were knocking them back, Bye!'

With that and an extra rev, off he went.

Nigel made a few more steps, before seeing the builder's toilet, 'need that!'

As he opened the door, the smell of the chemicals made him poorly yet again.

Need fresh air, and a drink of water, got a tongue like a Gorilla's flip flop.

Staggering to the Old House steps, he had to sit down. How long he was there, who knows? It was David who found him.

'Morning Nigel, you look poorly.'

'Yes, David I am a little. Could you please get me a drink of water?'

'OK,' David turned around and started to cross the front of the house.

'David, you can go through the house now.'

'No, I'm not allowed, Mary and Millie said if I need anything I need to stand by the back door, and they will bring it to me.'

David soon returned with a drink. 'Your friends are still here, they have finished breakfast, but Mary said: would you like a bacon sandwich, with fried bread and a snotty egg or these two tablets?'

'Excuse me, David. I need to go around the side of the house, I am not well!'

Nigel returned to the steps and sat rocking for a considerable time, before his guests started to leave.

As the group stood talking around him, stating how good yesterday had been, a success all-round, a great achievement, Nigel didn't feel any greatness and absolutely no achievement. The only achievement he felt was the fact he was still alive.

Each person, in turn, thanked Nigel explaining how proud they all were of him and his unselfish act. Each smiling at the poor man's predicament.

'Let's do it, again, next week,' shouted Raymond. 'Good idea,' yelled Helen. Cars revving and the sound of horns, the group left Nigel to slowly wither on the steps.

'Good afternoon, Nigel,' Mary said cheerfully, 'here, drink this, it will help.'

'What is it?'

'Never mind, get it down you!'

Nigel hadn't the strength to argue, down it went. Whatever it was, did not taste all that bad.

'You had better look better than that, Nigel, before Millie will let you in. Take yourself off for a walk.'

'Good idea. I will sit by the lake for a while.'

Whether it was psychological or not, but he started to feel a little better sitting by the lake, ensuring the soldier still had a view.

He reflected on the day before. Over all, his friends were right, the whole village had come together and achieved the start of a new brighter future.

Nigel started to walk toward the house, feeling strong enough to go in. After all it was his house, well his and Mary's and Millie's.

Nigel made his way over to the smaller bench, which was still wrapped in the polyethene. Taking out his pen knife he removed the wrapping to expose a beautiful oak bench, the same as by the lake only smaller. There in place of pride was a picture of Mum and Dad.

There it is Mum, you can now look upon a lovely old country house, and Dad you don't have to worry about cleaning the windows.

'Hi Nigel, I am surprised to see you today, what a state you were in yesterday.'

'Hello Paul, you should have seen me earlier. I am not too bad now. Do you fancy a walk?'

'What? To the Pub?'

'No, I don't feel that well yet.'

'Come on, then. You need to fill in the blanks from your story yesterday.'

'OK, where did I get to?'

'You left Raymond with those three.'

'Let's walk and talk, we need to have a look at your cash thermometer.'

'Oh yes! Well not much else to tell. As I said I knew about this place, because of visiting the graves, and asked Mr Parker to enquire.'

'Now, Wig played a blinder. As he discovered about the covenants, he was obliged by law, to inform the Auctioneer, who in turn had to announce it on the day of the auction.

'Well, we were the only bidders, we got it for a song, almost gave it away, which enabled us to reach out to the Pub, the builders and the farm.

'Helen worked alongside up-and-coming designers, and high-end suppliers. She talked with people and negotiated deals. Hasn't done her any harm, brilliant job, don't you think?

'Wig's son is now head Chef, that food yesterday was good, wasn't it?

'People have work and hopefully better futures.'

'You said 'we'. Who's 'we'. I thought you owned the Old House?' asked Paul.

'I do. I was able to pay for it all. The only thing I asked is a small return to help keep the place going, not unreasonable!'

'OK, I will come straight out with it. *Where did you get all that money*? You said Mr Parker told you, you did not have any?'

'That was correct, I signed every penny over to him, Wig and Helen, so they could execute all the work and purchases.'

'It's like pulling teeth, *where did you get all that money*?'

'Oh that. Didn't I tell you I won a record amount on the football pools? Biggest ever, and I put a cross in the box for no publicity.'

Nigel stopped and stared.

'Look at that sign post, look at the three arms, who wrote that?

Dot and Dab, Wet, Skimming.'

Heating Fund
Wet
Skimming
Dot and Dab

Acknowlegements

I have to offer my appreciation to my wife, Liz, for allowing me the time to write this story, and to June and Jim Stringer in offering more help than they realise. And to Our Daughter, Jeni, for laboriously readingover un-edited drafts.

I hope you enjoyed.

Ingram Content Group UK Ltd.
Milton Keynes UK
UKHW042200080523
421401UK00001B/38